"ROMULANS?" DR. McCOY ASKED. "WHAT HAVE THEY GOT TO DO WITH THIS?"

"They showed up at Starbase 16," Captain Kirk responded.

"Could it have something to do with the race? All those vessels gathered in one place?" the doctor suggested.

"I don't know," Kirk said. "A race is supposed to be entertainment. Sportsmanship. Competition. It just became something else."

"Maybe they just want to be in the race."

"I don't know," Kirk said finally. "But once the neighborhood bully shows up, you know the game isn't going to be fun anymore."

Look for STAR TREK Fiction from Pocket Books

Star Trek: The Original Series

Aboard the Romulan Cruiser *Scorah*

"VALDUS, YOU ARE A COWARD. I vomit on cowards. Cowards should be cooked and eaten. No—not cooked. And not swallowed. They should be chewed raw, then spat out. When we return to the homeworlds, you, your face, your body, your uniform, your helmet, your *smell*. . . will be removed from my Swarm, walked off this ship and stripped of rank. I never again want even to see you or any sons you may unexpectedly sire. If I had another pilot, you would be off the bridge already. Take your post and turn your eyes away from me. Anyone else who freezes at the controls will be put outside the ship and dragged home on a tether. Someone other than this worm step up here and give me a report on that vessel out there. And someone clear this smoke from here!"

The scorn in Primus Oran's voice was almost enough to move the smoke aside by itself.

Behind him, the object of that scorn, Subcenturion Valdus Ionis Zorokove, stepped away, actually stepped backward, and was particular about keeping his eyes down even after he turned to his helm. The Primus's blue

3

jacket and the red fur up the right arm seared his memory instantly.

Smoke obscured sight of his own feet, and for an instant he was disoriented. Malfunctions, malfunctions. Living and mechanical.

He maneuvered by simple habit through the cramped bridge—low ceiling, subdued light, shadows designed in, everything the colors of the smoke, bulkheads angled to make the crew always feel as if they were crawling about the underside of a giant insect. His comrades turned away as he squirmed past, partly for his benefit, partly for theirs.

For some reason he kept hearing his own name over and over in his mind. Before ten minutes ago, he had been the pride of his family. Suddenly he wanted to be anyone else, anywhere else.

The Primus is right. Cowardice endangers all. And I am a coward. I am the day's disease. Perhaps if I concentrate, I can find a way to go home in even more humiliation.

Already he had accumulated a demotion, on top of sitting on his backside in backspace, in the back of a patrol vessel, doing exploratory mapping work while the great war between the Empire and the Federation raged. There would be no guarding borders or putting down uprisings for this lucky Imperial Swarm. The wars would probably be over before the *Scorah* and its crew finished drawing pictures of the stars out here.

Valdus didn't understand it, but the war with the Federation planets was sucking the Empire dry. Conquest had seemed guaranteed against this foolishly open-handed, eager fledgling assembly of planets that didn't even have a dominant race among them. Surely, at first strike they would crumble, and the Empire would have control over vastly more space and resources.

But that's not what had happened. At the Empire's first strike on an outpost, the Federation had pulled together with an indignation never expected, and began to fight back. The Empire had attempted to skin a sleeping

STAR TREK®

THE GREAT STARSHIP RACE

DIANE CAREY

POCKET BOOKS

New York   London   Toronto   Sydney   Tokyo   Singapore

This book is a work of fiction. Names, characters, places and incidents are either products of the author's imagination or are used fictitiously. Any resemblance to actual events or locales or persons, living or dead, is entirely coincidental.

An *Original* Publication of POCKET BOOKS

POCKET BOOKS, a division of Simon & Schuster Inc.
1230 Avenue of the Americas, New York, NY 10020

STAR TREK is a Registered Trademark of
Paramount Pictures.

ISBN: 0-671-87250-8

First Pocket Books printing October 1993

10 9 8 7 6 5 4 3 2 1

POCKET and colophon are registered trademarks of Simon & Schuster Inc.

Printed in the U.S.A.

To Captain Tony Lesnick and the crew of the Official Star Trek Fan Club *Starship Intrepid* who, with their untiring work and above-the-call chivalry, give our ongoing trek a good name.

There is no danger to a man that knows
What life and death is; there's not any law
Exceeds his knowledge; neither is it lawful
That he should stoop to any other law.
He goes before them, and commands them all,
That to himself is a law rational.

George Chapman,
In Praise of Sailors

PROLOGUE

animal. Soft and slothful while dozing, the beast had awakened at first cut, ready to fight to the death.

"Unidentified ship is approaching," Commander Rioc reported. "A very old and simple design. Low warp capability only. No response to any hails."

"Move us closer," Oran said. "They could be a hostile ship in disguise."

Valdus chewed on his lip, and eased the *Scorah* forward. He felt the coldness of his fellow crewmen toward him. Somehow they were expected to work with him for a few more days without having anything to do with him.

Mutterings, orders, responses rumbled like thunder in the distance, but for several seconds Valdus could make no sense of it past the cloud of his personal shame. He dreamed of turning to the Primus, announcing how much he wished to leave duty on board the *Scorah* now. Almost as much as Primus Oran wanted him off. Almost.

But even after the Primus's condemnation and sentencing, he still didn't have the courage to do it.

Valdus started plotting possible pivoting maneuvers, just to be ready. In his mind Valdus saw the Primus's large sunken eyes and angular beard, and listened.

"Condition of our Swarm ships?" the Primus asked. "And distance—"

Then Oran tripped and fell onto his side against a support strut.

Valdus quickly turned away, like a dog that had been slapped. The other four crewmen occupying the small bridge paused, but no one moved to help. Even Tarn— their bold, dark, intuitive centurion who everyone said would command the sky some day—stayed back in the corner near engineering access. Along with cowards, the Primus had clarified to the crew that he loathed assistance for old wounds. He barely tolerated help for new ones.

Valdus gritted his teeth. *And I will give no help.*

Only Rioc approached the fallen fleet leader, but even he made no attempt to assist.

"Burn this foot," Oran grunted. "I should have had it cut off." He forced himself up onto an elbow, then over onto his knees, and managed somehow to grip the support strut and rise to his feet. "Condition?"

"All ships are on alert, ready to assist."

"Distance of the nearest ship? Don't make me bark, Rioc."

The commander gazed at him, and coughed on the smoke that was barely starting to clear despite the whine of ventilators. *"Worshipper* and *Whip Hand* are nearest, Primus. They can each be here in one-third day."

As he straightened, Oran glanced at the small sensor screens. "Alert to be ready."

The snapping, inaccurate, hard-to-read screens were near Valdus, who had to fight not to lean in the other direction, away from Oran. He felt the Primus's glare sliding past him like a creature of the deep caves.

The ventilators choked, and the smoke swirled around them again, antagonizing everyone. Improvement came slowly in the Empire. Too often their brightest engineers were penalized, demoted, even executed for failures in experimentation, so there was less and less experimentation. All that was left were the worst engineers, the timid ones.

Someday we will have better, Valdus thought, or *we will go out and take better.*

Shabby engineering. Poor manufacturing. Eccentric controls. Officers who were . . .

"I have more detail on that ship," Commander Rioc reported. "Not a ship, precisely. More like a long-distance, long-term capsule. Minimized living space, primary area is storage. Presumably food, possibly medicine. Three life-forms. Correction . . . four."

"Five, sir," the centurion corrected again. "This blip in the corner—"

"Very well, five."

Bluntly, Oran interrupted, "Dock with them."

Tightening his elbows against his ribs, Valdus blinked

and bit the inside of his lip. Yes, dock with them. Give no consideration to caution, no rein to the advance. That was the reputation of the Primus Oran. He was famous for this trait. He had won battles with it. His name was known in the Tricameron for it.

Valdus lowered his eyes and forced a swallow.

I will never again be cautious.

Roaring, the Primus demanded, "Do I have to say it again?"

"Prepare to dock," the commander related to his crew in a subdued tone, for they could not move on the Primus's command alone unless the order affected the entire six-ship patrol Swarm.

Rioc looked at Oran as though waiting for something else. Some clarification or meticulousness.

None came.

The bridge manipulation officer said, "Universal cowl ready, Commander."

Rioc nodded. "We are ready to dock, Primus."

"Have I gone deaf, Rioc?"

Rioc sighed and gestured a silent order to begin docking.

The procedure was awkward and irritating. They had to abort and approach again four separate times. Each time the Primus's face grew a shade grayer, until at last the crew was ready to crawl outside and force the cowl to fit.

Finally, by tilting their own ship until the thrusters whined, they were able to link up and make the "leakage" lights go off.

"Open the hatchway," the Primus snapped instantly. No sensor checks, no tests of any kind.

"What if their air is poisonous?" Rioc asked.

Now Valdus did look up, and so did everyone else. Poison?

The Primus snapped, "Then we hold our breath. Or shall we all be as priggish as you are, Rioc? I can send you to your quarters, where you will have more time to build those little replicas of ships you have battled. All those pointless Federation duplicates you have dangling from your private ceiling, as though you conquered them alone. Now, the hatch."

Commander Rioc seemed to shrug without moving. He gestured again for the crew to act, for the hatch to be cranked open.

Then Valdus heard Rioc quietly utter to the centurion, "Put the translator on line. Prepare to turn it off whenever I look at you. No more than a look, do you understand?"

"Yes, Commander, I understand exactly," the centurion murmured back.

"Hands on disruptors."

So the commander and the centurion would commit caution on the Primus's behalf.

The centurion motioned three of the bridge crew to back away, in case the foremost were attacked or struck down when the hatch opened. Valdus was one of them. He moved back without a word because now he knew what he was. Cowards always moved back.

His disruptor was cold, unassuring against his palm. He looked for fear in his mind, his chest, his limbs, but felt none. Perhaps it had been pushed aside by humiliation.

The hatch slid open, to the side, then upward, out of the way. Five faces stared at them, piled up like victims of a crash. Faces from yellow to copper, all with large wide eyes, innocuous, gawking, flat brows up, mouths open—how could five creatures all have the same expression?

Primus Oran huffed, relaxed visibly, turned to the commander, but swallowed a comment.

The visitors were already climbing through the hatch—

And the first one through plunged at the Primus and took him in a body embrace that pitched them both backward into Rioc, then all three against the pilot console.

Startled, Valdus also flailed away and bumped the bulkhead, and two others drew their disruptors.

"No!" Rioc blurted. "Wait."

Slowly Valdus realized that this was no attack. In fact, if it wasn't pure delight, it was pure stupidity.

Both, he decided as he regained his balance.

"Translator," the Primus grunted, canting his eyes toward Rioc.

Primus Oran didn't even push the visitor off. The visitor was just hanging there around the Primus's neck like a big decoration, giggling and babbling in a language Valdus didn't recognize. Nor, apparently, did the senior officers, who had been much farther and wider in their experiences than Valdus.

The other four visitors were through now, not even one staying behind for safety. No caution here either.

They came through, also babbling, grinning, and grasping hands with the *Scorah*'s bridge crew. Their clothing, a very basic space survival suit with hook-up accesses for . . . anyone's guess. Valdus hadn't seen a suit like that since early training, and for a few moments it stole his attention.

When he roused himself from this bout of curious nostalgia, the hatch was closed, Primus Oran was free from his manacle, and a bizarre standoff had begun.

The centurion held a medical unit up near the five big-eyed strangers, but only scowled at what he saw. An unimpressed kind of scowl.

"Weak," he said quietly, toward the Primus.

"I can see that. Is the translator on line yet?"

Rioc didn't answer or even nod. He touched the panel he had been preparing.

" 'Happy' . . . 'distance' . . . 'wait' or 'waiting'. . . 'population' or 'people' . . . 'alone' . . . 'astrotelemetry' . . . 'quasi-stellar' . . . 'galactic voice' or 'noise' . . . 'hopeful' . . . 'lost hope' . . . 'foreign search' . . . 'think' or 'thought' . . . 'unproductive' or 'fruitless'—"

The computer translated the foreigners' words, at least key parts of sentences, halting along in a grim, utilitarian monotone completely opposite to the motions and expressions of the people talking. It was entertaining, had Primus Oran been the type to be entertained.

Rioc glanced at the centurion, then at Oran as the translator snapped off.

"Can you get anything from that?" the Primus drawled.

"They've been looking for something and didn't find it," the centurion supplied from a shadow.

"They were looking in space," the engineer offered.

"The computer is confused," Rioc said. "Too many of them talking. Which is the leader? All their uniform markings are the same. They all look hungry."

"Engineering report," Oran requested.

The engineer leaned past a strut. "Their ship is basic early interstellar exploratory vessel, all equipment of a picture-taking or measuring nature. They have very weak sensor capability, no defenses, no weapons, only primary light speed and limited maneuvering capabilities at sublight."

The visitors were touching and laughing again, in fact almost dancing with delight.

Valdus smiled. His muscles had been welded by the Primus's excoriations, and now he was suddenly smiling.

But so was everyone else . . . was Oran smiling? A man who'd had those muscles surgically removed with his first promotion?

"Get them basic drawing materials," Oran said. His voice was lilting as he clasped the hand of the next shaggy-haired visitor who approached him. "Prepare a holographic star map. Get them to show where they are from. Location of their—" As he was engulfed in another embrace . . . "—engaging, resourceful little planet."

Several Empire officers smiled and bounced to action, backslapping each other in a manner reserved for weddings and only among clan members who trusted each other. Suddenly men who had never trusted each other were standing side by side. Tensions melted away. The joy of these idiotically naive visitors was infectious.

We're going to get credit for finding them! Valdus drew in a refreshing breath. He knew what was happening. The Primus would get that information, and this ship . . . would suddenly be crewed by heroes.

An unexploited planet. A rare prize with sufficient resources to support a culture intelligent enough to be turned into a workforce. A whole planet to be mined, milled, to provide materials and a reasonably skilled herd of people who could be taught to manufacture whatever the Empire needed in its war with the Federation. Advanced enough to be useful, primitive enough to offer no resistance.

An Imperial dream. A planet of slaves.

"Maps, maps," Primus Oran chanted, "this sector."

"Coming," the commander said.

An electrical fizz hurt their ears, then a pop, and abruptly a wall-size holographic star chart of this portion of deep space filled the center of the bridge. Rioc and two other crewmen were briefly awash in primary colors as they stepped through it to get out of the way.

Silence fell on the bridge. All gazed at glowing stars, hovering nebulae, streaking comets, overlaid by thin red navigational beams.

The newcomers paused, and the one who had first come through the hatch frowned at the holograph. He glanced at his shipmates, conversed briefly, but they were clearly confused. Not by what they were supposed to do, but by the picture they saw.

"They see nothing familiar here," Commander Rioc said.

Oran nodded. "Expand the grid."

The holograph swelled, grew more intimidating, demanding attention.

The visitors fell suddenly silent—startled. They blinked their large light-catching eyes and retreated nervously toward each other. The mood of joy began to slip.

Valdus felt his own smile fall away, and held very still.

Primus Oran motioned to the aliens, then at the holographic star map. "Well? Show us."

The visitors flinched, drew their shoulders inward at his tone. A steady tone, yes, but with a huff of threat.

They want to show us, Valdus realized, *but they don't know how to read the map. Have they ever seen a picture of space? Primus Oran wants that planet—*

"Can the computer explain," Oran said with his teeth tight, "in their language?"

The centurion leaned over a screen. "Insufficient primary vocabulary. Doubtful accuracy as yet."

"Don't we have a linguist on board?"

"No, Primus, there is not a linguist on board anywhere in the Swarm, and you know no one puts a linguist on any Empire ship that is not a diplomatic ship, and that in the current circumstances we have no diplomatic ships either."

Valdus stared at the centurion, who continued to stare at the small screen without apology.

Reaching out with one hand in a motion he hoped was unthreatening, Valdus caught the arm of the first visitor and pulled him toward the humming star map, pointed at the visitor's chest, then at the map.

Gaping at him, the visitor seemed to want to comply and moved forward again toward the star map, frowning and looking for a point of reference—

Then fate turned against them. The visitor's clumsy boot came down on Oran's old injury, and because of the thickness of the old-style space boot, the visitor didn't realize until too late that he was standing on his host's foot. Didn't realize—until Oran choked in pain and lashed out. His knuckles crashed across the alien's cheekbone.

Apprehension burst over the well-being. Thunder broke on the bridge. The alien flew backward and landed among his own kind like a gamepiece in some arena contest, and they all went down. The aliens sank back in fear.

"I will make them all die," Valdus spat. "I will make you all die! All my enemies will die!"

He crouched and fired his disruptor down the narrow open corridor, in wide circles, until there was nothing but sizzling fire and the access panels were exploding. One enemy who jumped out a hatch lay twisting in flames on the deck.

"Burn, burn!" Valdus choked. His hands shook so hard that the muzzle of the disruptor waggled and cut across the wall when he opened fire again. "You can't follow me now!"

Down through the *Scorah* he crawled, shooting wildly into each section behind him until its conduits exploded, then going on, locking hatches so he couldn't be followed.

Barely in control, Valdus slid into the long, thin access tube to the life pod, and was automatically dropped into the pod.

He smashed his palm against the controls. How did they work? Which control would launch the pod? Why couldn't he remember?

Finally he reversed his disruptor and smashed the panel with the weapon's handle until the pod began to buzz around him, bumped, and launched.

Alone in a pod meant for three, Valdus gasped for breath as though just coming up from under water. He crawled to the sensor screen and poked at it until the visual snapped on and provided a view of near space, of the *Scorah*.

As Valdus watched, the bird-winged patrol vessel shrank away, farther away, a metal button on the black canopy around him . . .

And with distance, the paranoia began to retreat from his mind. His thoughts began to clear, filter back to what they were before those aliens had been brought on board.

Crew . . . the ship . . . Commander Rioc . . . those aliens—

Those aliens . . .

The *Scorah* heaved like an animal in its death throes. Blue flame belched from the aft sections.

Before his eyes, the ship that minutes ago had been his home cracked and fell apart. Then the two halves tore themselves to bits in tandem explosions. First one, then the other.

Bodies appeared, spinning through the vacuum of space.

Valdus watched, his hands shaking, his mind clearing.

He pushed himself up onto his knees, still staring at the screen.

And he rasped, "What did we do . . ."

Seventy-four Years Later
The Last Whistling Post

"Asteroid! Collision course!"

The technician's cracking voice woke the senior scientist out of a good snooze so abruptly that she thought she was still dreaming.

"Look at the *size* of it!" Halfway out of his chair, the technician was pointing at the row of screens monitoring the solar system and as much space outside it as possible. One clearly showed a streaking yellow-green line and a blip moving from left to right at hideous speed. "It's almost a fifth the size of the planet!"

The senior scientist stumbled from her chair and pressed against her colleague's shoulder, deciding with every step that he was wrong, looking at the wrong screen, leaning on a dial—but he wasn't wrong.

A projectile was coming in, and coming in fast. Dead on course, right toward their planet.

"Beneon, what should we do!" her technician belched. "What—what—"

Terror spread across his ruddy cheeks, and his eyes contracted as he realized what he was seeing.

Beneon pressed her long unkempt nut brown hair out of her own eyes, thought for a painful instant how long it had been since she had made herself presentable—no one needed to be presentable on a moon station—and checked to be sure the garish yellow-green line was not a malfunction.

It wasn't. Out of nothing and nowhere, she was staring at her planet's death.

"Vorry, check . . . check the . . ."

"I did!" Vorry wailed. "I checked! Look at it!"

"Why didn't we see it sooner?"

"I don't know! It just dropped out of nowhere at us! How can that happen? How can it happen?"

He dissolved into sobs, tears streaming down his blotched cheeks.

"Whistling Post, Whistling Post, this is Planetside Assembly, do you read?"

Beneon forced her hand to move, to touch the communications panel. "I read."

"Dr. Beneon, do you see it? Are you tracking it?"

"Yes," she admitted, "we see it."

"We can't confirm the size . . . readings are fluctuating! How can it move that fast? Can we deflect it?"

Their request, and all their hopes, rested on her shoulders. For a second, it almost pulled her down.

"We have nothing that can deflect it, Assembly," she said.

The yellowish line grew longer, closer.

"Did you . . . not see it earlier?"

She almost choked. "We picked it up just as you did. At the same time."

"How can that be?"

"I don't know. I don't know how . . ."

Her voice petered out. There was nothing left to say.

Apparently Planetside comprehended that. The channel remained open, but no one spoke again. They were watching the yellow line, too, and they knew the words of their culture were about to come to an end. No point scraping up a few more.

As Vorry dropped into his chair and clawed at his

controls, Beneon drifted back to her own chair, sank into it, and stared at the yellow moving line until her eyes hurt.

Above the row of screens that so cleanly documented their death dangled a lovely handwritten note, and rather than staring at the terrible glowing line, she ended up staring at the note.

The long-range manned exploration program will not be reinstated due to diminished interest, past cost of lives and resources, and diminished hope of success. Thank you for your suggestion, but the Science Assembly's decision will have to stand. We are sorry. We are very, very sorry.

"I'm sorry, too," Beneon murmured.

Behind her own voice she heard Vorry's sobbing. She wanted to go over there, comfort him somehow, but the yellow line . . .

"What more could we ask of them?" she uttered. "We tend to draw back at first trouble. The best way to survive is to not do the dangerous thing. 'If everyone who goes into the valley gets eaten, then don't go into the valley.' But we had hope . . . we wanted to find someone out there in the black wilderness . . . we wanted to be neighbors with the galaxy. We wanted to find out we weren't the only intelligent life in the galaxy. Seventy-five, eighty, ninety years of long-range probing . . . good people, good ships, resources, donations, time . . . just to celebrate our centennial by shutting it all down . . . because we were listening to the silence in our own tomb. Because there is no one out there."

Beneath her narrow hips the seat was cold. It stayed cold somehow. No warmth in her body to affect it, probably.

She looked at Vorry, broken and miserable, horrified and sobbing. The yellow line had completed one screen and had branched over to the next screen.

Inside the solar system.

She was sobbing too, inside. She was just too wrapped with hopelessness to release what she was feeling. So she sat on the cold chair, feeling every bone in her pelvis and remembering the childhood lessons about evolution that built those bones over millions of years, and she felt every muscle in her thighs and her hands, resisting every impulse she had to run.

There was nowhere to run.

I wish we had found someone . . . this would be so much easier. Can this be all? We come out of the slime, live for a million years, and now we die. Without the support of the planet, the colonies will never survive. Is this all the galaxy has to whisper to us? That intelligent life might have been a mistake all along?

Sobs wracked inside her, not coming out, until she thought she would suffocate on her own fear.

The two of them were alone, the last two Whistlers. The ones who hadn't given up. The last two.

"The last," she murmured. "And now we have to be the first to see that . . ."

That. The slaughter of their culture. A comet, asteroid, something big enough to decimate the planet, coming directly at them at almost the speed of light.

Plenty of size, plenty of speed.

The yellow line daggered toward the center of the second screen. When it got all the way across—

Something happened to the screen. The line began to falter.

Vorry gasped, "It's slowing down!"

Beneon licked her cracked lips. "Something's wrong with the tracker."

"I read a change of mass," Vorry said. "It's disintegrating!"

They watched their screens and listened to the pounding of their own hearts.

Mopping his wet face with one hand, Vorry slumped forward across his panel and fingered his controls. "No . . . it's slowing down! How can it slow down?"

Pushing to her feet and moving on legs that almost

folded beneath her, Beneon checked the controls herself before her assistant blew himself into a dozen frantic pieces.

"It can't slow down," she said.

How clumsy—reassuring him that they were definitely going to die and that there were no miracles.

"Whistling Post! Did it slow down?"

She struck communications. "Do *you* read that it slowed down also?"

"Yes! How can it slow down?"

Beneon grabbed the messy braids hanging down her chest and pulled her hair to be sure she was still alive and this wasn't some bizarre afterlife delusion, even though she didn't believe in such things. She also didn't believe asteroids could stop in flight.

"It can't," she said. "It didn't disintegrate either . . ."

"But we read that it's shrinking!"

"We never adjusted our instruments to read apparent mass at near light-speed. Why would we? Nothing moves that fast . . . nothing other than light . . . no *mass* does . . . Vorry, what have you got now?"

Her poor technician had his fingernails deep in the foam cover of the control panel, which was chipped and torn from their months of picking at it during their isolation.

"Only three hundred thousand tons now," he rasped. "More or less. But how can it slow down?"

Beneon twisted sharply, stumbled across the lab toward the broadcast/reception center, tripped on her own panic and slammed to the floor, staggered up, pushed the crated equipment out of her way so violently she was bleeding when she got to the auriscopes and crossover coils. As her hands clutched at the close-range broadcasters, she could barely remember how to turn it on.

"Turn it on, turn—turn—turn it on—" she gasped.

"The tape!" Vorry spat from across the lab. "Put the tape in!"

"Yes, I know, tape, yes, tape, tape . . ."

She dropped it twice.

Somehow she finally crammed the prerecorded information tape about her planet, her race, her history, her culture, and rudimentary language into the slot.

"Work! Work!" She pounded it with her fist.

Vorry gulped, "The switches! Turn it on! I'll—I'll help—"

But he couldn't even move.

Half blind with shock, Beneon knew she would have to do it by herself. She jabbed at the controls until the lights came on and the steady flashes told her the message was broadcasting.

Sending . . .

And then, receiving.

The computer didn't have much of a voice, but it could have been singing to these lonely listeners.

They flinched at the sound.

"Attention . . . sending culture . . . this the hood . . . want to meet . . . do welcome us?"

Beneon stared at the receiver. A computer's voice. The voice of the galaxy. The tomb wasn't empty.

Begging to believe, she murmured, "The 'Hood' . . ."

"The 'Hood,'" Vorry whispered.

They looked at each other.

Suddenly the scientist and her technician broke into cheering, screaming, jumping up and down so hard and for so long they forgot they'd just been asked the most important question in the history of their world.

"Ans—ans—!" Vorry was gasping, his voice on a high pitch of panic.

Beneon shoved him away, stumbled to the broadcast keyboard and typed in permission for the computer to translate any incoming messages and respond to them. Her fingers were frozen and tangled up. She had to type the commands three times—four times—

Her chest constricted. Frustration was a stupid way to die. She took deep breaths and forced herself to do the work, symbol by symbol, digit by digit.

"Wait . . . don't leave . . . please wait . . . please don't leave us . . ."

Somehow Beneon finished the order, somehow committed it, and pushed back.

The computer worked silently, except for a few crackles left over from poor repairs and antique parts. It worked hard, for a machine.

A moment later—

"We would . . . speak together to faces . . . shall we visit you?"

Vorry's fingers dug into Beneon's arm. Her fingers dug right back.

Just like that, after a million years of nothing but past, suddenly—they had a future.

Beneon tapped out another word, and committed it. *Yes.*

The computer swallowed the order, and winked and blinked pathetically, without the simplest idea of the cruciality of what it was doing.

Drawn-out seconds later, a message came through in the computer's voice.

"Thank you . . . we will be there in one minute."

Vorry almost collapsed.

Out of habit and a sense of responsibility, Beneon clasped his arm and said, "It can't be. Must be miscommunication. The computer's translator is too old, Vorry. They'll need time to listen to the tapes . . . to learn about us . . . learn our basic vocabulary."

"I think I'm going to throw up," Vorry said.

Beneon shuddered through a smile. "How would that look to them? We should occupy ourselves while we wait . . . we should make ourselves presentable. Change suits or—"

An electrical whine pinched her ears. She and Vorry both winced, and glanced around for the source. What was happening? Were they being attacked?

The whine grew louder, and the room started to shimmer as though lightning was striking.

Beneon stared at the lights, and Vorry had to yank her back, try to protect her—

As the lights began to take shape.

22

Shape!

Elongated oval shapes—then the shapes of living beings!

Beneon almost dropped to her knees, but Vorry held her up somehow. They both stared impotently.

The lights settled and began to fade. In their place, they left four beings. Four *people*.

Two eyes, two ears, hair cut short, two legs, two arms—

Like us, Beneon thought distantly, *but not exactly. More like the birds in the hills. Sharp, quick, aware.*

The creatures didn't approach or make any threatening movements. In fact, their expressions were cautiously hospitable. They wore clothing that was exactly alike except for the bright solid colors. Their faces were different too, Beneon saw instantly. Small eyes, different shapes. All the fiction described aliens as nearly duplicates of one another. Imagine all the fiction being wrong . . .

Two of them held small boxlike tools that hummed and beeped.

The one in front nodded—a simple gesture.

His eyes seemed small to her, but all the newcomers were like that. His hair was short and black, his face lighter than hers, and he seemed too young to be in front.

He fixed his eyes on Beneon and Vorry, as though they were his sole purpose. He held up a silver mechanism to his mouth, and he stepped slowly toward them.

His lips made a different movement from the sound that came out, and Beneon understood that the mechanism was some kind of general translator—much more advanced than anything she could have anticipated—and even his translator had a friendly voice.

"I bring greetings to your people," he said, "from the United Federation of Planets. I am Captain Kenneth Dodge, commander of the *Starship Hood.*"

THE
CAPTAINS'
MEETING

Chapter One

Twelve Years Later
Starbase 10

"IT'S NOT FAIR. There's nothing fair about it."

"If you want fair, don't enter races."

The room was full, decorated with ship's pennants and flags, and very bright. The restaurant at one of the Federation's farthest reaching starbases.

Uneasily situated between the two people snapping at each other, Starship Chief Surgeon Leonard McCoy felt fundamentally out of place. He was the only person in the room who wasn't a ship's master, or a line officer.

He crushed his hand into a fist to keep from reaching over, restraining his captain's arm, and whispering a phrase of caution.

"Don't enter races?" What kind of thing is that to say at a time like this?

Usually the doctor didn't hesitate to tag along behind his captain into command briefings. No matter the glares he got, he was used to glaring back and knew nobody would have the gumption to tell the captain of the *U.S.S. Enterprise* he couldn't have his doctor, his dentist, his favorite carpenter, or his dog groomer at his side if he wanted to, security clearance or not. And Leonard

McCoy was known as a man who could glare as good as he got.

But this was the first time McCoy had been among shipmasters who weren't all dressed in uniforms of the Fleet and who didn't have to abide by the same regulations he did. Or any regulations. After a twenty-year career in Starfleet, he realized how awkward it might be for him to step outside again someday. He who had always claimed to be out of place in the Fleet . . .

Captains, captains everywhere, but only four of them from Starfleet. Merchant captains, alien captains, privateers, yachtsmen, and any other description of ship's master he could come up with—and looking at this crowd, he could come up with quite a few.

So McCoy was still out of place, even at this time of bright conviviality, with captains of every stripe gathered over fruit and doughnuts, winking and beaming at each other as though they had a secret. At least half of them had spoken to him, but even so, he got the feeling he was just being tolerated.

Interrupting from a table on the other side of the dining area, near the huge windows, backdropped by docked spacecraft and floating workbees, Captain Buck Ames leaned his bulky frame forward, and spoke.

"Look, fellas," he boomed, his heavy voice filled with zest and anticipation, "apparently some of you don't feel this way, but I for one am tickled pink about racing against all these vessels, including whatever Starfleet can throw at us."

He pointed boldly at the three uniformed men and one Vulcan woman. The Vulcan's eyes—only her eyes— grinned at him in amusement. She was elegant, yes, subdued, yes, but still she was amused. The human Starfleet captains were trying to be gallant and restrained, but the Vulcan lady was canting an almost-grin at Ames.

McCoy knew that look.

No feelings, my backside.

Somebody else made a crack about not really wanting to tickle Buck Ames pink, and the other captains smiled collectively.

Most laughed when somebody added, "Or any other color."

Captain Nancy Ransom didn't. "It's supposed to be a sport, but how can it be with *them* here?" she snapped in a deep southern accent. "Those Starfleet ships change the whole texture of this race. They've got heavy shielding, reinforced framing, automatic reaction control, combat-trained crews—"

McCoy frowned. Ames sat back again and shoveled himself a handful of complimentary chocolate-covered raisins. "Consider it a challenge, babe."

Ransom glared. "Build a successsful corporation without government help. Then you can 'babe' me, porky."

Grumbling threaded with laughter throughout the room, and even Buck Ames chuckled, "Got a point, babe."

Everybody laughed, and Nancy sat down.

A six-foot-four man in a baseball cap with a dark beard and cheerful narrow eyes proclaimed in a Virginia accent, "Now, darlin', I'm glad they're here. I'm looking to show 'em up."

Somehow Pete Hall's "darlin'" wasn't as compromising as Buck Ames's "babe."

McCoy felt a sense of agreement ripple across the room. Captain Ken Dodge of the *Hood* pointed at Pete and said, "Somebody shake him. He's dreaming."

At the front of the room a broad-chested man in his forties, with black hair, bright eyes and a salt-and-pepper mustache, stood and waved both hands in the air for attention.

"Okay, Captains, let's keep this on a gentlemanly plane, all right? As most of you already know, I'm John Orland, chairman of the Race Committee. I'm here to pass out some information and answer your questions. Sure, this race is public relations, entertainment, whatever else you want to call it, mostly a way for our hosts to drag some attention out to that black tundra where they live—"

The gathering of captains, shipmasters of every description, and one uneasy doctor, chuckled again, but kept listening.

Orland smiled like a salesman and shrugged. "This is the first real exchange of culture, a kind of coming-out party for the Rey. Before twelve years ago, when Ken Dodge and the *Hood* answered a little blip out in the middle of nowhere, the Rey were all alone. Not that they were lonely, mind you. Population's over five billion, and every one of those is friendly. Captain Dodge can tell you—you never saw such hospitable people, people so excited about becoming part of the Federation. Up until now only diplomats, a few natural and medical scientists, and cultural transition teams have interacted with these people, hoping to prevent the usual future shock that can happen when a new race rushes too quickly into the Federation. But these people," he laughed, "we had to hold 'em back for their own good. I swear they've organized this race just to get the Federation to hurry up letting 'em in."

Sudden warmth and an extra measure of eagerness touched each face. Orland seemed to notice that, and got a little more serious.

"But it's also a real race. Don't forget that. Like the Interstellar Olympics, the New Braemar Highland Games, the Pentathlon of Alpha Centauri, the Rigel Passage d'Arms, the Triple Crown, the Grand National, the America's Cup, the Great Tea Race between the clippers Ariel and Taeping, the Grand Prix . . . it's a strict and real competition. There's going to be a winner, and the first winner of the Great Starship Race will be remembered forever, ladies and gentlemen." He paused, scanned the room, and said, "The acceptance of Gullrey, and its associated colonies, into the United Federation of Planets almost doubles our perimeters."

He opened his mouth to say something else, but was

blasted down by applause—a solemn applause, not the sports-event rattle from before. The captains were absorbing the scope of what they were doing in the next couple days—and what they had done in the past twenty-five years.

Orland took advantage of the pause to hand stacks of red leather folders to three stewards, who began distributing them to the tables.

"In these packets you'll find a list of ships participating, their flaggings and captains. You all know by now that any ship within specified gross tonnage and thrust brackets can join the race. We might get a few more coming in at the last minute, but I don't think that's going to be very many. We'll have some non-Federation entries meeting us out at the starting line at Starbase 16, but we pretty much know who they are. A Tholian entry, a couple from Federation protectorates, and candidate members like Sigma Iotia, and a few others who didn't want to make the trip all the way here to Starbase 10 just to turn around and go back to 16. Also, I know some of you have a problem with gambling, but there's nothing we can do to stop it. The area between Starbase 16 and Gullrey isn't officially Federation space yet. If you have some moral objection to gambling, better get out of the race here and now."

Coffee cups clinked and shoulders shifted, but nobody got up and left. McCoy knew that in this crowd, they would if they wanted to. Orland moved his eyes from side to side, then relaxed.

"Okay, good," he sighed. "Had to ask." He squinted toward the right side of the room, where the Starfleet captains—and McCoy—had gathered. "The rules of communication for this race are going to be basic Maritime Standard. That'll be comfortable for the civilian vessels, but you Starfleet people will have to do some adjusting."

From McCoy's right, Kirk spoke up: "We'll adjust."

Three tables over, a robust dark-haired man of fifty

with a black beard winked and said, "You're a wolf, Jimmy."

McCoy blinked at Ben Shamirian.

Just like that. We'll adjust. Snap a finger and undo years of training in our people. Start talking like barge drivers.

"We'll have no problem," Ken Dodge added. Dodge was still as dark-haired and pink-faced as he had been when McCoy had first met him eight or so years ago.

"There won't be any Starfleet channel," Kirk said. "No one has to feel intimidated when talking to any of our ships."

"Don't intimidate me none, spud," Buck Ames's deep voice announced from behind.

Eyes shifting, James Kirk turned and resettled himself so he could look back there and rest one arm across the back of his seat.

"We've made it a Starfleet Academy tactical exam to devise something that does intimidate you, Buck," he said.

"That's why Starfleet's in the race," Captain Dodge said. "To intimidate Buck."

As the room's laughter cushioned him, McCoy sank back against the soft chair. He wasn't used to this kind of frivolity coming from lone wolf captains—and all captains were lone wolves in their ways. That much he was sure of.

"And right here," John Orland continued, "is a copy of the rules."

As attention floated back to the front of the dining room, he held out a piece of paper. It was blank. He turned it around for them to look at, and held it high.

Also blank.

"As you can see, there's nothing on it," he pointed out. "That's because there aren't any rules you don't already know. Just basic, run-of-the-mill maritime rules of the road. This race is taking place outside of Federation space, so there isn't even any law that applies across the board. I mean, you can't take potshots at each other to disable a contestant or anything, but this is like one of those strongest-survive field tests. Whoever comes out first . . . wins."

Someone from the other side of the room asked, "When are we going to get some details about this 'host' planet?"

A high-pitched elderly voice toward the front of the room demanded, "Do *they* have any laws we can apply out there?"

"A background of these people is in the command packets. They don't have any interstellar laws because they hardly have interstellar travel, never mind regulations about it." He pointed at Captain Dodge. "Hell, when Ken Dodge first contacted these people, they were shutting down their space programs and just sending signals. Lucky for them we caught them when we did. Maybe you can corner Ken on the way out, but don't bug me about it. If he's gonna be the guest of honor, he oughta pay."

All eyes brushed briefly over the man who had started it all by answering a faint blip twelve years ago.

"I'll get you for this, John," Dodge promised.

A surly-looking, overweight red-headed young man with a short beard suggested, "Sneeze on his lunch."

Through the laughter somebody else added, "Class act, Ian."

"Look," Orland said, "I'm just up here so I don't have to drink that coffee."

More laughter allowed for a pause while stewards milled around filling coffee mugs and offering trays of fresh doughnuts.

Orland looked at a list, nodded to himself, then chose a subject, and continued.

"Oh, there's no cargo transporting allowed."

A very young, dirty-looking captain in a patchwork jacket moaned, "Aw, what's that for? I'm carting textbooks."

"Can't do it. Can't take any chances of contraband or border disputes. You'll have to present your ship's bill of stores to the Consul of Foreign Ports for holding until the end of the race. Any cargo being carried will be stored in a bonded warehouse on Starbase 16, which is as far out as Federation jurisdiction goes to this new system."

"Just how far out is it?" Nancy Ransom persisted.

"Trust me," Orland said. "It's far. Now, as I said, there aren't any rules, but I'm going to impose one here and now." He widened his eyes in a manner more amusing than threatening, but no one chuckled this time. He was serious. "When there's any vessel dead ahead of you, the following vessel must either alter course or power back to adjust for ahead reach. We don't want anybody cramming into the back of the ship in front of you, got it? Anybody not understand that?"

McCoy almost raised his hand out of natural bullheadedness, but stopped himself. He tried to glance around without moving his head. Everybody else seemed to know what all that meant. He'd have to choke an explanation out of a junior engineer later.

"There are beacons and buoys placed throughout the sector to mark dangerous areas," Orland went on, "and don't forget there are plenty of those. Don't go around hawking, 'I know this space,' because you don't. Nobody does. Globe topmarks are for gravitational anomalies, diamonds are electrical clouds, triangles are sensor blind spots, and flashers mark storms. All of these are as close as possible, but we're not infallible. These suckers move around. Starfleet patrols double-checked the markers yesterday and already had to move five of them. Now, these are *not* coasting markers!"

The room heaved with collective laughter. McCoy grinned like a cat and pretended he had some idea what Orland meant.

"Please do *not*," Orland added, "attempt to follow these things from point to point! Or somebody's gonna have to throw a big chain into some goddamned twister and pull you out, okay?"

More chuckling.

A movement at McCoy's side made him flinch. Jim Kirk's hand was up.

"What's the distress frequency?"

Orland nodded and pointed at him. "Good! Thanks. Damn, I knew there was something I'd forget. The distress frequency is five thousand megacycles subspace. Just having your equipment on that channel will constitute SOS, so if you leave your lights on, even by mistake, don't be surprised if somebody knocks."

Apparently Kirk wasn't satisfied, because he pursued, "No safety ships or draggers?"

"Aren't any. The only vessels who can respond to trouble will be your fellow competitors or the spectator ships that will be dotting the routes here and there. But those are big, clunky cruise ships and I wouldn't hold my breath. If you get in trouble, just put yourself on the distress frequency, as Jim pointed out, and we'll try to determine your EP and come get you."

McCoy watched his captain intuitively. He knew what the problem was.

Race or not, competition, sport, fun and games or not, the lack of official safety nets meant that the Starfleet ships would be the lifeguards unofficially. Everyone would expect that.

Seeing the way Dodge and Kirk looked at each other and at the other two Starfleet captains, McCoy realized the raw joy of sport had just slipped an inch for these commanders, and the tempting danger just hiked up. He couldn't tell which of those two they would rather have—but he had a suspicion.

Then Nancy Ransom stood up.

"I still protest the participation of Starfleet," she insisted. "We were told this was a general public competition. Why weren't we told these enforcers were going to get to run the race?"

Suddenly uneasy, Orland shifted back and forth and rubbed his hands on his thighs, then held them out in a pacifying manner.

"Look, Nancy," he began, "even at this moment the Starfleet ships are being handicapped for just the reasons you're concerned about. They're in spacedock or box docks, being mechanically deprived of hardware advantages and having their power reduced across the board by twenty percent. They're big ships, but they'll have to swim with their legs tied. Don't know what more we can do for you."

"I do," she said bluntly. "It's not fair for us to have to go up against spacehawks like *him*."

She turned and thrust a pointed finger toward Jim Kirk.

Kirk's face took on the demeanor of the hawk she accused him of being. He shoved his command packet into McCoy's hands and stood up to face her.

"I'll be a good sport and shed my bars when my ship crosses the starting line," he said, "but until then, you watch your sportsmanship. Fairness doesn't get anybody anywhere. Every running river knows that. Some rocks get washed away. Some hold their ground and eventually they turn the river. Why run a race where everything's 'fair'? You'll never know how you really did."

The room fell silent.

There was wordless applause in the eyes of not just his Starfleet comrades, but in the eyes of other captains as well, who understood what he meant.

McCoy knew from past experience there was either adoration for James Kirk or hatred, but no middle ground.

And Nancy Ransom wasn't in the middle.

"I still think the starships shouldn't try to win," she barked.

Kirk's eyebrows flared.

"What you think," he snapped, "is your problem, Captain. I've got advantages, but so do you. You've got full power. This is a test of smarts as much as it's a test of ships. And it's supposed to be *sport*. The losers won't get executed, the winners won't gain ultimate power, so relax and get ready for a good hard game we'll all remember for the rest of our lives." He leaned forward on the table and spoke to her as though they were alone in the room. "Or withdraw now. Because I don't enter any race not to win."

Officers' Lounge

A vital place, somehow.

Carpeted, soundproofed, trimmed with cherry molding and rough-hewn ceiling beams, decorated with paintings—not pictures—of ships through the ages, from Federation planets far and wide.

But in spite of the heartwarming decor, it was the big viewing wall, a great clear wall divided only by the smallest and fewest possible support threads, which was the real attraction of the place.

McCoy strode in slowly, scanned the lounge, found what he was looking for, then crossed the spongy carpet and sat down in the lounge chair near the viewing windows.

In the chair beside him, feet up on the low window ledge, Captain James Kirk didn't move, glance, sigh, or in any way acknowledge that he wasn't alone anymore. He just kept gazing out the viewport, at the busy black canopy of open space. Gazing and grinning.

This wasn't like the dining room viewing windows that looked inward at the core of the starbase, the "inside", where ships were docked for tours and interior maintenance. This was the outer rim of the starbase, where the view outside was a view of space. This view stirred a cathedral reverence and a certain library quiet in the lounge.

Kind of like the difference between looking at a swimming pool and looking at an ocean.

Jim Kirk was looking at an ocean. A young man with electricity in his eyes. One side of his mouth was pulled up in that grin.

McCoy gazed briefly at the few other people milling quietly around the lounge, some also just sitting and looking out.

Some were captains. Some were people trying to get away from captains.

"So," he bridged, "what're you doing? Waiting to see a green flash?"

Kirk didn't move a muscle. He was looking up, out, and slightly to the left.

McCoy sat down next to him, pivoted in his chair, and followed Kirk's gaze. Together, they looked.

"That's how she was the first time I saw her," Kirk said. "Hovering in a box of lit-up red girders like some kind of living thing. Not a machine at all, Bones."

McCoy nodded. From below, the ship had a stirring effect upon the men who served her, who relied upon her, and who time after time had insisted she press on through the hell of space. A kind of courage seemed to glow from her white plates, with strips of shadow lying across her underside cast from the box dock's hexagonal struts. She looked as though she was almost breathing.

"How did it go in there after I left?" Kirk asked.

McCoy blinked at the sound of his captain's voice. "Hmm? Oh . . . you mean after you strode out, leaving your handprint on Nancy Ransom's face? What is it with you and her anyway?"

"She hates me."

McCoy crossed his legs and scowled. "Does anybody besides us *like* you?" he drawled. "How far do we have to go into space before we find somebody whose eggs you haven't cracked?"

Kirk shrugged. "She washed out of the Academy. She was in my command competition team. Blamed me for bad leadership."

"Was she right?"

The captain smiled devilishly. "Who knows? Not even the Academy can replace hard experience. I might've been 'perfect' back then, by the book, but I wasn't 'good.' A few years ago, I told Ransom that. But it didn't help.

She hates my guts, and she's not going to stop. So if that's how she wants to play the game, that's how I'll play it."

He sounded casual, and a lot more indestructible than McCoy knew he was.

"Don't worry, Bones," he said, "It's just a race."

The doctor didn't buy it. "It is when you say it fast."

Without looking at him, Kirk said, "Ships have been racing for centuries. It's a tradition. That's what made me accept the invitation. Even the fishing vessels out of Gloucester or Portugal had to race. They raced to be the first back to port. It wasn't the fullest ship that got the best price—it was the fastest."

"Want me to find you a pipe to smoke? Take your boots off. That story would sound better if you had bare feet."

Kirk chuckled. "I can see myself whittling on the corncob pipe now. Open that folder," he said, "and see if there's a manifest of ships and masters."

"It's right on top." The doctor dug into the leather packet, and handed the paper toward Kirk.

But the captain didn't move, didn't look away from his ship. He leaned back and sipped a drink. Looked like ice water.

"You still on duty?" McCoy asked.

"Until fourteen hundred. Read the list off to me."

"Oh." McCoy sat back awkwardly. "Well, all right, let's see here. It starts with Helmut Appenfeller commanding the *Drachenfels,* flagged for Colony Drachenfels—I remember when that ship was launched. It's a German legend or Norwegian. Means 'Where the dragon fell.' Somebody killed a dragon, and that's where they built a town or dug a hole or something. Course, if there was a dead dragon lying there, I'd dig a hole too."

"So would I," the captain chuckled. "Read, man, read."

"I'm reading, Jim, don't be a midshipman. Buck Ames, *Haunted Forest,* a private yacht . . . Hunter, *Dominion of Proxima* from Proxima Beta . . . Sue Hardee on *Thomas Jefferson,* Federation Museum Ship . . . Lar

—Legarr . . . Leg-something in command of *Orion Union* . . . Nancy Ransom, *Ransom Castle,* from Ransom Carnvale Interstellar Mining Company . . . Ben Shamirian, *Gavelan Star,* private explorer . . ."

"Yes," Kirk said. "Good to have friends in the line-up."

"Yup, nothing like beating the drawers off an old friend. What else've we got here . . . Leo Blaine—isn't he Starfleet retired?"

"If so, it's before my time."

"You're only thirty-six. Everything is before your time. I think he retired as a decorated captain. They offered him a starship, but he turned it down and went off on this thing he calls—"

"Cynthia Blaine. Named after his mother. Flagged for the company she started."

"Why did you ask me to read you this list if you already memorized it?"

The captain grinned. "I like the sound of your voice."

"Who's this Ian Blackington? Says 'private.' Must be a yacht."

"No yacht," Kirk said, sounding slightly offended. "Working ship. Merchantman. At least, that's the legal term for what he does."

"What's the illegal term?"

"Pirate."

McCoy cleared his throat, then found out he probably shouldn't make a comment on that, and retreated to the list. *"Alexandria,* Captain Pete Hall . . . I met him once."

"He's kind and capable," Kirk said. "Has a lot of finesse."

"Irimlo Si, from Zeon, Captain Loracon . . . *Bluenose IV,* Captain Mitchell Rowan, Earth . . . oh, this is interesting—I'd like to see this one myself. The Hospital Ship *Brother's Keeper* under Surgeon General Christoff Gogine. I didn't know that General Gogine was a licensed captain."

"He's not." Kirk leaned forward and peered suspiciously at a work pod as it approached and attached itself to the engineering section of the starship. "He's got a flight master who does the actual maneuvering. Gogine just gets the credit. That's one thing you'll find out, Bones. Credit is negotiable . . . blame isn't."

McCoy looked up.

"Now, where did that come from all of a sudden?"

The captain's expression suddenly changed as he eyed his ship. "Look at that ship, Bones. Look at her. Only twelve of those in the Fleet, only twelve people in the galaxy who get to drive them . . . and this time I get a chance to show her off. Win or lose, the *Enterprise* is going to be seen by people who only hear about her. The people who paid for her."

The doctor felt as though a curtain had parted and the mystery dropped away. In spite of the swaggering that went on when more than one ship's commander was in a confined space, in spite of having been dragged off patrol for what seemed at first to be a silly public relations game, Jim Kirk was looking forward to showing off his favorite girl.

All at once McCoy understood the captain's eagerness to participate, to seeing old friends, dressing the ship in rainbow fashion, soaking up a little appreciation and drenching the crew in some well-deserved merrymaking while somebody else faced off with the unknown for a while.

Kirk was looking forward to this. The best leave—a leave when he could enjoy the ship. No planets, no music, no women—well, maybe women. But most of all, the ship. Out in space where the public followed for a change, where attention of the Federation was focused on the starship, with tourists flocking by the boatload to have a look, the captain could do something very rare. He could puff up and show off, and nobody would expect anything else.

A ruddy pride flushed in the captain's face, and in his eyes too.

"Hm," the doctor sighed and went on skimming the

list. "That's a relief . . . deep space can do without us for a while. I could use a break from roughhousing with the warring Birdbathians as they clash with the Knobheads of New Wherever. Jim, look at this—seems a lot of these are ships representing systems or planets that I know for a fact don't have any spacefaring technology of the required tonnage and thrust yet."

"They're flagged for those systems. Like Argelius," Kirk pointed out. "They want to participate, so they hire a ship, muster a crew and captain, and put their flag on it. The Tellarites aren't coming at all, in spite of their insistence upon joining the Federation."

"Snubbing us, are they?" McCoy drawled. "Well, they've got the faces for it."

"The Klingons don't want anything to do with it either. They say competition without solid reward is a waste of time."

"Gosh, I'll miss them. Look at this—Charles Good-year the Ninth with a ship he calls *The Blimp*. Better be a fat ship." The doctor let the list drop into his lap and rubbed his eyes. "You know, I'm beginning to think there's nothing somebody won't name a ship."

"No one's done the S.S. *Rest in Peace*," Kirk tossed back. "Guess that's yours."

"No one's done the S.S. *Butter Cookie* either, but I wouldn't go scanning manifests. Jim, take your eyes off that ship before you go blind!"

The captain sighed and said, "I don't get to see her much, Bones. We spend all our time trying to get from here to there and live to tell it." He leaned forward and rested his elbows on his knees. "She's my ship . . . but I never get to see her from the outside."

"Never thought of that," McCoy admitted.

In contemplation they sat together for many seconds in silence, gazing at the starship, its shadows and its lights.

Then the captain said, "That's because you're not a sailor."

* * *

"Welcome back, everybody. We'll try to keep this session short. Lord knows I don't want to look at this collection of faces any longer than I have to."

John Orland pawed through his Race Committee information and huffed impatiently while a steward set up a computer access panel next to him.

Once again sitting beside Jim Kirk, Dr. McCoy ducked as two more stewards bumped past him, carrying a computer screen the size of a tabletop. They set up the screen while the last few captains settled back into chairs and the room calmed down again.

"Okay," Orland said, and clicked it on. "Take a look at this."

The screen came alive with a beautiful schematic of simulated open space. He clicked his panel a couple times until the picture was overlaid with pulsing lights in a jagged formation that only in a child's imagination could be called a line, and only because they started in one place and generally ended across the screen from there.

"This is a Klingon's-eye view of the racecourse," he said. "Now, it's just a representation! Don't go out there and start saying to your crew, 'Hey, on the picture the course went in that direction,' because this thing on the screen is just intended to give you a *general idea!* I mean, if we showed you what the actual course looked like, there wouldn't be any game here, right?"

He scanned the room with a schoolteacher glare until he got nods from most of the captains, but still didn't look satisfied when he jabbed a finger at the screen again.

"The point here is Starbase 16, where the starting line is." He indicated the only dot that wasn't blinking. "These other blinking lights are beacons put in place by Starfleet and the Race Committee. Basically, they spiral out from the starting line."

An old man with muttonchop whiskers and bright red cheeks laughed and rasped, "Bet them beacons ain't sittin' on lightships, right?"

"Hell, no!" Orland boomed. "They go right through

the middle of all this trouble and strife. Real tricky space, most of this, and the course is laid out to make use of all the tricks. There are twelve beacons altogether. Each one has a different frequency. At the starting gun, we'll give you the frequency of only the first beacon. When you're within a hundred thousand kilometers of it, you broadcast your ship's recognition code, and the beacon will log your arrival and transmit the frequency for beacon number two. When you're within a hundred thousand kilometers of beacon two, you'll get the frequency of beacon three, and so on. So don't try to skip a beacon, or you'll be totally lost, not to mention disqualified. We've done all we could to tricky-up finding the beacons. It's gonna be like being in a canyon and somebody rings a bell. You'll have to decide which is the echo and which is the real sound. The faster you go into warp speed, the more the distortion. The course goes in a spiral that bends way out, then comes back to the finish line, so don't assume you can just head for the finish line and win. You can follow somebody else, but there's no guarantee that guy won't be on a wild-goose chase himself. You're gonna have to use crazy thinking, wild guesses, deceit, subterfuge, lies, witchcraft, and my mother's knitting patterns to get those signals."

"'Scuse me, John?"

"Yes, Ian?"

Everybody looked at Ian Blackington as he asked, "What if nobody can find every beacon?"

Orland shrugged. "Let's just hope we didn't make it *that* hard!"

A sporting roar of camaraderie lifted across the room. Bantering threats and jokes rippled in a dozen directions.

"Hey, it's the first time we've done this," Orland said. "Maybe it'll be perfect at the *next* starship race, right?"

More laughter.

McCoy took the moment to glance at Kirk, but the captain gave him a bastard wink and didn't say anything.

"After beacon number twelve," Orland went on, "head straight for Gullrey. The finish line is between two committee markers. First ship between them wins," he said, pointing at the far right of the screen.

He scanned the faces of the captains.

A pale woman in a bright red robe grinned cattily and asked, "What do we win?"

"You get to be Byorn's bosun for a week," Ken Dodge said, flashing a grin at a Norwegian man in back, who shook a fist and grinned back at him.

"His *personal* bosun," the woman accepted, and waved at the Norwegian.

McCoy leaned to his side. "Who's that woman?"

"No idea," Kirk responded. "Look at the list."

Trying to be subtle, the doctor scanned the list, but was confounded by aliens' names. "Zeon, maybe?" he whispered. "Or Lauru ifan Ta from New Malura."

"Not Zeon," Kirk said. "Zeon's in the far corner. Gray uniform."

"What about Eliior—Eminiar. Say, weren't we there once?"

"Shh," the captain snapped.

They fell silent as John Orland raised his hand. There was something between his thumb and forefinger.

"You get this," he said.

He held the small item up before them for a moment, then brought it down to be scanned by the computer panel, and the screen changed abruptly. Now it showed a fairly accurate picture of his hand holding a gold coin with rough edges, a royal crest on one side, and a bird on the other.

"A little chunk of gold?" Ian Blackington boomed. "I wouldn't cross my bathtub to sell that!"

Orland smiled and waited for the chuckling to stop. "You don't *sell* it, flybrain, your sponsor *possesses* it. Until the next race."

"When's that?" Kirk spoke up.

"We don't know yet. A year, five years—depends how this race goes."

"Well, what is that thing?" Blackington pursued.

"This," Orland said, "is a doubloon. It was part of the

treasure found aboard the galleon *El Sol,* sunk off Spanish Wells in the Abaco Islands of the Bahamas just as it left for Spain. Spanish Wells, the last place where the Conquistadors could get fresh water before crossing the Atlantic. It's theorized that their heavy coffers of water contributed to the ship's turning over in a storm. Possibly a white squall that they didn't see coming, because according to the way the spars were arranged, there's evidence that the vessel went down in full sail. Apparently they didn't see trouble coming. They didn't reef in at all. For the benefit of you non-Earth people, that means pull their sails in part way," he added, nodding at the Andorian, the Orion, and a few other aliens.

McCoy leaned sideways and grumbled, "As if all the Earth people know what it means."

"Treasure hunters looked for *El Sol* for almost a hundred fifty years, until it was found nearly a thousand miles from where it was thought to have gone down. Tales of a great treasure kept the hunters going decade after decade. Lives were lost, techniques invented, fortunes risked, to find this ship . . . and they did find it. All that was recovered other than the ship itself, ladies and gentlemen, was this single gold doubloon."

Empathic silence fell across the dining room.

Jim Kirk's brows drew into an expression that could've been anger in another situation. "Nothing else?"

"Not a thing else."

"That's mighty sad," the old man with the mutton whiskers said.

"It's sad," the race committeeman agreed. "They figure the ship was plundered by natives, because it went down in less than forty feet of water. Would've been easy to find, if anybody had been looking there. Nobody did. It's been in private hands until now, and the team who found it wanted to do something encouraging with their one little find from Earth's seafaring age. They didn't want to just put it in a museum. Didn't seem a fitting memorial to all those who risked everything to find a treasure that wasn't there. So here it is. The purse of the Great Starship Race . . . our doubloon."

He held the gold piece before them for a moment longer, then placed it in a purple velvet bag. Then he put the bag into a magnetically sealed box. A burly Starfleet guard stepped out of nowhere, and Orland handed the box to him.

Orland cleared his throat, gazed at the collection of ship's masters from the far reaches of space, and nodded as though finally satisfied.

"Good luck, everybody," he said. "Let the race begin."

THE
STARTING
GUN

RACE MANIFEST

VESSEL	COMMAND	FLAG
Drachenfels	Helmut Appenfeller	Colony Drachelfels
Haunted Forest	Buck Ames	Private
Dominion of Proxima	Hunter	Proxima Beta
Ytaho	Legarratlinya	Orion Union
Ransom Castle	Nancy Ransom	Ransom Carnvale Int. Mining Co.
Gavelan Star	Ben Shamirian	Private
Cynthia Blaine	Leo Blaine	BlaineAerospace Inc.
New Pride of Baltimore	Miles Glover X	Baltimore, Maryland, United States, Earth
Blackjacket	Ian Blackington	Private
Irimlo Si	Loracon	Zeon
Bluenose IV	Sinclair Rowan	Canada, Great Britain, Earth
U.S.S. Hood	Cpt. Kenneth Dodge	Starship, Starfleet
U.S.S. Enterprise	Cpt. James Kirk	Starship, Starfleet
U.S.S. Great Lakes	Cpt. Hans Tahl	Frigate, Starfleet
U.S.S. Intrepid	Cpt. T'Noy	Starship, Starfleet
Brother's Keeper	Christoff Gogine	UFP Hospital Ship
The Blimp	Charles Goodyear IX	Goodyear Inc.
Unpardonable	Lauru ifan Ta	New Malura
Thomas Jefferson	Sue Hardee	UFP Museum Ship
Eienven	Thais	Andor, Epsilon Indi
Alexandria	Pete Hall	Alexandria, Virginia, United States, Earth
Yukon University	James Neumark	Yukon University, Earth
Specific	Im	Melkot Sector
552-4	Kmmta	Tholus
Chessie	Samuel Li	C & O Spaceroads Inc.
Valkyrie	Bjorn Faargensen	Skol Brewery, Rigel IV
River of Will	Eliior	Braniian College, Eminiar
Forbearant	Steve Daunt	Argelius
Ozcice	Sucice Miller	Host entry

NOTE: LIST MAY BE INCOMPLETE. OTHER ENTRIES EXPECTED.
SOME COMMANDS MAY CHANGE ALSO. PICK UP FINAL MANI-
FEST FROM RACE COMMITTEE AT STARTING LINE. THANK YOU.

Chapter Two

U.S.S. Enterprise

"WELCOME ABOARD, CAPTAIN,"

The distinguished baritone voice warmed the bridge and blended so naturally with the blips and whirrs of the starship's command center that James Kirk and his ship's surgeon almost forgot to respond.

Dr. McCoy blinked as the two of them paused on the quarterdeck and heard the turbolift doors gasp shut behind them.

Kirk inhaled as though to draw in the aroma of the bridge, looked at the forward viewscreen's breathtaking picture of the box dock girders as they peeled away, then he turned to their right.

"Thank you, Mr. Spock," he said. "Ship's condition?"

A bit of the night came toward them from the upper bridge.

First Officer Spock was ten legends in one—not all from the same planet. Triangular eyes and upswept black brows, olive complexion, and ears that came to points, all framed by the black Starfleet collar and blue Science Division shirt. Even for McCoy he was an oasis of familiarity on the bridge.

With a twinge of annoyance, McCoy noted how incomplete any starship's bridge would seem to him without a Vulcan hovering about.

A light from the ceiling glowed in a purple band across Spock's slick black hair as he approached them with his hands clasped behind his back.

"Leaving spacedock as ordered, sir," he said. "Preparing to leave the jurisdiction of Starbase 10 and set course for Starbase 16. All propulsion and maneuvering systems are down by nineteen percent. Despite his somewhat understandable disgruntlement, Engineer Scott is striving for the extra one percent, as requested by the Race Committee for Starfleet vessels. Sensors are reduced to merchant level, as are any other applicable systems. A complete report is in your office, ready for review."

"Thank you again," the captain said.

"And the host observers have been beamed aboard and issued guest quarters."

Kirk's glare sharpened. "The *who?*"

"Host observers. Every ship has at least one citizen of Gullrey on board, as specified by the Federation diplomatic corps."

"Since when?"

Spock frowned as though he didn't understand the question. His voice had a shrug in it. "Since twelve hundred thirty hours, sir."

McCoy bit his lip on a snide remark and waited.

"Who are these individuals?" Kirk asked, somewhat sharply.

If Spock was disturbed at all by the tone, it was only with a faint curiosity.

"Their names," he said, "are Royenne, Osso, and Tom."

"All right, if we have to have them on board, I want them assigned two yeomen whose duties—" The captain paused and blinked at him. " 'Tom'?"

"Yes, sir."

"As in Tom Sawyer? Tom Jefferson?"

52

"Yes, sir," Spock said. "These people were highly enthusiastic and emotional upon joining the Federation. Tom took an Earth name several years ago."

McCoy leaned past the captain's shoulder and asked, "Why would he do a thing like that?"

Spock raised one eyebrow. "This culture had to be talked out of changing the name of their planet. They were debating among 'New Earth', 'Earthfar,' and, I believe, 'Earthvale.'"

"They shouldn't do that!"

"We did succeed in convincing them not to, Doctor, but only with the intervention of Captain Dodge, who is highly revered on Gullrey."

Moving from one band of shadow to another, Jim Kirk stepped away from them. He trailed his hand along the red rail that separated the upper bridge from the command center and gazed at the large forward screen, at the picture of distant space and the dozen vehicles peppering the vicinity of Starbase 10.

"Gullrey," he murmured.

The word settled peacefully around the bridge, and it seemed silly that anyone would want to change the planet's name from something so melodic.

Spock didn't follow him. "That is the English equivalent. Phonic only, and somewhat clumsy. The word appears in the Western alphabet as something quite other."

He stepped to his library computer console and waved a magician's touch over the controls, then looked up. A series of letters appeared on one access screen.

d g u i b b e a l e a i c h a i e r e u w

"That's the name of their planet?" the captain commented. "And it's pronounced Gullrey?"

"Call Scotty," McCoy said. "That looks like Gaelic to me."

"Observant," Spock agreed, "but I doubt Engineer

Scott is any more proficient in ancient Celtic linguistics than you are in Middle English."

McCoy pressed his lips. "Spock, you're the only man who can give a compliment and take it back in the same breath. What do these people look like?"

"I have yet to encounter them personally," Spock said as he cleared the screen. "The developmental parallels are remarkable regarding the arts and sciences, though much slower. Their flight and space programs took nearly seven hundred Earth years to reach low warp capabilities, while Earth took less than a century and a half."

"Captain," a resonant voice interrupted from the back of the bridge. As the three turned, Lieutenant Uhura's exotic eyes swept over them from the communications station. "I'm receiving coordinates from the Starbase, sir."

"Those are for the starting line-up at Starbase 16, Lieutenant," Kirk said. "Log and acknowledge."

"Aye-aye, sir, logging."

"Then feed them through to the helm."

"Aye, sir." She played her equipment lightly, then nodded at the Oriental lieutenant at the helm. "Mr. Sulu, can you confirm for me?"

Using his hand like a pointed spade, Sulu stabbed his controls with the abruptness of a construction worker. His method was very different from the coaxing touch of Uhura or the fluidity of Spock, but the machines happily purred in response.

"Confirmed," he said, "and laid in."

"Clear us with the dockmaster," the captain said. "Prepare to leave the Starbase area. It's very crowded around here today, Mr. Sulu, so be aware of all-points incursion into our drift sphere. Uhura, broadcast intent on merchant channels and make sure none of those other ships are moored in the departure lanes. I don't want to clip some amateur's tail section as we pull out."

Sulu barely nodded. "Aye-aye, sir."

Uhura echoed him so closely that the sounds blended

and almost camouflaged the breath of the turbolift doors as they opened and closed at the back of the bridge.

The captain turned to Spock and leaned a leg on the bridge rail.

"Now, Mr. Spock," he said, "why don't you tell me what happened twelve years ago that started all this?"

McCoy stood beside the captain and glared at Spock, hoping the Vulcan would feel on the spot, but the first officer didn't respond. He simply gazed between them at the turbolift vestibule.

Together the captain and the doctor turned, and they too stared at the back of the bridge at three beings, not quite human.

"Oh, Captain," one being said, "can't *we* tell you?"

Three shadows of humanity's past, gentle biped ghosts of humanoid ancestry. Clothing of different styles, complexions and haircuts all different, but the expressions all alike.

Adulation, anticipation. Joy.

Their most striking characteristic was their eyes—very large, with almost no whites showing, like the light-catching eyes of a horse or a deer.

His medical background gurgling with delight, McCoy noted right away that the bridge lights didn't seem to bother these newcomers. Of course, the bridge wasn't all that bright. Still, he was instantly curious about the evolution conditions that produced these people.

The one who had spoken had shaggy wheat-blond hair that licked at his shoulders and made his dark brown eyes very obvious. His squarish face was bright and changed expression almost by the second. Delight bubbled his cheeks and his lips trembled around a nervous smile. He was moving toward Kirk as though he thought the bridge would crack under him.

"Captain," he gasped. "I'm so honored to be here!"

He put his right hand out easily—either he'd been practicing or handshakes had been adopted on Gullrey along with other Earth habits.

Kirk took the hand. "Welcome aboard, Mister——"

"I'm Tom. Please call me Tom . . . do you like it? I tried to choose a friendly name."

Feeling as though he'd suddenly opened a nursery, Kirk stabbed a glance at Spock, then said, "Yes, I like it very much. It's what we call an old-fashioned name."

Tom turned rosy with pride and asked, "What's your name?"

After another pause, Kirk said, "Jim. And this is my first officer, Commander Spock, and our ship's surgeon, Leonard McCoy."

Tom didn't grab for Spock's hand, but he did manage to get ahold of McCoy's.

Only now did McCoy notice that the Gullrey people were all fairly tall and somewhat gangly. That and their delight seemed their only common trait. Tom was the fairest one, while the other ones had black and chocolate brown hair respectively, and their clothes were all different. The two lagging back were wearing some kind of long shirt—not exactly tunics—and the black-haired one had a baggy knitted vest with pockets.

Tom's clothes could have come off the rack at any wilderness outfitter back on Earth—a red-and-black buffalo plaid shirt, blue jeans with suspenders, and moccasins.

He saw McCoy looking at his clothes, and grinned. "Catalog service. Mountain man clothes. Did I get it right?"

McCoy laughed and suddenly relaxed. "You got it right for any mountain I've ever been on, that's for sure."

"These are my associates," Tom said, and motioned the other two forward. He gestured first to the one with black hair and the vest. "This is Royenne, and that is Osso. We're proud to be guests on a starship. To be able to ride on a ship like the one that ended our loneliness——"

"You said you'd like to tell me about that," Kirk prodded. "Why don't you start now. We'll all listen."

Tom looked at his two friends, who silently encouraged

him to move forward start talking. Tom swallowed a few times, as though the story was too wonderful and he didn't deserve to be telling it. Only when he realized the eyes of all were on him—at least for the moment while departure arrangements were being cleared—he nodded and forced himself to speak.

His English was flawless, yet he treated it like a golden charm discovered in the dark.

"We live far out in space," he said, "in a lonely sector of the galactic arm, well past your farthest starbase. We have a very unimaginative sun, and only lifeless rocks orbit it. We crawled up through evolution, then through many halting civilizations to an age where our science matched our visions of hope, and we looked into the sky. We reached to the nearest planets in our system but found they were rocks. We sent robotic probes into deep space to see if anyone else was out there and to beg for a response."

Osso prodded, "Tell them about the stories, Tom."

"Yes, we wrote stories," Tom said. "Thousands of tales about space travel and meeting alien life and what it would be like the first time. It was the most popular mode of literature for almost a century. Since first our long-range telescopes peered into the unthinkable reaches, our children went to bed with toy spacemen."

If Tom was unsure of himself, he wasn't unsure of his tale and its quality. His smooth maple-sugar face took on a flush of excitement.

Definitely red blood . . .

McCoy found himself smiling at the visitor's un-quenched enthusiasm, and saw the captain smiling beside him.

And everyone else was smiling too. Even Spock had a subdued smile on his face and a glimmer in his eyes as he brought his arms around to the front and folded them across his chest.

Tom saw the motion and might have been intimidated, because he paused for a breath before going on.

"It was all through our culture—in our minds, in our

hopes, our hearts—every day it was with us. We were so sure there was someone to hear our call that we spent our work time preparing and our spare time making fantasy visits in our books and papers, so we would be ready to participate in interstellar culture! For decades we reached and probed and called," he finished on one breath, "but in nearly two centuries of hope, we saw . . . not one sign of life."

The three aliens' big soggy eyes blinked sadly. The smiles around them faltered.

Tom shook his head. "We had lost many adventurous crews in the attempt to fly to nearby stars, but they found . . . nothing. After lifetimes of spinning fabulous tales of space travel and alien meetings, of straining to unify our nations in order to be ready, our dream began to starve."

Now glad to be standing a little behind the captain, McCoy instinctively battled down a shiver of empathy and thought he saw Uhura do the same. Just empathy—just Tom's ability to spin a story. Beside him, he saw the captain go tense, and he sensed they were all taking this too hard.

"We mourned heroes lost in the attempt to reach out," Tom said, "for they had apparently died for nothing. The sacrifice lost its nobility and became too much for us to bear. Literature of space travel died away. Enrollment in space science fell off. Funding of out-system exploration dissolved. Planetwide disappointment settled over us."

"The story must get better," McCoy interrupted, desperate to make the cold feeling go away. "After all, we're here."

Tom's large eyes swept to him. "Yes! You are here. You came to us and you answered us . . . one day, in the last decade of our interest in space, when there was only one little outpost left listening. The last outpost . . . they heard an answer and thought they were imagining what they heard." He spread his lanky arms and said, "It was a call from a race calling themselves the Hood."

Decorum folded and laughter broke out on the bridge.

"The 'Hood'!" Sulu repeated.

"I like that!" Ensign Chekov burst from beside him at navigation.

The three aliens smiled as though they were about to boil over, and seemed overwhelmed by the welcome they'd received here.

And the feeling of cold loneliness melted into sudden community warmth.

"Does that make us the 'Enterprise'?" Sulu said. "What would you call us?"

Tom fell silent for an instant, then stepped down to the command deck. With three of his long fingers he touched the point of the helmsman's shoulder.

"You," he began, "who were devoted to seek out distant and lonely cultures like ours. You, who appeared before us in a brilliant white ship . . . who were bold enough, who were confident enough in yourselves to answer our tiny fading call . . . you, who are generous enough to make the Rey part of yourselves . . . what should we call you?"

Sulu gazed at him uneasily, not moving a muscle.

Tom's eyes glowed, then creased with smile lines.

"We call you saviors," he said.

Chapter Three

Approaching the Starting Line at Starbase 16

"Yellow alert. Yellow alert. All hands to battle stations. Prepare for emergency action. All hands to battle stations."

James Kirk skidded around a corner and down the corridor of his own ship, gratified in this moment of emergency to see his crew leap to action. There were times when running was a good idea, if only to bring the crew to the right mental level for what they might have to do.

He plunged into the turbolift and the doors closed behind him. He grasped the control handle and turned it.

"Bridge," he said.

The lift surged through the veins of the starship, a ship within a ship, carrying the lifeblood of decision to the place where he would decide. But for these few moments, he was the least active person in his crew of nearly five hundred.

Least active except for his mind. In his mind he was preparing for the wildest, the most horrid, the most draining of possibilities, for any of those might be awaiting him on the bridge. This turbolift ride would be his last peace, until events came to an end under his phasers, under his fists, or by strength of will.

Yellow alert from a Starbase this far out could mean any of a dozen problems. Structural breach, terrorist activity—and with a fleet of racing vessels pushing for position, last minute supplies, anything might happen. Collision, power loss, dispute. Whatever did happen, a starship in the vicinity had authority over starbase administration.

That means me. Me and the other Starfleet masters, if anyone else is here yet.

And a call for battle stations was mystifying, as much as the mustering of all hands on deck.

Those could only come from Spock.

He could buzz the bridge and get details, but he stayed his hand from the comm panel and let his adrenaline build, his senses sharpen, the tension rise. Whatever was happening, he would never assume it was nothing, maybe just a mistake, somebody's bad judgment. Starbases were run almost as efficiently as starships, but still there was that added danger—accessibility. Starbases could be visited with little more than a request. Starships were private terrain. The captain's terrain.

Anticipation boiled in his chest until his uniform shirt felt tight around his ribs. When the turbolift slowed and the doors blew open, he felt as though he were being shot out of a cannon.

He dropped to the center deck and put his hand on his command chair. "Status, Mr. Spock?"

"Approaching Starbase 16 at warp factor four, Captain," the Vulcan said from where he bent like a vulture over his readouts. "ETA, twenty-eight minutes current speed. They report an enemy presence."

"Enemy?" Kirk turned. "We're not at war, Mr. Spock."

Spock straightened and faced him. "Apparently there is a vessel of hostile configuration approaching the starbase at high warp. Contestant ships and others are scattering. I requested specification. No response as yet."

"Go to warp five."

"Warp five, sir," Sulu echoed. "Revised ETA, thirteen minutes, ten seconds."

Kirk settled into his chair and gestured over his shoulder to Uhura. "Broadcast general alert of our approach and recognition codes, Lieutenant. Warn off any trouble."

"Aye, sir," she said. A moment later, her melodic instructions to the starbase provided an undercurrent to all other sounds on the bridge.

"Scanning the area," Spock said. "Picking up movement from several vessels."

"Broadcast a regional all-stop. See if they comply. Give me a visual on the hostile as soon as you can."

"Yes, sir."

"Identify exhaust emissions of every ship you can pinpoint. Get me a list of power ratios. I want to know who's there. Winnow out any non-Federation presence in the sector."

Spock nodded, this time to Ensign Chekov, who had been looking at him, knowing at least half of those orders would be his to fulfill. A moment later, both of them were hovering over the science stations on the bridge's starboard side, struggling to make use of the ship's diminished sensor capabilities.

Frustrating. Kirk watched them, empathizing. Still, starship personnel were trained to deal with whatever they had, even if it was a twenty percent power down.

He felt the struggle in the ship itself as she gathered as much power as she could find and funneled it into the warp-five order. Not quite full speed, and she was already sweating.

He knew she was . . . because he was.

Eying his science specialists, seeing their frowns and glowers, their shoulders go tense over instruments that should've had the answers within the first ten seconds, he tried to think up more for them to do. Something that would give him a clue about what was going on in such a way that he wouldn't have to hail the starbase for answers.

He wanted to know the answers already when he hailed them. It was one of his tricks. Know the answer before you're supposed to.

He wanted that answer.

Repressing an urge to get up and go stand behind them as they worked, Kirk grilled them with a silent glare—and they felt it, he could see that. The sounds of the bridge had slightly intensified. The Rey guests wouldn't have noticed if they'd been here, but the captain did, and he knew the bridge crew did, too. That information was being yanked into the starship's system through reluctant power grids and a damning distance.

Chekov stepped over to Spock and for a moment their heads were together over a monitor, then Spock straightened and snapped an order. Chekov dropped from the upper deck to stand beside the captain's chair and brave the expression Kirk could feel on his own face.

"Sir," the young Russian began, "twenty-three vessels identified by intermix exhaust, including twelve capable of thrust above warp four. No Starfleet vessel identified as yet," he went on, struggling past his halting accent, "so Mr. Spock concludes we will be the only starship present at the moment."

"I'll assume that. Go on."

Chekov looked at Spock.

The Vulcan stepped to the rail and gazed down. "Subspace intermix formula readings suggest several definitions of thrust engineering, and I have isolated ships that I deem unfamiliar to Federation emission control. Those would be the Melkot vessel, the Andorian vessel, the New Malurians, and two others that I can pinpoint but not identify. Of vessels now moving both away from and toward the Starbase, I'm picking up one level of emission residue that the computer correlates with an intermix formula currently being used by the Klingons."

Kirk glowered at him, then at the forward screen. "Klingons?" In his mind he saw Starbase 16 dangling out there in the invisible distance. It made a lovely picture except for the crane-in-flight ship speeding in from another place, its wings angled back, its long neck and the bubble on the front somehow threatening just by pointing toward the starbase. It angled in without invitation, to a place where it didn't belong, at a time when it wasn't wanted. He couldn't see it yet, but it was out there. He knew, because Spock told him it was. That was enough to start him stewing.

Spock's steady face bore an untrusting scowl as he, too, gazed at the forward screen. Kirk knew they were looking at the same picture in their two minds.

"Klingon design, Captain," Spock agreed, "but the emission ratio is eight percent richer."

James Kirk pushed himself out of his command chair, and his teeth clenched tight. "Romulans."

The other side of trouble. As aliens went, Klingons were temperamental, surface-thinking, hot-blooded and gruff, and could be outthought and outfought by someone who kept his cool. Romulans were stiff, mean, quick on the trigger, but cunning. They would outlast someone trying to outlast them. Cool judgment made them formidable.

Suddenly Kirk felt betrayed, his peace and everyone else's blowtorched. The Great Starship Race had been robbed of its luster before it even had a chance to begin.

He glared at the forward screen, pacing back and forth behind the navigation and helm consoles. He knew Sulu and Chekov were deliberately not turning, not looking at him, because the atmosphere here had become so suddenly tense.

"Red alert," he said. "Maintain general quarters. Plot an intercept course."

The lights on the bridge changed. Everything went rosy and more active. Alert panels on the bulkheads went from amber to red and flashed faster. Uhura's voice pounded through the vessel.

"Red alert . . . all hands maintain battle stations . . . this is not a drill."

Like his ride in the turbloft, the next few minutes were grilling frustration. Kirk wanted to be there already, to know what was happening, to stand over a dangerous situation and demand that it hold itself together.

"Approaching the vicinity of Starbase 16, sir," Sulu reported. "Contacting several vessels vacating the area."

"Enhance magnification, Mr. Sulu."

"Aye, sir. Full magnification."

Race vessels, spectator ships, touring yachts, cruise ships—vessels of every purpose and design suddenly shot toward them like some kind of interstellar boat show. No—as though somebody had set off a bomb at a boat show. Kirk read panic in the trajectories of these ships, heading out toward nothing in particular, just away from the starbase, shooting past the *Enterprise* without even the simplest of ship-to-ship signals. There should've been an industrial grandeur here, but in fact, for James Kirk there was only a sense of overcrowding and a knowledge that whatever he did, success or mistake, would involve all these ships.

A situation that could be instantly ugly, dozens of ships beating for the rear, seeing the starship racing past them to brace the storm . . . a hobbled starship . . .

A minute later there were fewer ships, and the starship was briefly alone.

"Starbase 16 on visual, Captain," Sulu said, and adjusted the magnification to show the beautiful light-dotted spool of the starbase floating in the middle of nothing.

"Spock, anything?"

"Incoming vessel is unshielded, Captain, weapons systems off-line. They are broadcasting interstellar truce. It is your choice, of course, whether to believe them."

"Confirm shields up."

Sulu glanced down to see what he already knew was there. "Shields are up, sir."

"Arm phasers."

"Phasers armed, sir."

"Continue intercept course, Lieutenant," Kirk said, relying on tone and innate familiarity with his crew to tell them all which lieutenant he was talking to. "Demand that they full-stop immediately, or reverse course. If they encroach Federation territory any further, we will open fire."

"Aye, sir," Uhura said. She made the broadcast with interstellar codes, but they all knew she was simultaneously sending the same message in computer translation in the Romulan language as well as Federation linguists had been able to piece it together.

"Contact, Captain!" Sulu said suddenly. "They're reducing speed . . . coming to full-stop, sir . . . there they are."

A Romulan battlecruiser, caught just close enough to the starbase that both it and the starbase showed at opposite ends of the big screen. Not the little bird-of-prey fighter type, but the big, long-necked design the Romulans had stolen from the Klingons and redesigned for stealth and bursts of power.

"Ship to ship, sir?" Uhura asked.

"Not yet."

Kirk prowled his command deck. His eyes never left the pale green ship hovering on his screen. He familiarized himself with every line, every running light wink, every shadow.

He would have felt better if the ship hadn't been aimed right into the heart of the starbase, as though it meant to fire up thrusters and ram its way through.

"Close the distance. Put us between them and the starbase. Stand them down."

"Closing distance, sir."

The Romulan ship grew larger and centered itself on the viewscreen like a piece of art in a frame.

"Come nose to nose with them, Mr. Sulu."

"Aye, sir."

The great sallow green ship angled toward them, head-on against the black of space. Kirk gazed at it, considering the present, unlikely circumstances. Under normal conditions, the *Enterprise* could have sent them begging, but powered down twenty percent, the other ship had any mechanical advantage it wanted to have.

That meant relying on other advantages.

"Ship to ship."

Around him he felt the crew putting on their resolute faces, hiding whatever they might have been feeling, determined that the Romulans not see a shudder, a blink, a flinch.

"The Imperial Subcommander, Captain," Uhura said, and swiveled to look at the screen just as it began to waver.

The Klingon-style vessel dissolved, and the picture formed into a severe face with all the expected elements, and a few unexpected ones—drawn angular brows shading carefully governed eyes, hair blown back and even a little shaggy, cheeks somewhat pale today.

"I am Subcommander Romar," he said. *"You have questions for me."*

"I'm James T. Kirk, commanding the *U.S.S. Enterprise*. What is your purpose here?"

"We come under the order of my commander, who wishes to greet you in person, on your starbase. We have deactivated our weapons, as requested by your starbase personnel."

"We have no treaty with you," Kirk said bluntly. "You don't want one. When you do, then you can start making requests to approach, and not before. Do you have an emergency?"

"There is no emergency," the Romulan admitted. *"May we approach the starbase and speak with you personally?"*

"Why won't your commander speak with me here and now?"

The subcommander shrugged. *"He has an arbitrary*

67

habit of wanting to look into the eyes of others. He doesn't like viewers. It's a habit I must deal with. After all, he is my commander. Please let us approach, Captain."

Kirk sensed more than tension on the other side. The subcommander's voice was relaxed, his posture rounded, a certain yearning in his gaze.

Kirk followed his instinct and said, "Keep your shields down, your weapons off-line, and your engines powered down to point five sublight. Follow us in, and we'll arrange for a mooring. Our weapons are armed and we won't be taking a mooring. We'll be ready to act on the half-second if there are any aggressive or destructive moves. I want your commander ready to talk to me within five minutes of my direct order."

"I will tell him," the Romulan said without pause. *"He will explain our presence."*

"That's right. He will. *Enterprise* out."

The screen faded back to the view of the Romulan ship, but somehow Kirk had the lingering sensation that he was still being watched.

"Clear with the dockmaster, Mr. Spock. But specify that we won't be taking a mooring. We're at red alert. Lieutenant, hail the starbase, code five."

"Aye, sir," Uhura responded, but drumming up such an uncommon code took her a few seconds longer than usual. The extra seconds proved she understood what he meant and would mask the communication with double and triple guards. If anybody was listening, they wouldn't hear much more than electrical whistles and coughs.

So listen if you want to, Kirk thought as he stared at that ship.

"Captain," Uhura said, "Helen Fogelstein, starbase magistrate, and Mr. Orland from the Race Committee."

"Visual."

"On visual, sir."

The screen changed so smoothly this time, moving between compatible systems instead of struggling with two separate technologies, that for an instant it looked as though John Orland had a Romulan ship growing out of his ear. Then it was just Orland and a very approachable-looking woman in her fifties with short black hair and a single worry line across her brow.

"Captain Kirk," she said, *"welcome to Starbase 16. I wish I could offer you peace and quiet."*

"We'll have peace and quiet, ma'am, if I have to get it at phaserpoint. What's going on? Why did you let that ship past your border outposts?"

"They came in broadcasting interstellar truce, and since they complied with all weapons deactivation regulations for approach, I had to let them come in."

"No, you didn't," Kirk told her casually. "The Federation isn't a candy store, Ms. Fogelstein. You have an entire starbase and three security outposts at your administration. You might consider reviewing the regulations manual regarding approach of non-treaty contacts. You shouldn't have to feel intimidated by anybody."

"But I didn't have any reason to turn them down. Part of our purpose for being out here is—"

"Part of the *advantage* of being out here," Kirk interrupted, "is the ability to act at your personal impulse regarding friction in non-self-governing regions. You've got the power, Ms. Fogelstein, and you should use it."

The woman blushed, swallowed a couple of times, sighed, and nodded. *"I wish I'd told them that."*

Kirk took a step forward and asked, "Mr. Orland, what do they want to talk to you about?"

Orland wasn't any more at ease than the magistrate. He shifted back and forth so nervously that the screen seemed to be swinging. *"They seem to want to join the race, Captain Kirk."*

"Join the race?" That was their story? A Romulan heavy cruiser moves across the neutral zone, and that was the best they could do?

He studied John Orland's face to see whether or not he bought that story. How offended would the Race Committee be if he laughed in their faces?

"Do you want them in the race?"

"No, not really."

"Why didn't you say so?" He let them squirm a few seconds, realizing his bridge crew was squirming too, with empathy. "Why didn't anybody speak up before the situation reached this point? You people shouldn't be waiting for a Starfleet presence before you drum up the resolve to act on the power you *do* possess." Too often that only leaves Starfleet with a disaster to clean up, he added silently. Clean-up wasn't the purpose of a starship as far as he was concerned, and he didn't like doing it.

The two people on the viewer suddenly dropped their helpless expressions for one of shame.

"I know that," Orland said. *"You're right, Captain. But they came in and now we're stuck with them. I know I'm the big shot from the Race Committee, but I'm a chemist by trade. What do I know about these kinds of people? I could give them a ruling and they'd blast my face off for not offering them the right interstellar nose-picking ritual or something. The only reason I'm on the Race Committee at all is that I run a youth rally on Rigel 12, and my brother-in-law is a UFP diplomat, and he wanted to get me back for not arranging for his kid to win. I mean, this is his idea of a good-natured joke, you know? Nobody ever said I'd have to deal with Romulans. Will you come over here and deal with them, please?"*

"I'm going to have to," Kirk said flatly. "Tell their commander to meet me in Ms. Fogelstein's office in ten minutes."

Ms. Fogelstein dropped some of the reddish terror out of her face, but still looked nervous about telling the Romulans they'd have to leave their ship and do the bidding of Starfleet, but she didn't argue or ask for a different arrangement.

"Thank you! she gasped. *"I'll tell them!"*

The screen dissolved to the view of the Starbase and the Romulan vessel, and Jim Kirk got a mental vision of what the *Enterprise* must look like to the Romulans. Big, white, armed, angry, and coming in at high warp—maybe they were having second thoughts too. Maybe he could play on that.

Eying the screen, he leaned back toward Spock and lowered his voice.

"They're not here to run a race," he droned. "I know that, you know that, and they know it."

Spock only nodded, and also watched the big intruder hovering there among all those race contestants.

"Do Romulans have kamikaze missions?" Sulu speculated from his helm. "All they'd have to do is open fire, and they'd cut up a dozen ships and a starbase before we could even blink."

Kirk glanced at him. "I assume that means you've plotted your firing pattern, Mr. Sulu."

"Oh—" Sulu blinked and grabbed at his controls. "Pattern plotted, sir. I'm sorry, sir."

"Rule number one, Mr. Sulu," Kirk said. "Never be too fascinated with the enemy."

"Yes, sir. It won't happen again."

Kirk watched for a few moments while the Romulan ship approached the starbase and was accepted by the mooring detail in what appeared to be a series of deceptively ordinary movements.

"Spock," he began tentatively, moving to the ship's rail and lowering his voice.

The Vulcan turned in his chair, and Kirk realized this was the first time today that Spock had sat down at his controls. Maybe this underlying twinge that things had been going a little too right and had to snap wasn't just in Kirk's command imagination.

Maybe Spock felt it too.

"Speculate," Kirk said. "What would Romulans want in all this open space? I understand that Starfleet pre-exploration charting reported almost nothing here worth having, and certainly not much worth fighting over. These Gullrey people, and that's about it, correct? No other notable star systems?"

"Few," Spock confirmed. "If Gullrey is accepted into the Federation, then the UFP gains access to an area of open space equal to eighteen percent of current Federation holdings. A very large acquisition, even if it is empty space with very little mining or strategic use. Even as colonization possibilities, the vastness of the area between Starbase 16 and Gullrey is substantial. The Romulans may not covet the area, but may simply be suspect of Federation purposes. That alone would be enough to make them wary. They may simply take our interest in the area as a reason to covet."

"They don't buy the idea of the Gullreys wanting to join us for their own betterment and protection."

"The Rey, sir," Spock corrected dryly. "And that is true."

Kirk leaned his back on the rail and pressed it with both hands, again glaring at the forward screen. He tried to talk himself into what he had just heard and what he had just said.

"I don't like this. This is piecrust diplomacy. It's pretty, but it crumbles. The Romulans aren't that stupid. There's something else going on. I don't like the fact that they happen to show up when the Starfleet vessels are hobbled. We'll be easy pickings if trouble erupts. Maybe they're looking for a reason to erupt."

Spock nodded. "This could be an opportunity for them to get into that sector without going to war with the Federation over it."

"Which leads me to ask," Kirk said slowly, "what the Romulans know about this sector that we don't." He grasped the arm of his command chair and nailed the comm panel. "Sickbay."

"Sickbay, Nurse Chapel."

"Get me Dr. McCoy."

"Yes, sir, one moment."

That one moment lasted thirty years. By the time it was over, Kirk was grinding his teeth.

"McCoy here."

"What took you so long?"

"A compound fracture, Captain," McCoy responded, sounding irritated at having to explain himself.

"Interns should be setting broken legs, Doctor, not you," Kirk barked. "I want an analysis of our Rey visitors from you. Physiology, anthropology, history, and any attraction they might have for Romulans."

"Romulans? What've they got to do with this?"

"They showed up at Starbase 16."

"Could it have something to do with the race? All those vessels gathered in one place?"

"I don't know. A race is supposed to be entertainment. Sportsmanship. Competition. It just became something else."

"Maybe they just want to be in the race. Use it as an excuse to have a look at us. Since we don't have anything to hide, then what's the harm?"

"I don't know," the captain repeated, his fists sweating at his sides. "But once the neighborhood bully shows up, you know the game isn't going to be fun anymore."

He knew the Romulans were here for some other purpose than curiosity about some competition or other, and there wasn't any clue yet. Clues had to be dug for, coaxed, weeded out, sometimes from between the nerve endings of people who should never have gotten so close to each other.

The Romulan ship could cut the *Enterprise* in half with the present power ratios, and he assumed they knew that. A spy, a cousin, a coaxed barmaid—information couldn't be held down, and no one had made any particular efforts to keep quiet the fact that the Starfleet ships were being handicapped for the race.

"Captain?"

"Yes, Mr. Spock?"

Well, he'd been expecting this.

"I do not mean to question your judgment," Spock began.

"Yes, you do, but go ahead anyway."

"Is it wise to offer them mooring? And I presume, since you did not decline, that you intend to meet their request of personal contact with their commander."

"I'm curious," Kirk admitted.

"And is it possible," the Vulcan added, "that you are curtailing their arc of movement by bringing them in?"

Kirk glanced at him, and a smile pulled at his mouth.

"That's right. Spock, contact our Rey guests down below and ask Tom if he or his planet has ever been approached or even scanned by Imperial ships to the best of his knowledge, and then I want to know how he thinks his planet will feel about hostile participation in the race."

Spock pulled himself away from the view on the screen with obvious effort.

"I assume you mean participation of hostiles," he said.

"You know what I mean."

"Yes, sir."

The computer's remote earpiece went in, and the Vulcan turned to his console. His deep voice murmured behind the bridge noises, short questions, terse and complete, efficient. Kirk watched and read his first officer's posture, as he had learned to during their years of service, and noted that Spock wasn't any more satisfied with the situation than Kirk was.

After not very long at all, the Vulcan swiveled in his chair and said, "The Rey guests have absolutely no awareness of any Romulan interests in their planet, economic, scientific, sociological, or hostile. No approaches whatsoever. In fact, Tom insists he has never heard of Romulans. However, he does mention that if the Romulans wish to join the race, the Rey have no compunction about their planet's open-armed welcome, but will defer to your judgment."

"Oh, wonderful," Kirk drawled. "Let's all try to handle the Romulans with valentine cards. See how well we do."

Spock raised a brow, frowned, and nodded. "I understand," he said.

Somehow that was comforting. Annoying, but comforting. Spock felt the same way, or at least knew what Kirk was feeling.

Just a race. Just an event for fun. For showing off and making dares. Just a race. That's all.

Now it was suddenly a breakable situation.

He turned to the viewscreen, which showed him the enormous Romulan ship, with several race contenders now warily returning to the area.

"I didn't come here as an umpire," he grumbled, "but I'll hold the scales if I have to. The Rey have bad judgment. It's unwise to reject basic caution. Spock, don't you have any hypothesis about this . . . presence?"

"I can only extrapolate on your own suspicions," he said quietly. "The Rey are somehow the key. Their advancement into space travel was suspiciously sudden, given the slowness of their cultural developments."

Kirk felt his brow tighten. "You mean . . . the Romulans might have tampered with the Rey already?"

Shifting fluidly from one foot to the other, Spock drew a long breath.

"Everyone tampers. Many cultures have joined the Federation and, by doing so, made a leap ahead that would otherwise have taken generations. Billions of lives have been saved which would otherwise have been sacrificed to the normal development of medicine and science."

Kirk grasped the rail and pivoted himself up onto the quarterdeck to Spock's side.

"But that's us, Mr. Spock. We're like that. That's our . . . way. We found out a long time ago that we all profit from it. If I didn't believe in it, I wouldn't be out here. But the Romulans—that's not their way. So why are they here?"

"Is it possible they have something hidden in this sector that they wish left undiscovered?" Spock offered.

Diane Carey

Kirk grew suddenly speculative and quiet.

"Anything is possible, Mr. Spock," he answered finally. "Especially where the Romulans are concerned."

Tribal masks, pub signs, and whiskey mirrors decorated Starbase 16's transporter room walls. Beaming in was like waking up from a nice neat dream into a travel brochure.

"—irk, I'm Helen Fogelstein."

She had her hand out toward him and was speaking even before the transporter process had cleared enough to let him hear her start talking.

Kirk stepped off the pad and scanned the room. "Looks as if somebody's been exploring."

"My husband and his brother," she said. She waved her hands as she talked. "They go all over. My office is right down the hallway. Mr. Orland is meeting the Romulan captain and taking him to a waiting room until you can get to my office. We're going to make him come to you, instead of the other way around. We thought that was kind of . . . would give you a psychological advantage."

"Good thinking. Did he come alone, or does he have guards with him?"

"Oh, no, we told him he'd have to come by himself."

"I wish you'd summoned that kind of resolve two hours ago."

"Oh, so do I, so do I. They didn't like it either, his coming by himself. But now that you're here it just seems easier to set conditions."

Her office was a muddle of decor, a pub sign here, a decorative egg there, a terra-cotta pig by the door. She offered him a seat, but he shook his head and she immediately understood. She waved her hand over a tea set whose pot was in the shape of a 1900s iron stove, but again he declined, determined to communicate that he was here for only one purpose and wanted to get it over with.

Finally Ms. Fogelstein shrugged and blinked, then

76

shrugged again, couldn't think of anything social to say, and tapped the communication unit on her desk. "Toby, have Mr. Orland bring the Imperial Commander in, please."

There wasn't any response, but Ms. Fogelstein didn't seem to think that was odd. She rubbed her hands together in a nervous manner, then held them out and shrugged again.

"I'm sorry about this," she said.

Ordinarily, Kirk would smile and let her off the hook, but he resisted. Anyone running a base this far out of the mainstream needed to learn how to handle the dangerously unexpected. He'd seen the remains of outposts who were unprepared in attitude or arms to deal with the antagonisms in sectors of space that could seem perfectly established, but become disputed at a stranger's whim. Apparently, Starbase 16 had been lucky until now.

As the hope fled in his mind that luck would not slack today, another door opened and John Orland appeared, markedly less lighthearted than the last time Kirk had seen him.

In that instant Kirk's reflexes got the better of him and he straightened his shoulders, flexed his arms, and inhaled. He knew the reaction was like a little boy defending a street corner, but it came out of him anyway. He wanted to appear as capable of subterfuge as honor. He wanted the Romulan to see him not as the ribboned commander, but as a swindler, a tactician, a manipulator, a human gauntlet. As whatever he had to be to get a rise out of him.

The Romulan leader was bearded like a medieval knight, neatly deported and dressed in unfamiliar gear, maybe an older style uniform, a simple blue jacket with amber trim and a sash over one shoulder. Or maybe it was just their version of off-duty clothes.

The two civilians stepped apart and the two commanders came together, gazing firmly, plumbing for vulnerabilities, finding damned few.

Jim Kirk stared at the face of his Romulan counterpart

and endured a thunderclap of distrust—and other things he couldn't quite define.

"Captain Kirk," the commander said fluidly. A mellow voice for his kind. "I've heard of you. A remarkable record for one so young."

"I'm backed by remarkable support, Commander," Kirk said. "What's your purpose here?"

The Romulan's eyes didn't falter—something the captain always looked for. "We heard of a great race. We demand the chance to participate."

"You demand?"

"Forgive me—poor choice of words. I stumble over your language from lack of practice. My people tend to learn harsh words first. May I request that we be allowed to participate in your race?"

Kirk turned his head a little, to allow for a sidelong glare. He parted his lips and slowly asked, "Why?"

The commander licked his lips and allowed—Was it shy candor?—to show through in the form of a smile.

"I see you aren't easily maneuvered, Captain. Would it help if I admit to you that my presence here is unsanctioned by the Empire?"

Kirk's gaze bore into the Romulan. "You breached Federation space on your own authority? Risked a death sentence from your own government just to run a race?"

Out of the corner of his eye, Kirk saw Orland and Ms. Fogelstein huddled together, backing away an inch at a time. The farther the better, as he closed the inches between himself and the commander.

"I'm going to ask you one more time," he said. "Why?"

The Romulan smiled in a reserved way, not really a smile so much as a tightening of the lips, an accenting of the cheekbones.

"There is no challenge left for me and those like me," the visitor said. "There are no questions, no conquests, no unknown territory in Empire space. All we have to do is to go around and around, Captain. As you see, I am no longer a young soldier, hot for adventure as I once was.

But I crave a challenge, one chance to go up against . . . legends." He made a consciously passive gesture toward Kirk. "I only want to run the race. Perhaps to push the boundaries of Federation thought about my kind . . . to know I have altered the galaxy just a little. I cherish the last challenge of my career and want it to be something other than . . . one more circle."

Caught for a moment between suspicion and his oath to break down barriers between cultures, Kirk felt thorns of denial pricking at him. He knew what had just become his obligation. Provide an example—be bigger than his reflexes, even bigger than his instincts. Be gallant. Be polite. Give the answer time to show itself.

"I don't believe your story," he said. "But for now, it'll do. If you and your ship qualify according to Race Committee specifications, and your ship is handicapped to the level of Starfleet ships, then I won't order you out of the sector."

"Order us? Captain, the race is being run in free space. You have no jurisdiction here."

Kirk handed him back one of those not-quite-smiles and added to it a half-swagger. "Want'a bet?"

The Romulan chuckled openly and said, "No, I would prefer not to make a bet with you."

"Believe me, Commander," Kirk stomped over the chuckle, "if I don't want you in that free space, you won't have time to run a race."

There were subtler changes logged away in his file of expressions to watch out for, but this Romulan was different a second later. A difference like the color of clouds deciding whether or not to rain.

"Understood," he said. "Accept my apology again."

Too fast.

Fast and personable, way too much. Starfleet would just have to make a new set of rules about dealing with smiles and quiet words that couldn't possibly be true.

"Report to the starbase maintenance dock for handi-capping. Keep all your personnel aboard. You stay here and sign up with the Race Committee. I want to know

Diane Carey

your ship's specifications, fuel and weapon capacity, and its name in the English equivalent."

"Yes," the commander said. "I will provide you with that information. My ship is called *Red Talon*. It happens to translate directly."

Kirk choked back a snide remark about the vicious nature of the ship's name,—a remark of the kind that no ship's master deserved, no matter how ragged a past between civilizations.

"And your name?" he asked.

"Oh, of course," the Romulan said. "My name is Valdus."

Chapter Four

Imperial Cruiser *Red Talon*

"ANSWER THEIR QUESTIONS. Be direct. Be very short, but be polite. Humans read politeness as a clue. I'll join you in a few minutes."

"Yes, Commander."

Valdus stood alone before the viewscreen as his ship's centurion went off to handle the committee regulations, to tell the humans what they needed to know and not one syllable more.

Until his eyes ached, he gazed at the gleaming white Federation ship, with its powerful warp drive nacelles and its glowing forward section hovering above the starbase and above him.

His purpose had seemed simple until this moment. Perhaps it was still simple, and this churning within his innards was not a complication but a clinging memory of that other captain's glare. That glare—boring and prying into him like some kind of drill.

That man, that piece of fire. James Kirk. He had not been merely handling an annoyance, or even handling a potential threat. He had been thinking hard, trying to think like the enemy alien before him, to dig into them and know what their minds held.

Valdus knew humans were not soft-hearted as rumor preferred. He knew they could summon steel willfulness; that had been the only way they'd beaten the Empire behind a neutral strip and held it there these generations.

And that young man over there was the kind who had done it, that James Kirk and his sort.

"Dangerous," Valdus uttered.

"Commander?" a voice came up from behind him.

The sound of his subcommander's voice was at once comfort and challenge.

Valdus, realizing he had been slumping, straightened. "Yes, Romar, yes."

He turned now and the two of them sank into a shadow together.

"You have something to tell me?" the subcommander asked.

"Yes," Valdus said. "I'm hungry."

"You're always hungry when you're tense."

"Oh, you misread me."

"I'm the one who must order your meals to the bridge, remember."

"No, I don't recall that."

"I shall point it out next time. This is not a sanctioned encroachment of Federation territory," Romar said, speaking very softly, but in a casual tone for the sake of others, as though discussing a menu for the officers' table. "It makes me uneasy, Commander. We have no orders to do this."

"Nor orders not to," Valdus pointed out.

Romar shook his head. "Please don't smile," he sighed. "You know I falter when you find me amusing."

"There are age-old reasons for my actions," Valdus told him quietly. "Older than you. And you're not that amusing."

"Let me bring weapons up."

"Oh, yes. Let's fly into unfamiliar territory burgeoning with Federation vessels, including at least one Starfleet battleship, and let's power up our weapons so their sensors can read the surge. I wish I'd thought of it."

"What *have* you thought of?" Romar persisted, still keeping his voice down. "You haven't confided in me yet."

"Perhaps I never will."

"Yes, you will. You don't like keeping secrets. You never make me guess like this." Romar stepped closer to him and eyed him squarely. "You're uncertain of what you're doing here, aren't you? You're here to discover something, not to do something. Yes?"

"I will do something," Valdus assured him. "I have clear actions to take, once I make up my mind. This is their idea, Romar, not mine. I use the other man's methods whenever possible. This competition is the best way I can get an entire battle cruiser near that planet."

Romar paused and thought for a moment. "The host planet? Why should you want to be near it?"

A chill rammed down Valdus's spine at those words. To be near such a place, with such people . . . to put himself and his ship and crew near such creatures—

I was wounded. I was confused. Can a mind be stripped of sense from outside forces? How can I be sure my memory hasn't fogged over the years? Many humanoid species look alike in the galaxy. What was I seeing? Do I know how to answer his questions? Will I know any better in a few hours?

All around them, officers and bridge personnel engaged in pointless work just to keep from standing still and staring into the screen at that starship, but also to keep from glancing too often at their commander and his second, over here in the corner, muttering about the secrets of this mission.

Valdus felt their tensions and the pounding of all their hearts. It took his best inner control to resist them.

They would sense what he sensed when he looked at news pictures from the Federation and saw the Rey people. Most of what he sensed, at any rate. For how could they know that his one great animus had been discovered in the wilderness? Was it really the same group of people who sent that one small ship out all those years ago—could it be?

Could it *not* be? He would never forget those eyes of theirs, wide and round and dark—how those eyes changed from friendship to fear, and poisoned him and his crewmates.

He had searched space for the source of that ship, and never found it.

Now, the Federation had found it. But the Race Committee had denied him a host guest aboard his ship, so he couldn't be sure.

Sure . . . he must become sure.

"Do memories ever lie, Romar?" he murmured. He focused again on the Federation ship before them. "Do fears fester?"

The low bridge lights passed in patches across Romar's reddish brown hair and light brown eyes.

"Such questions," he said, frowning now with concern. "What are you asking yourself?"

"I may be looking at a demonic image through a haze of a young crewman's fear," Valdus admitted. "The years may have left me only a cloud of suspicion. I may be entirely wrong, but I am driven to find out. I must know," he added, "if these are the people who destroyed my ship and murdered my crewmates . . . so many years ago."

Romar studied his commander's face, the echo of youth that still lingered in those gray eyes that had seen so many campaigns, the graceful way Valdus had aged, suggested only by threads of silver in his dark hair, an old scar across his left temple, and a certain touch of fatigue in his voice from time to time.

But this other thing that was in his voice—this was something Romar hadn't heard before.

"You had better tell me this story," he said, "because if you're making arbitrary decisions for your own sake instead of the Empire's, then . . ."

Valdus gave him a sidelong leer. "Then?"

In his own usual manner, somewhat less severe than most of their order, Romar offered an almost imperceptible shrug. "I will have to stop you."

"And I will have to kill you when you try."

The words were crushing, but neither of them was surprised.

Romar nodded and pressed his shoulder to the bulkhead. "Then we shall have an interesting few days."

His leader barely reacted. But there was something in Valdus's tone when he spoke.

Something precarious.

"Oh, yes," he said. "If we live."

Chapter Five

Bridge of the *Enterprise*

ROMULAN. An Earth word. Earth legend.

The word might as well have been chiseled across the screen as Jim Kirk prowled the view of that other ship. How had an Earth word become so alien?

Somehow he was outraged at the theft, even though it was just a word.

He crossed back to the science station.

"Spock," he said.

The slim blue-and-black clad form pivoted toward him, the black eyes severe, yet tolerant of things Vulcans weren't supposed to understand. The style of the man himself overcame those stereotypes. Spock and his kind were often described as stiff.

There was nothing stiff about him.

"No record of encounter with anyone named Valdus," Spock said, "other than a Federation agricultural intermediary from Daran V who died six years ago. If this Valdus has gained any particular renown beyond the Romulan Empire, it has escaped Federation notice.

"Meaning he's either extremely bad at what he does,"

Kirk said, "or extremely good. Did you notice what he said? That running this race was his own idea?"

"Plausible deniability," Spock agreed.

"Yes. He admits he's doing this on his own, and the Empire can deny everything if trouble arises. That proves to me that trouble's about to break. Get ahold of McCoy. I want that report on our guests. Are they in their quarters?"

"I've been monitoring their movements since this problem developed, sir," Spock told him, "and apparently they sleep very little. They've been touring the ship constantly since their arrival, though slowly and with somewhat irksome appreciation."

"Irksome?"

"I only report the crew's reaction, sir."

"Yes, I understand," the captain allowed. "There certainly is such a thing as too much adoration."

Spock nodded and resisted reacting, but part of a grin surfaced anyway.

"They have been adoring us copiously," he said.

"Restrict their movements. Keep them away from the propulsion systems and any computer accesses over level four. I'm not ready to trust them yet. Not with this new development."

"I would hesitate to characterize them as spies, Captain," Spock said. "The Rey have gone out of their way to learn English planetwide and have even made it their second international language. This is documented by the Federation and fairly accepted as genuine brotherhood. It's difficult to convince an entire planet to perform espionage. The purpose of their interest in Federation membership seems genuinely to be education and advancing their culture's capabilities and contributions."

"Somebody else might have to teach them."

The blunt statement set Spock to silence for a moment. He stood and stepped down to Kirk's side.

"Captain, I wish I could offer you more reassurance

regarding the Rey. Or the Romulans. Or this sector of space. Regarding the first two . . ." the Vulcan shrugged. "As far as the third is concerned, unfortunately, this race was organized before the sector could be secured. As such, the event will prove to be as much exploration as sport. This, of course, provides the added possibility of vessel damage and accidents, without the safety of marked space lanes."

Kirk shook his head. "I'm not worried about the contestants. Those people don't need baby-sitters. I just hope one of those spectator ships doesn't get caught in a vortex. Those are the ones I'm worried about." He glowered at the screen again. "They also carry hundreds of potential hostages."

"Captain," Spock began.

Then he was suddenly quiet, and Kirk had to turn and look at him to get the rest of that sentence.

"Yes, Spock?"

"I've received a list of additional entrants to the race as provided by the Race Committee. A vessel representing Harrell Hullworks, from Catula, Theta Pictoris, two from the First Federation, one from Ardana Exports—"

"All right, all right," Kirk cut him off. "Have the list available in my quarters. I'll look at it later."

"Yes, sir."

But Spock didn't turn away.

"Captain, I would like to remind you of something," he said.

"Well," Kirk prodded, "go on."

"While we are here, you should not forget to . . . enjoy the race."

Kirk felt his shoulders and the muscles of his stomach relax a little.

"Why, thank you, Spock," he said. And suddenly, Kirk found himself breathing a little easier. Maybe it would be all right. Maybe this really was just the curiosity of one Romulan commander. Whatever it was, the only advantage the Romulans would have was that secret. The starbase engineers would bring their ship down to the power level of the starships. That in itself was a gamble. Starbase people were used to peace that was provided for them by the starships and other vessels of the Fleet, who took the brunt of trouble, like the army that went into the frontier before the pioneers.

"Well, we'll see," he murmured.

Spock blinked. "Sir?"

"Nothing, Spock, nothing. I was just wondering if it's . . . I guess the word is *healthy,*" he said, "to run some races."

From behind them a welcome voice interrupted. "This from a man to whom a salad is green peppers in a taco."

They both turned in time to see McCoy step down to stand behind the command chair between them.

"Doctor," the captain greeted. He felt a grin tug at his lips and realized suddenly that Spock's effect on him was holding. "You have a report for me regarding the Rey?"

"More or less," McCoy said. "I talked to them, I looked at them, I invited them to have a look at sickbay and got them to 'ride' the diagnostic beds—"

"Which gave you a medical checkout," the captain hurried. "What did you get?"

"I got a lot of thank-you's. They keep repeating how happy they are at having outside contact. Apparently they wanted it very desperately. They're highly social and the idea of being the only intelligent life in the galaxy sent a cold shudder down their collective spine."

"I can understand that," Kirk commented.

Spock nodded. "Earth went through the same apprehensions in the early 2000s."

"You have a conclusion on those observations?" the captain prodded.

"I would say they're not predators, not built for hunting at all," McCoy replied. "They're runners, generally slender, high metabolic rates, herbivorous—they keep asking about our galley and that's where I sent them. They like to cook. Blunt teeth, good hearing, good eyesight, strong sense of smell, tend to be clever, quick, good at hiding—"

"Can you get to the point?"

McCoy shrugged, and plowed ahead.

"I'd say they're antelopes," he said.

Kirk and Spock eyed each other, and the captain took solace in the fact that Spock didn't seem to understand that either.

"Elaborate," Kirk picked.

McCoy spread his hands as though the whole thing should be clear by now.

"They're deer, Jim. That's their place on the evolutionary scale. They were never hunter/attackers on the food chain. They were always gatherers and scavengers. They come from a planet where all the predators were brutes and the intelligence developed in the secondary levels of evolution—the large prey. Eventually they gained control of the planet and got control of the predators with science and medical means of containment. But they're pretty twitchy. They don't sleep much. They wander around the ship all the time, afraid they'll miss something. These people's advancement has been very slow according to Earth standards. It took them centuries to get up to warp drive, and they never made it beyond warp one point five. Then they just . . . gave it up. They're very shy on the scale of advancement, and they tend to give up easily when things get uncomfortable."

"Comfort doesn't make strong souls, Doctor," Kirk commented. "If they were never predatory, they never had to be strong. That's why humanity went to space. Because it's hard and uncomfortable and it builds character."

"The strong survive? Maybe," McCoy said disapprovingly. "I'd have to say these people are more interested in the character of others than themselves. When they received a response to their last couple of calls, and Captain Dodge flew in with the *Hood*, and the Rey discovered that not only was life out there but humanoid life that almost looks like them—why, hell, they almost broke down and had a planetwide sob. The galaxy suddenly opened up to them and they're desperate not to miss anything. To find life like themselves that acted strong and powerful, decisive, willing to share—they've been wrapped up in humanity like some kind of big hobby ever since. They think we're . . . nifty."

Kirk shook his head and that grin finally broke out as he looked up at his chief surgeon's cocky, friendly face under the cap of brown hair, and absorbed the touch of Atlanta in his old friend's voice.

"Yes, we're nifty. Not one of your more helpful reports, Bones."

"Well, Jim, look at it this way. It's a chance to put on your Napoleon suit and start giving orders, because this time you'll have an audience. These people are quailing and kind of spooky, but they're thrilled to be here."

"*Spooky* is a non-descriptive term, doctor," Spock pointed out.

"Not if you have Halloween on your planet, Bub," McCoy tossed back.

"Captain," Uhura spoke up from behind him. "Race Chairman Orland is hailing us from the starbase."

"Not a moment's peace," Kirk said. "Put him on audio, Lieutenant."

"On audio, sir."

"*Captain Kirk? Are you there?*"

"Affirmative, Mr. Orland, you're audio."

"*Thank you for that—it seems to be all worked out with . . . them.*"

"I'm glad, Mr. Orland. As long as 'they' don't provoke any incidents."

"*Well, they've agreed to run the route without any race committeemen or host visitors on board. We just plain told them we didn't want anyone but their own people on their ship.*"

"I was going to suggest that," Kirk said. "I'm glad you thought of it yourselves."

"*So am I. And they've let us harness up their ship and bring it into the maintenance bay. We'll have those power reductions done in about six hours. By then the other*" *contestants should be here and we can all go outside the solar system and take places on the starting line. Everybody's anxious to get the race started, so we're going to fire the starting cannon at nine o'clock base-standard time. Okay with you?"*

"I'm just here as a contestant, Mr. Orland," Kirk told him. "You don't have to check with me."

"Well, I just figured . . . you know."

"I understand. Let's hope my job is done regarding . . . you know."

"I sure hope so too. Thanks very much again, Captain. We'll start polishing the cannon!"

"Fine with us. Kirk out."

He motioned a cut-off to Uhura, and in the corner of his eye noted that she had smoothly terminated the communication. To his right, he felt Spock's silent gaze again.

"Fine with us," he grumbled, so that only Spock could hear. "Let's hope we don't have to start polishing the phasers."

The starting line was a sight to see. Dozens of beautiful ships, new ones, old ones, plain and painted, a half dozen ugly ones, all standing at broadsides to each other, waiting for the sound of the cannon to come over their sensors.

And there, studding the line-up, were the Starfleet entrants. Two more starships and a frigate. The *Hood,* the *Intrepid,* and the *Great Lakes*—big, beautiful, white ships gleaming along the line of merchant vessels and representative ships.

All the ships were "dressed," lit up, all running lights and exterior spotlights on, all hull decor sparkling, flags and pennants strung wherever possible. It was a glittering display.

It would have been especially invigorating, except for the dominating presence of the Romulan battle cruiser, hovering a third of the way down the line, dwarfing most of the ships around it.

Except for the four Starfleet vessels, the *Red Talon* would've been the largest ship participating.

Suddenly Jim Kirk was glad Starfleet had accepted the invitation to the Great Starship Race.

"Ship to ship," he ordered, "Starfleet frequency code three, Lieutenant. Shield the communications as well as you can. Starfleet vessels only."

"Code three, sir," Uhura complied, but it took her a few moments to do what he wanted. "Captain, I have Captains T'Noy, Tahl, and Dodge."

"Put them on visual."

"Aye, sir. Visual, screens seven, eight, and nine."

Kirk stood up, and by the time he turned to the small upper deck scanners between the science station and the communication station, three faces were gazing at him with bridges of other ships in the small backgrounds.

"Captains," he greeted as he stepped up there and Spock came to his side.

"Hi, Jim," Ken Dodge cheerily said first.

"Captain Kirk," the relaxed-looking Vulcan woman offered with a glint in her eye. Behind her, her Vulcan bridge crew watched the screen with practiced dispassion.

And Hans Tahl only smiled and nodded because he heard the others beat him to saying hello. He was a very blond, very friendly man who always looked as if he was about to sneeze.

Dodge, on the other hand, was a dark-haired former field soldier who had come up through the ranks very fast and without any Academy boost and was very tough to surprise.

"Jim, you sure you want to bother running the race now that we're here?" he asked.

"I was going to ask you the same thing," Kirk said.

"Come on. When have you ever beaten me at anything?"

"Do I have to remind you about summer, oh, about eight years ago?"

"Oh, you got lucky!"

"But I won."

"But it was plain, dumb dog luck!"

"But I did win."

Dodge grinned widely and paused to let his bridge crew laugh at him. *"Good point."*

Kirk could tell they were working at their high spirits more than should have been necessary under the circumstances—circumstances which had been changed by the intrusion of a certain ship and crew.

"I'll have the coffee ready for all three of you when you get to the finish line," Tahl said from the low-lying, heavily armed Starfleet frigate.

Kirk smiled. "Who says you're going to get there first, riding in that warmongering bucket?"

"Hey, this is a frigate, boys! No tender labs or science crew to weight me down, and all our power's tight. You should've commanded one of mine, Jim. What a frigateer you'd have made!"

A foxy smile lit Kirk's flushed apricot face. "Then what would you do for a living?"

"Lounge in a starship, what else?"

Kirk heard something to his left and realized it was Scott moving on the upper deck. The engineer had come to stand against the rail, and together they gazed at the tightly built power-packed Starfleet vessel off their bow.

"Lord, I love a frigate," Scott admitted. Then he blinked and added, "But don't tell him that."

"Too late," Tahl said. *"I heard it. You're mine now, Scotty."*

Scott smiled, and Kirk chuckled outright. Spock's brow rose at them, but he didn't say anything.

"You're sunk, Kirk. The race is mine," Tahl crowed. *"After all, ladies' men never win. They're too easily distracted."*

"I'll take that as a compliment."

"You might as well," Dodge laughed. *"You can't win. There's no way to just get lucky."*

"Oh, fine," Kirk drawled. "Dignity between captains. I'm glad this is a private line."

"You mean you're lucky it is. I'm glad you're here, given the . . . changes of the last half day."

"Yes. After the cannon fires," Kirk said, "use of these Fleet frequencies will be grounds for disqualification. However, I wanted to have a word with all of you about those 'changes.'"

"Understandable," T'Noy said.

Tahl nodded, and Dodge rolled his eyes.

"I guess," Dodge sighed, *"it shouldn't be a surprise that somebody would take advantage of a public event like this in an open sector."*

"I'm surprised," Tahl flipped. *"Aren't you surprised?"*

With a serious snap, Kirk told them, "Let's just hope the other contestants are sufficiently distracted by the details of the race. That way, we can probably maintain the peace of this event. But if trouble does erupt, we'll be the ones expected to deal with it. I suggest we keep our eyes open and our Starfleet channels on standby."

"Agreed," Dodge said.

Tahl folded his arms saucily. *"We'll muscle the peace if we have to. Hell, I got a frigate."*

Dodge's first officer leaned into the picture and popped off, *"A friggin' what?"*

Jim Kirk chuckled and scratched his ear, and he and Dodge exchanged a glance across the viewscreens.

Tahl was about to respond when the Vulcan woman on the far screen interrupted.

"We should also be on guard for tensions from otherwise friendly vessels," T'Noy suggested. *"These crews and commanders are not trained in dealing with hostiles. They may misread movements or approaches and react prematurely. Obviously all are aware of the Romulan ship, and some apprehensions have been voiced."*

"I've authorized a communiqué to everybody this morning," Kirk told her. "I explained the situation and that we're on top of it. Hopefully, that'll head off any provocations."

"Very good," she said, and seemed to be satisfied.

"I just got the memo," Tahl confirmed. *"It'll probably*

keep the other contestants from taking any action unless they're acted upon. Very well worded, Jim."

"It should be." Kirk nodded back over his shoulder. "Spock composed it."

"Mr. Spock," Tahl greeted, *"it's good to see you again."*

"Welcome, Captain," Spock said with simple grace.

"You're a comforting fixture standing next to that guy there. At least we know there's somebody on that ship with some self-control."

Spock nodded, but only once, unwilling to take a compliment that cost his captain a point.

"Perhaps we can get together when this is all over," Tahl added.

"Our pleasure, sir," Spock said. "We shall have the coffee ready."

0900 Hours, Starbase Standard Time

"Attention contestants. This is John Orland from the Race Committee. Prepare to receive the frequency for the first homing beacon on the racecourse. When you get to that beacon—that is if you get there—you'll receive the next frequency, and so on. The spectator ships will already be there at Gullrey when you come between the committee markers at the finish line. I'll be there, too. Good luck to everybody. Stand by for starbase navigational specifications."

"Lieutenant Uhura," Kirk said, as he settled into his chair, "receive that on the main viewer, please."

"Ready, sir."

"Mr. Spock—"

The turbolift interrupted him with its breathy whisper, and he turned to see Tom and Royenne come onto the bridge, their enormous brown eyes wide and shifting. They stepped onto the upper deck as though the bridge would fall away under them if they moved too fast or stepped too hard.

Tom blinked around with those big foallike eyes and finally fixed them on Kirk.

"Captain!" he said, as though he hadn't expected Kirk to be here. "May we watch? Do you mind if we watch from here?"

"No, I suppose not," Kirk said. He managed a sigh that took some of the tension out of his shoulders. "Where's your other friend?"

"He wanted to watch from the VIP lounge," Royenne said. "He was enjoying the food. He's a cook by trade, and your ship's cook was sharing techniques about feeding a whole starship crew."

"All right . . . well, you make yourselves reasonably comfortable and—"

"And stay out of the way." Tom smiled broadly, and his eyes picked up about six lights. "We understand."

Even though he didn't really want it, Kirk felt a sense of excitement brush over him. Suddenly he was a little more eager, a degree prouder than he had been a moment ago. "Mr. Spock, adjust the bridge viewers and viewscreens all over the ship."

Spock tapped one button—only one—and suddenly the bridge staff, and on the lower decks anyone else who looked up, saw a surrounding scape of the race vessels hovering before, behind, and to the sides of the starship, near and far, all itching for the race to begin. It was as if the whole bridge had become surrounded by windows.

Whatever Spock had done, he'd done it right, and all for people who hadn't suspected him capable of such poetic stage direction. The screens compensated for each other, making the regatta look as though it was right "outside"—even to leaving slices out of the scene where there was bulkhead between the screens. Warming engines on dozens of ships preparing for light speed caused a fluorescent glow along the starting line.

Lieutenant Uhura started a round of applause, and after that first instant of thinking they might be breaking a rule by clapping in church, the rest of the bridge crew joined her and smiled at Spock. The two Rey hammered their palms together better than children at a circus.

"Oh, very nice," the captain murmured as he looked

from side to side and forward at the tails of the private vessel *Gavelan Star,* the *Starship Hood,* and the scattered others who had drawn line-up positions forward of them.

"Thank you," Spock said.

He nodded for the applause to taper off, then allowed himself a few moments appreciation of the beauty of the ships, the tableau of dozens of vessels that wouldn't otherwise be gathered in one place at one time.

"Captain, receiving subspace," Uhura said. "Transferring visual to the screen."

"Relay the subspace to Mr. Spock."

"Aye, sir."

Spock bent over his small viewer, and the soft blue mask of light played across his eyes.

On the forward screen appeared a picture of a small brass cannon about the size of a water carafe, backdropped by a simple drape of red velvet.

A voice came over the audio system.

"Ready . . ."

"Receiving directional, Captain," Spock said.

"Set . . . tune to frequency one point nine six . . ."

A human hand approached the little brass cannon on the screen and touched it off.

Firing a plume of black smoke, the tiny cannon make a deep-throated blast a lot louder than anyone expected.

It echoed, and it hurt Kirk's ears.

"Go!"

Chapter Six

"WARP FACTOR TWO, Mr. Sulu. Let's race."

"Aye, sir, warp two!"

For solar miles around, vessels of every description streaked from their places and glittered into a formless dance against the backdrop of space-like lanterns lit from within.

Some ships bolted away at warp three or four, betting that their fix was a clear one, willing to risk the chance that they were chasing a distortion into the depths of night. Others lagged behind at warp one or two, betting they could "hear" the beacon better at low speed and risked being left behind.

Jim Kirk took both bets and both risks. Maneuvering speed, sensor flexibility. Of course, that also meant he could end up lost *and* behind.

In the next instant, *Gavelan Star* flashed into high warp. Then the *Starship Hood,* and the Starfleet Frigate *Great Lakes.*

"Looks like Ben Shamirian thinks he found something," Kirk commented. "Dodge and Tahl are tailing him. That's what we like to see . . . starships dogging private yachts. Don't make me look."

"Several spectator liners are beginning to pull away from the starbase, sir," Spock reported.

The captain nodded. "They'll be there for the honors and jubilees when the race is over."

He moved quietly to the upper deck. He and his first officer stood with their elbows almost touching and into the science station sensor access, but they weren't just looking for the race lane beacon. Not yet.

"Are they tracking the committee beacon?" Kirk asked, keeping his voice low. "Following the race-course?"

"It seems they are," Spock answered, but he sounded uncertain. He grasped the viewer with both hands, squinting into the blue light as it played across his eyes. "The beacon is confounding any attempt to triangulate. I believe it is sending an intermittent signal. When we are nearer, we may have to slow down even more in order to read it with any hope of accuracy."

Kirk pressured him for a glimpse into the monitor. "Looks like there's interference of some kind. The Race Committee downplayed the trickiness of this area."

"How long is the race expected to take, Captain?" Chekov asked.

Kirk straightened so quickly that a muscle in his neck cramped. He ignored the knot and said, "As long as it takes, Ensign. Races are like that. Someone will go over the finish line first, second, third, then the body of the contestants, then the stragglers or the lost entrants will be scooped up from wherever they are, and the Race Committee will declare a finish."

He barely heard his own voice. Why was he so nervous? Nothing was wrong.

Nothing was wrong, nothing was wrong . . .

On the port screen across the bridge, aft of the middle of the bridge, just over the engineering station—where Mr. Scott would be standing if he weren't in the main engineering section complaining that races were a waste of time for starships with serious business to do—was a sensor image of the entrants *Irimlo Si, Ransom Castle,* and *Blackjacket.*

And beyond them, barely more than a sliver of lime in the night, was the only ship he really had any interest in other than his own.

Turning away from the Rey gentlemen, away from the crew, Kirk leaned toward Spock, but didn't look at him.

"They're using the race for cover," he uttered. "Why else would they come into the sector when almost everybody else is here for a public event?"

Spock remained deceptively still. "We are not on patrol, sir."

Kirk probed his own deepest thoughts, his needs and instincts that told him to dog that ship and not let it just fly off, their jurisdiction or not.

"No," he said finally. He gazed at Spock in a way that they both understood. "Get the best fix you can on the beacon and let's run the race. But keep that ship under surveillance."

"Yes, sir."

Kirk stepped to the lower deck and slipped into his command chair. It felt particularly comfortable, the seat and back cool through his clothes, impressions in the cushion recognizing the shape of his thighs and his back.

The Romulan wasn't doing anything untoward, the race had started smoothly, the seat felt good . . . he resisted the needling doubt at the back of his mind, though he knew it was a signal.

He was about to say something just to break the silence when he was interrupted from behind.

"Excuse me . . ."

Tom was looking at the forward screen. His fair hair touched the collar of that incongruous lumberjack shirt, and for the first time Kirk noticed that the other one, Royenne, had been given a Starfleet casual uniform to wear. The olive green shirt was wrapped somewhat loosely around his lean rib cage, and the sleeves hung a little short on his gangly arms, but he looked very happy.

They both looked completely out of place and absolutely delighted.

"Yes?" Kirk prodded.

"Oh!" Tom shook himself from watching the panorama of ships either matching their speed, rushing past them, or dropping away at their sides. He glanced at Royenne and pointed forward, but didn't say anything.

Royenne poked him. "Ask."

Tom nodded. "Why can't you just tell your computer to pick out the beacon?"

Spock straightened, flexed his shoulders slightly, and said, "Ninety-nine point nine nine nine percent of radiating objects in the galaxy are natural. The computer can't discern between natural and fabricated radiations."

"That's our job," Kirk added proudly. "It's one of the reasons robot ships have limited use."

Sulu smirked and muttered, "If we told the computer to find those beacons, it'd start drooling."

Royenne drew in a breath and laughed along with the crew. "I love these answers you give!"

Kirk grinned, and asked, "Are you having a good time exploring the ship?"

Tom almost gagged in his rush to answer first. "Oh, yes! It's so strong!"

"It's so *orderly,*" Royenne punctuated.

Everybody was smiling. Well, not Spock, but he was *almost* smiling. His eyes were smiling.

Kirk was about to make a joke about that when Spock eyed his console and spoke up. "We're being passed by the private vessel *Haunted Forest,* sir. Captain Ames is winking an acknowledgment at us with his hazard lights."

"Wink back at him. Then increase speed to warp three." The growl in Kirk's voice gave away his playful exhilaration. And he didn't mind a little immoderate showing off, either.

Everyone paused in a moment of silence as the *Enterprise* launched herself with incorruptible purpose into a higher level of hyperlight.

There was a beautiful sound, a beautiful feeling, and sense of being surrounded by power—which, of course, they were.

Just before the sensation faded, Kirk capped it off by saying, "Chekov, get a net on that beacon."

"Trying, sir."

"State of Maryland vessel *New Pride of Baltimore* coming up on our starboard," Spock said, "immediately flanked to port by the Blaine Aerospace entrant *Cynthia Blaine*. Hospital ship *Brother's Keeper* is falling slightly behind us, as are the Andorian entry and the museum ship *Thomas Jefferson*. Romulan vessel is running abeam of us to port at some distance."

"They're not making any unexpected moves?"

"None at all—sir, sudden increase in speed, several vessels—"

"Captain!" Chekov yelped. "Contact with alternating fixed and flashing marker! Relative bearing, broad on the starboard beam, z-minus four degrees."

Kirk leaned forward. "Take a running fix on it, Mr. Chekov, then log the contact. Hold onto that beacon!"

"Aye, sir. Computer, note running fix."

When the computer spoke up with its metallic voice, Tom and Royenne almost hit the ceiling.

"Noting running fix, alternating F-and-F marker, Stardate 3223.1, zero nine thirty-eight hours. Contact logged."

"Mr. Sulu, increase to warp three point five toward that marker."

"Warp three point five, sir!"

"Keep alert for other ships. We'll all be converging on that point. Sensors on maximum. Full alert."

"Full alert, sir," Sulu said, and an instant after Chekov echoed it.

"What does all that mean?" Royenne asked.

As the ship hummed with effort to comply, Kirk pivoted his chair so he could answer before anybody else did. He was starting to enjoy all this showing off. He'd have to be a stone pillar to not like these people.

"It means we found the first beacon. We have to come within a hundred thousand kilometers of it in order to get the clues to the second beacon. With a field of other ships trying to get the same signal, it'll be like threading a needle. A hundred thousand kilometers is a *very* small area in spatial terms."

"But what is all that . . . fixed and flashing?"

"Oh, I see," Kirk chuckled. "On Earth—where a lot of our terminology originated—fixed and flashing meant an alternating light of one color varied at regular intervals with a flash of a different color. Out here, of course, it's flashing a subspace signal."

"And your navigator can see it?"

"With the ship's sensors, yes. We're taking a running fix, which is a fix taken at two or more different times as we pass the marker."

Tom interrupted, "Is that how you know your heading?"

Royenne pushed forward. "And what's—"

"Ah!" Tom erupted. "You stepped on my foot!"

"Oh—pardon me."

"I shouldn't have been in the way."

"No, no, I'm sorry. We're sorry, Captain . . . what's a bearing?"

"Gentlemen," Kirk chuckled, "don't try to swallow too much at once. The heading is the direction the ship is going. What you mean is the course. That's the direction to be steered. Relative bearing is the direction where something is in relation to the ship." He leveled his right arm out at the one-thirty angle from the bow of the ship. "That's broad on the starboard, and down one, two, three, four degrees is the z-minus. So the fixed and flashing marker is down this way, relative to where you're standing. Now we're turning toward it and working to hold the signal."

With infectious enthusiasm Royenne pursued, "Why can't you hold the signal?"

"But what's a fix?" Tom insisted at the same time. "I'd

really love to know! Should I take a class in space navigation?"

"Does Starfleet have a class?" Royenne asked.

"I'm not sure," Kirk said. "We'll check for you. A fix is a position taken without any reference to a former position. We take the time and our location of contact with an object, even a natural object in space, and log it. If another ship has logged it, we may be able to find it on a chart. If we're the first, then we could use it to find our way back."

"Same as dropping breadcrumbs," Sulu commented, still grinning.

"And we're having trouble holding the breadcrumbs," Kirk said, "because the Race Committee made the racecourse difficult. There are sensor blind spots and interference everywhere in this sector, and the committee beacons are designed to be tricky on purpose. That's the sport of it."

Tom drew a long appreciative breath. "Beautiful!"

Suddenly, Chekov shouted, "Look out! Ships coming in!"

He pointed at the board between himself and Sulu, and the helmsman twisted his lean body against the controls. The ship surged to starboard and whined with effort.

"Hang on, everyone," Kirk warned, mostly for the two in back.

Before them on the screen, and to the sides on the auxiliary monitors, space was suddenly crowded with hulls of every configuration. Streaking out of the darkness to haggle for the eye of the needle, they dove viciously for one spot in space, the hundred thousand kilometers around that flashing marker.

Within sixty seconds almost the entire field of contestants were plunging for that spot, converging like bees.

"Continue at warp three point five," Kirk snapped. "Do *not* reduce speed, do you understand?"

"Aye, sir," Sulu responded through gritted teeth, his

body still canted to one side as though he were pushing the ship himself.

"I'll play chicken with all of them to be the first one to the first marker," Kirk said. "That's it, Sulu, don't give an inch."

"Not inching, sir," the knotted helmsman grunted.

A gleaming sable ship with a broad sulfur yellow stripe from nose to fantail and fake gunports painted onto her hull dropped out of nowhere in front of them. It consumed the forward screen so sharply that Uhura gasped and Chekov pushed back in his chair. On the aft deck, Royenne almost fell down, and Tom shouted something, but Kirk instantly forgot what it was.

He was busy.

"Get in there, Sulu! Get under him!"

"Trying, sir!"

"Not good enough! Push! Make him move aside!"

The ship screamed around them, dragging up every ounce of power she'd been left and insisting she should have more, like an amputee refusing to believe her limb was really gone.

"Who is it?" Tom gulped.

"New Pride of Baltimore," Spock supplied. "Unlikely to give way."

"We'll see," Kirk cracked.

"Other ships approaching, Captain," Chekov said breathlessly, but he needn't have bothered.

There would be no efficient way of describing the shocking thunder of vessels converging on this spot, and even Chekov forgot his caution of senior officers and quit looking at his monitors. He just stared, as all around them on the screens a swarm of ships dipped toward the same spot.

"Don't sideswipe anybody," Kirk warned. "Remember, we're one of the biggest ships."

Sulu didn't respond. His concentration was full-up.

"Collision!" Chekov came halfway out of his seat and pointed at a starboard screen behind Spock.

On the screen, sparks were spitting between *Irimlo Si* and *554-2*.

"Ask if they need assistance, Miss Uhura," Kirk said. Cleanly he added, "Mr. Sulu, do not give an *inch* yet."

The two officers each muttered a separate response that made the bridge sound very efficient, but no matter what anyone might have tried to claim, this just wasn't business as usual, or even emergency as usual.

This was something very new and different for the *Enterprise* crew, and no one knew how it would spin out. Excitement for kicks—

"Increase speed, Sulu," he insisted. "Get under the *Pride*. Turn on your ear if you have to, but squeeze past him."

"Captain Turner isn't easy to squeeze past, sir," Sulu commented, but it was only a comment. He proved that by pressing the *Enterprise* forward, galling the speed out of her that was dangerous for these quarters, and turning up on a nacelle, somehow managing to skirt past *New Pride*.

Chekov gawked at his console and choked, "Less than five hundred meters to spare!"

"Sir, receiving a frequency for beacon number two!" Uhura said. "Frequency eight six six."

"Log it!" Kirk barked. "Sulu, veer off!"

The starship howled furiously around them, and turned herself inside out to change direction violently.

On the main screen and the screens all around the bridge, the panorama of vessels suddenly changed. Several other ships changed course too, adjusting to their own readings of the second beacon.

How true was the signal? Were the readings coming in to *Enterprise* clear at warp three point five?

"*Irimlo Si* reports minor damage only, sir," Uhura said. "And *554-2* claims no intent to drop out of the race. Both are jockeying for position. And Captain Glover is hailing from the *New Pride of Baltimore*. He wants me to inform you that he had right of way."

"Well," Kirk tossed off, "tell him to go on back to the starting line and look up the rules, then let me know."

Uhura smiled, and had to wait a beat before she could respond without laughing. "I'll tell him, sir."

On the starboard upper deck, even Spock's practiced impassion was suffering. Kirk saw it as he glanced up there, for some reason impelled to keep an eye on his first officer.

Spock's voice had an unexpected lilt when he glanced up at the main screen.

"Sir, the Melkotian entry is bearing off slightly, but reducing speed. *Starship Intrepid* is moving away firmly on a new course. Six other ships—correction, seven—are following her, apparently assuming Captain T'Noy has discovered a clearer trace of the signal. Ransom Carnvale Mining Company entrant *Ransom Castle* is taking a course on the z-minus port beam. The field is beginning to draw apart and widen—"

"Romulan vessel just increased speed, sir," Chekov interrupted, and he said it so quickly that Kirk heard Spock draw a breath to say the same thing and just get beaten to it by his junior officer.

"Correct," Spock allowed. "He is pulling away, sir. Moving on a descent plane."

Kirk eyed the port screens. He wanted to tell Spock to keep a finger on the Romulan ship, but he also didn't want to appear to be hawking another entrant for no good reason, and the Rey, so far, apparently didn't perceive all the good reasons.

"*Red Talon* is blending with the lead vessels," Spock said, reading Kirk's posture, obviously. "Difficult to discern which vessels those are any longer, however. Interference is thickening . . . I believe I read the *Blackjacket,* possibly *Ransom Castle* . . . at least a half dozen others are blurred readings, some pulling forward, others falling back."

Hesitation battled in his face, in his voice. He didn't like what he saw on his monitors.

But Kirk noticed something else. Never mind that

Spock didn't like what was happening, there was another struggle going on. Spock's brows would tighten, then he would raise them and try to relax, try to keep in mind that this was all supposed to be for fun.

"They're taking the frequency for the second beacon and moving off toward it. Let's do the same. Mr. Spock, feed that frequency through to the navigational computer . . ." He leaned forward and allowed a naughty grin to break on his face. "Mr. Sulu," he said firmly, "helm alee."

The quick-fingered Oriental officer who could steer a ship through a curly pasta noodle—and just had— suddenly looked lost. He peered back over his shoulder.

"Sir?"

Spock turned an amused attention on the helmsman, raised both of those upswept black brows, and said, "Mark eight, Mr. Sulu."

Sulu's face lit up and he got the idea that all this machinery, all this fabulous science was still being run by the same kind of folks who invented it in the first place.

A mischievous delight took him over. "Aye-aye, sir. Helm's alee!"

The Federation's first heavy cruiser began to hum as power and directions were fed through the systems, through the engineering section and up into the great nacelles where the brittle and brilliant warp science boiled to do its job, and the ship changed course, veering off toward the flickering second beacon on the corkscrew racecourse.

The captain pressed forward like a man facing into the wind.

"I always wanted to say that."

Red Talon

"What they have done is clever."

"I beg your pardon, Commander?"

Subcommander Romar approached Valdus from behind, but stayed an arm's length back.

"These beacons," Valdus said, gazing at the field of racing ships shifting and fading in and out. "Somehow the race people have devised tricks with which they disguise these beacons. A maze, Romar. They will make us climb the walls and look out. Signals read false and more false on certain speeds, and leave the truth of their locations for us to devise. We cannot rely on our navigational equipment. We have to be cunning. We have to guess. If, of course, we wanted to win." He inhaled abruptly. "What is the condition of the vessel now that we are under power?"

"All systems have been impressed with powerbacks by the starbase mechanics. There are bottlenecks on our thrust systems—"

"Begin work to take them off."

"I beg your pardon?"

"Start taking off the bottlenecks *now.*"

"It will take hours, sir!"

"Let it take hours."

"We'll be disqualified."

"I don't care about their race," Valdus said through his teeth. "Get my *power . . . up.*"

Studying the unconciliatory determination that suddenly flared on his commander's face, Romar held still and quiet for a moment until control returned.

He knew Valdus as well as anyone and had watched over many cruises as the commander had driven his crew on the singular key of cowardice.

Subdued, introspective, but ruthless, Valdus was willing to accept shorter odds than most, was merciless with underlings who showed any sign of putting their own lives before their Imperial duty, and had no particular interests outside of his own command. He had tolerated whole civilizations he completely despised because it was in the Empire's interest. It was said he had grown his beard to disguise himself from himself. He didn't even have any particular interest in the United Federation of

Planets. Rather than seeking renown, Valdus simply did a job with somber and sometimes ghastly deliberation.

Until today.

So Romar was treading carefully, with all his senses on alert. He didn't want to do the wrong thing and end up scrubbing photon shells below decks. Too well he remembered the low point in their relationship when he had tried to prevent Valdus's destroying the career of a centurion who had balked in the face of danger. It had taken months for Romar to regain Valdus's trust.

Red Talon was known as the worst ship to serve in the Imperial Fleet because its quiet commander could become suddenly merciless with weakness in others. Promotions and demotions went up and down like a bouncing ball. No one envied Romar his nearness to this one unreadable commander.

But Romar stayed. Part of his perseverance was due to curiosity. Valdus was a mystery, and Romar couldn't resist a mystery.

He knew Valdus's career had been somewhat lackluster in its early years until he was the only survivor of an attack and boarding by an unknown enemy. Valdus had managed to escape and, when all was lost, had destroyed the ship rather than let these hostile superior beings take it. The story had been vague, Valdus in medically documented mental confusion, and speculations had run rampant while investigations thrashed without evidence.

Patrols had been sent in and worked the area for years, but nothing had ever turned up. For years the Empire searched for this powerful enemy that could come out of nowhere and end up consuming a ship of an Imperial Swarm. But wherever the boarding party had come from, they had disappeared. Ultimately, the Empire lost interest and decided that such a violent civilization must have destroyed itself somehow.

By then, Valdus was considered a hero. Time had done that too.

Only Valdus's shunning of accolade continued to let Romar believe the story, or some part of it, was true.

Valdus had been offered command after command, but had accepted only the ones that left him haunting the same unremarkable sector where he lost a ship long ago.

Perhaps that, too, is part of my loyalty, Romar thought as he looked at Valdus from behind. *I know he is merciless with himself too. He carries the demeanor of a man who has looked too close at the face of death, who has been purged of pointless ambition, and who is somehow hungering to look at that face again to see if he can make it blink.*

Pushing his thoughts back for the moment, Romar determined to get at least part of an answer about this odd event, which normally Valdus would avoid, even laugh at.

He stepped closer.

"May I ask you," he began, "how long do you intend to participate in this activity of theirs?"

Valdus cleared his throat and shook away his stare at the screen.

"Until I decide which ship to track."

"Which ship," Romar echoed, to see if it made any more sense coming out of his own throat. It didn't. "Very well . . . which ship do you think you may target? What type of ship?"

"I refrain from telling you because you would then be obliged to dispense a recorder marker to the Empire regarding our movements."

"Yes," Romar admitted tentatively. "And I would do so, of course, being an officer who knows the course of operations . . ."

"If we weren't running under silence now, yes?"

The subcommander laughed but kept the sound private between them.

"Yes. Thank you for looking after . . . me. Your order of silence keeps me from such a troubling choice. Which ship are you targeting?"

"Romar, I will tell you when I am ready."

"Why do you want to corral another ship, Commander?" Romar persisted, in a tone that said he would get at least part of the answer before leaving his leader alone again.

Valdus very well knew that tone. Now that he heard it, he felt somewhat relieved. There was a certain complex security in knowing he was being watched, as he always had been, as was the way of their kind.

"Because the suspicious Starfleet field leaders would not allow me to have a host guest on board this ship. And I want one of those people."

"The leaders?"

"No—not the leaders," Valdus snapped. "Those . . . people."

"The Rey?" Romar's brow drew tight. "But why? They are—weaklings. No one considers them a threat. They're just another whimper in the night the Federation will have to protect. Why do you want one?"

Valdus let his facade of nonchalance slip from his expression. He watched the starlight peel away before them on the dominant main screen and found himself wishing for the days when there were no such screens at all in these ships.

"Because," he said, "I know they are the most dangerous people in the galaxy."

Chapter Seven

"VERY GOOD WORK, all of you. Be assured that was the easiest we'll get."

James Kirk flushed with pride as he beamed at his crew, and on top of all this, they had witnesses to their wonderfulness.

He glanced back at Tom and Royenne.

When he was a child, his mother had told him that winning didn't matter, it was the game that counted, the fun, the exercise, the teamsmanship.

Like hell. He wanted to win.

He'd nodded at her like a good little boy—even though he really wasn't a particularly good little boy—because he had known not very deep inside . . . winning was more fun.

"Readings on beacon number two are already becoming sketchy," Spock said. He came to the rail and looked down at Kirk. "Our twenty percent power down is costing us sensor distance and accuracy. While the vast majority of this space is empty, this one particular region is dotted with anomalies of various types: nebulae, spinning stars, pockets of electrical action, communication dead zones, and so on. Long-range sensor readings are already distorting and diminishing. Soon it will become awkward not only to trace the beacons but other ships."

Kirk gazed up at him, then glanced back at the two Rey men again, and lowered his voice. "No wonder nobody found these people until twelve years ago."

Spock nodded, but didn't say anything.

"John Orland downplayed the trickiness of this area," Kirk went on. "They probably took all that into consideration when they decided how far to power down our ships, adjusting sensor capacity to make sure this area remained a challenge for us." He lowered his voice. "Just keep track of the Romulan for me."

Not making any obvious acknowledgment, Spock held his captain's gaze a few seconds—just long enough—and turned back to his monitors.

On the small screens to port and starboard, the field of ships still in this area was beginning to widen, to stretch away as each ship's crew sought its own science and instincts, followed its captain's whim, experience, or passion, as the case might be. A portion of the field was invisible already, having rushed from the first beacon at higher warp than others, but there was no way to tell if they were still ahead, or if they were off on a wild-goose chase in the wrong direction, chasing sensor shadows.

When Tom and Royenne began muttering to each other and pointing at the forward port monitor at a glimpse of the Canadian entry *Bluenose IV,* Kirk took their distraction as an opportunity.

"Where is he, Mr. Spock?" he asked quietly.

Preoccupied with the surging and broadening of the race, Spock didn't look up from his monitor. "So far, abeam of us at flank speed . . . distance increasing. Ambassador Shamirian's ship *Gavelan Star* just pulled out of sensor range."

Kirk rubbed at a cramped finger on his right hand and said, "Doesn't mean he's not lost."

"Also losing contact with *Blackjacket* and the *Haunted*

Forest. We are outdistancing several other entrants. I will specify them if you wish."

"I don't."

Chekov's face was almost buried in the cuff of the science station auxiliary monitor, so close that his voice sounded muffled. "Captain . . ."

"What is it, Ensign?"

"Host entry *Ozcice* is passing us . . . but they're going in the wrong direction. They are heading . . . in that direction, sir." He stood straight and pointed to port aft, over the heads of Tom and Royenne, who suddenly thought they were doing something wrong. They ducked and glanced at the ceiling.

"The contestants are scattering," Spock said. *"Ozcice* could be following a bounced sensor reading, or they could be seeking the third beacon."

"The third beacon?" Kirk shot back, suddenly relishing the challenge. "They're already a beacon ahead?"

Chekov looked at him. "But, sir . . . I thought I saw the Tholian ship going under *Ozcice,* heading directly back toward the starting line. How can it be?"

"That's how it's going to be from now on, Ensign," Kirk added. "And it'll get worse. It's like a road rally. Clues everywhere, being interpreted and misinterpreted. Beacons can fold back on each other. As long as we don't try to follow anybody, at least our mistakes will be our own. Any sign of the second beacon?"

Chekov plunged for his monitor, knowing that was supposed to be his job.

"General reading, sir," he said, "not settled down yet. I will try to make it settle."

Kirk tried not to smirk. He was feeling a lot better than he had expected to feel. Flank speed . . . he hungered to increase his own speed and nose the Romulan out. Actually run a race with him, beat him. On the other hand, would it be a nobler show of sportsmanship to let the visitor slip ahead?

He had an unprecedented chance to be cosmopolitan

if he wanted to avail himself of it. Take Valdus at his word, think back on that face and look for affirmation, sift faith out of the skepticism he'd trained himself to rely upon, read Valdus as an independent person rather than tagging him collectively—he wanted to do all that. The Federation expected him to be able to do that. To let the visitor win, possibly move the plate tectonics of separate civilizations a little closer.

If he could believe Valdus.

The trained Federation representative wanted to take the galaxy at its word, but the kid inside—the one who wanted to win—didn't.

"Bring us back up to warp three, Mr. Sulu. Pull ahead. Take your course from Mr. Chekov."

"Warp three, sir."

"Sir," Chekov called, apparently feeling pressured now. "I have interference on the beacon frequency."

Kirk swiveled slightly. "Spock?"

Spock left his monitor, sat down, and tapped into another monitor that a moment ago had only been showing part of the racecourse. Now figures and a window graph appeared.

"Beacon two is being scrambled by what appears to be a spinning neutron star. Pattern of the static tells me that the beacon is behind the interference."

"Behind it?"

"Yes, sir."

Chekov looked distressed. "Then how can we track it?"

Kirk shrugged. "Find the ripples, and you'll find the fish."

"Sir?"

"Rather than looking for the beacon, look for the source of the interference. You're the navigation specialist, Ensign. Reach out there and get me a course."

Chekov's round young face went blank for a moment, then he blinked, muttered a vague, "Yes, sir," and turned back to hunt for that spinning neutron star.

"Captain?" Tom asked tentatively.

Kirk turned. "Yes?"

"How long is the racecourse?"

"It's about three thousand linear light-years, if you stretch it out along a string. As they've designed it, it's bunched up into a corkscrew that bends out into deep space, then bends back to your planet, if you can visualize that. Didn't they fill you in when you were accepted as a guest on a contestant vessel?"

"We received a packet of information," Royenne said, "but . . . I haven't read mine yet."

Tom smiled sheepishly and added, "We were so busy looking at all the ships and meeting everyone . . ."

"There were people *everywhere,*" Royenne muttered.

Embarrassment raged across both their faces.

"That's all right," Kirk said. "I haven't read mine either." He smiled, and had a sudden thought.

Relief drenched the two visitors as they saw that they hadn't insulted him, or the race organizers, or Starfleet or the Federation or any unmentioned deity.

Again everybody was grinning.

Kirk smiled, and had a sudden thought. "Would the two of you like to sit down?" he asked, realizing that they were the only people on the bridge without chairs. Off their eager nods, he continued. "Lieutenant, notify the quartermaster and have two chairs brought up here."

Uhura's smile disappeared and surprise struck her flawless face. She uttered an acknowledgment and turned to get some chairs onto the bridge, but she still looked surprised.

Kirk knew why. He'd never done this before. Guests had always been allowed to take a look at the bridge, then politely invited to go to the observation lounge for snacks and beverages and generally to stay out of the way.

But what the hell. This was time for entertainment, right? He had a chance here to show off and push the envelope of interstellar perception.

Right?

* * *

"Searching for beacon number five, Captain," Spock said. "Reading seems clear at the moment. The signal is occulting, however . . . appears to be overlapping shadows. I seem to be reading two beacons."

Kirk could tell the Vulcan was dissatisfied with his own answer. "We haven't got all day, Spock."

Seeming almost affronted, Spock straightened and looked down at his captain. Spock said, "They are identical, sir."

"Can you differentiate between the signals?"

"Captain, I believe we are looking at a gravitational lensing effect. A beacon and its identical echo."

"Mm," Kirk murmured, "good trick. Which one do we follow? Can you detect what's splitting it?"

"Not yet," Spock admitted. "This sector of space is devoid of life-sustaining bodies, but also cluttered with adverse naturalia which, as you pointed out, have been responsible for turning back many early explorations before ships were capable of dealing with them. With our sensor power reduced, these natural distractions tend to drag our signals off course. I'm attempting to map them and compensate for them, in case any of the beacons turns us back on a course. Mr. Chekov is tracking the competition."

Kirk nodded, then pivoted as casually as he could. "And where's our friend?"

"He is at the extreme of sensor range, having increased to flank speed again."

"That's the fifth time he's fallen back then come up on us again. Am I haunting him, or is it the other way around?"

"I would say there is a mutual haunt in progress, sir."

"But I don't have a reason, Mr. Spock, other than the race. He does."

Spock stepped down to the command arena and stood at Kirk's side, but said nothing to scratch the mood.

They stood together, gazing at the main screen and its image of a few racing ships moving in and out of visual range, some matching time with them, wondering which ship would next flash off into a higher warp speed or drop to a lower one.

Spock's voice was deep and melodic, almost as though he was reading poetry. "Immediately behind us are *Haunted Forest, Unpardonable, Hood,* and *River of Will.* Slightly ahead of us are *Blackjacket, New Pride of Baltimore,* and *Alexandria,* sir. Flanking us are—"

"Alexandria," Kirk said as his eyes fixed on a bulky working trader humming two points off the starship's starboard bow. He propped an arm on the back of his command chair and said, "My father used to talk about her. He served on her as a deckhand when he was a teenager. Tough old ship. Some parts of her interior are made of the wood from the original *Alexandria,* a Baltic trader schooner. The pieces sat in a Chesapeake Bay museum for almost two hundred years until somebody bought them and built them into that ship out there. Lots of stories in her bones."

Spock shifted near him. "In her bones, sir?"

As nostalgic mist came over his eyes, the captain said, "That's right."

Spock let a few seconds tick by, then droned, "Captain Hall would do well to have them scraped out."

A laugh boiled up in Kirk's chest, and he tried to stuff it down but couldn't.

"You're a pirate, Spock," he chuckled.

"Sir," Uhura said, "Captain Dodge hailing from the *Starship Hood.*"

"Put him on."

"Kirk, this is Dodge. Do you read?"

Raising his voice to compensate for the crackle of interference in the communication system, Kirk said, "Poorly, but you're on audio. Can you boost the gain?"

"Already on maximum. The whole area's full of this garbling and clicking. Where are you?"

Kirk's eyes glittered as he glanced at Spock and lied his tail off. "We're looking for beacon six."

"Six! How the hell did you find four! We can't find it anywhere!"

"We shut it off as we went by."

"Kirk, you son of a dirty, lying, sidewinding— somebody cut me off before I say something I'll have to apologize to him for."

Uhura smiled and said, "Captain Dodge has terminated the communication, sir."

"Well, now that I've told him we're looking for six, we'd better hurry up and find five." Kirk leered at the screen, and prowled toward the starboard rail. "Chasing shadows . . . is there any way we can pick out the real beacon with any certainty?"

"No," Spock flatly told him. "We may take the fifty percent chance, if you like."

"Something's going on," Kirk said, still glaring at the screen, which refused to give him facts. "I can smell it."

Spock's elegant head tilted a bit. "Intuition?"

"Damn right."

A year ago Spock would've frowned with teeming arrogance. Disbelief, disrespect, probably both. Today that intolerance was nowhere nearby. He only nodded with what could've been approval, but was, at the very least, understanding.

"Mr. Sulu," Kirk said. "Take a fix on one of those two signals, and increase speed toward it by one half. Swing past *Alexandria* and take the lead. Give her a wide berth, or she'll try to cut us off."

Sulu looked doubtful. "They'll try to cut off a starship?"

"They might," Kirk said. "That's a strong ship. She's taken a lot of punches in her time and shook them off. Pete Hall's a tug captain by trade."

Sulu shrugged acceptance. "Can't beat that combination."

Kirk ticked off the right number of seconds, then stepped forward and stood next to his helmsman. A hot glitter showed in his eyes.

"Sure as hell gonna try, though," he said.

Red Talon

A race. Vessels rushing this way, that way, chasing blips and echoes. Small-minded business, the living abnegation of worth.

Romar paced across the back of the bridge, turned, and paced to where he had begun. This he had done before and would again before he summoned the courage to step to the command level and confront Valdus.

His shoulders tensed within the padding of his uniform. Strong shoulders, his father's shoulders. Shoulders that could break a door. Legs that never ached, no matter the strain, though he might climb a pyramid.

Muscles turned against his ribs, his fists coiled, his feet—it felt as if there were splinters of glass in his boots. He was a subcommander of the Imperial Fleet and he knew his duty. Take over if the commander is insane.

There was no menace to men of their kind like the menace of the mind. When a trained mind began to stray, seek its own purposes above the primary causes of the Empire . . .

He looked down in the command ring.

Down there was no pyramid, only Valdus. A quiet commander as that kind went, a man of surpassing contemplation and scant hardness in his face. He sat with his own shoulders rounded even in the padding of his uniform and his hands folded between his knees. His posture said he wouldn't fight.

What good was this? If any other ship hailed them and they went to visual, others—Federation people—would see the Imperial commander sitting there with his shoulders down and his hands folded, forlorn as a lost thing, and that would be the new view of the Empire. For decades people would tell their children and grandchildren of the time they saw a commander in his ship, slumped and sorry looking, and how the rumors weren't true. How there was nothing to fear across the neutral zone, and all was empty legend.

Could he let that happen? The Empire turned on the fear of others. Did he dare stand by in case the stone wall should crumble?

Romar had paced since the starting gun while they went from one beacon to the next, as politely as anyone could please, mustering the nerve to go down there and ask questions. He had to do it. He had to find out if there was madness.

He counted to three and demanded of himself that he go down and not have to shame himself by counting again. One, two—

"Three," he murmured. His feet were numb from the glass.

Trying to look casual, he sat on the deck riser next to the commander's chair. He looked at Valdus, but the commander didn't turn his eyes from the main screen, from the field of ships moving in the nearness and in the distance.

Romar swallowed twice, cleared his throat once, then swallowed again. Folded his hands, unfolded them, and finally became angry enough with himself that he would either speak up or not look in his mirror for many, many days.

"If you die in your sleep," he began, "it would do well that I should know . . . what your plan is."

"To run the race," Valdus said bluntly.

"Until?"

"Until they believe I'm only running the race."

Almost with an audible moan, Romar sighed, "Commander . . ."

Valdus smiled suddenly and looked sidelong at him. "If I *happen* to die in my sleep?"

Romar felt heat rise in his face and almost got up and left, but the commander's smile held him down.

Looking tired and careworn, like a man waiting to see if his crops would grow or if he would starve this year, Valdus changed position to stretch the muscles in his back and looked again at the forward screen.

"I have never thought about dying in bed," he uttered casually. "I've been prepared in my life to die in every situation, but never in my sleep. I have been ready to die for most of my career. That's what happens when you skim past death at close quarters and you feel its breath upon your neck . . ."

Confused even more now, Romar fretted beside him. "Commander, won't you talk to me?"

"I *am* talking to you," Valdus said. "I can't tell you the plan yet. I'm revising it."

"Why are you revising it? What has changed?"

"The simplicity has gone out. Things are different. You should have come with me when I went to meet the captain of the *Enterprise.*"

"I would have been honored to go, but they told you to come alone and you complied. You said there was nothing to fear on their starbase."

"I should have defied them. That is how a firm will is displayed, but I failed to think of it in time. You see, I had no fear of going alone, and that cost me a show of strength. Remember, Romar, fear can do you service in the right circumstances."

"I'll try to remember. Why would you wish me to meet him?"

"To look at his eyes."

Romar's spine started to ache. He wished he could take his boots off. Curiosity chewed at him, but he would gladly ignore it if the commander would agree to turn back, abandon this unexplained movement into claimless space, and simply be part of an unfinished story in a Federation history book.

Brittle and acute, he tried to be cold-blooded. "Eyes are eyes, Commander."

Vigilance kept Valdus very still as he gazed at the screen. Moments crawled by in silence, with the commander's face creased by things he had seen, perceptions he had distilled since leaving the starbase.

Quietly he said, "Oh . . . no."

And he said nothing more.

The bridge made haunting noises around them. Other crewmen did not look at them. They all realized how bizarre this movement was, and they were all worried.

Romar knew he was being unimaginative, and that somehow he had failed to inspire trust. Suddenly he felt twice his own weight.

"What do you want me to do about this race," he sighed, "while you decide upon your action?"

Enchanted with the view of space and its activities, Valdus didn't respond immediately. Romar's suspicion that the commander might not be sure of their purpose was strengthened when Valdus didn't resent the structure of that question. Others might have called this behavior weak, but Romar noted a valiance in how hard Valdus was to embarrass.

He would remember that, too.

"Try to win," Valdus said. "At least, appear to try. Run their race as best you can. When the opportunity arises that fits my purposes, I will act upon it. The moment will have to offer us privacy, solitude, even separation, because we must put off confrontation as long as possible."

He stood up, impassive, perhaps withdrawn, but he continued to gaze at the screen, and back in time a few hours, to the eyes that had changed his plans.

"I do not want to have to deal with that man."

125

Chapter Eight

Ransom Carnvale Mining Co. Vessel *Ransom Castle*

"HERE YOU GO. Bonafide one hundred percent gen-u-wine down-home Confederate breakfast. Eggs over medium, Smoky Mountain sawmill gravy, sourdough bread, Ozark grits, and chilled apple cider, unstrained. Ship's specialty. We try not to leave out any Southern mountain range. Now, here's how you eat it. Take your grits and spoon 'em on top your eggs. That's right. Now, take and chop it all up with the side of your fork. Ataway. Go ahead, be mean to it. Now hoist yourself up a shovelful of it, and you'll have a dilly of a breakfast recipe to take home to Golleray and teach all your pals."

As First Mate Mike Frarey directed the breakfast like a musical jamboree, he got what he wanted from the sweet little lady perched on the bench at the mess table with the off-watch crew—he got a whopping big smile.

He straightened and asked, "Did I say something wrong? Ain't that how you pronounce it? Golleree?"

"Yes, that's how," the girl said.

He knew she was lying, but it was one of those kindhearted lies, the sort meant to make somebody else feel good.

126

And being the somebody else, he did. Feel good, that is.

"I'm not mispronouncing your name or nothing, am I?" he asked.

"Oh, no," she said.

"Say it again for me, just once, so I'm sure."

Pushing aside a lock of her platinum hair, she plunged her fork into the mountain meal. "It's Turrice Belliard Roon. But I like the way you call me Turry. You won't stop, will you?"

"Oh, no!" Mike boomed. "Sure won't."

"Where is your captain?" she asked. "I haven't met her yet."

Mike jabbed at a fellow crewmate and jolted the man to one side so he could squeeze in beside Turry. He got a couple of nasty, teasing looks about it, but nobody made any cracks. Good thing too. He'd have cracked 'em back.

"Well, I dunno," he said. "Nancy's kinda particular about having strangers on the bridge. Not that you're strange or nothin'—in fact, gotta say it's kinda pleasant having you around here. Can't quite explain it, but you're dang pleasant to have around."

Mike smiled and felt his face go red as Turry pursed her lips and tried not to laugh. As first mate, he was informally assigned to taking care of their host guest. He was a big guy, rough-hewn, self-conscious about his size, and embarrassed about the gap between his front teeth, but he'd been told by more than just his mother that his eyes had an animated crinkle about them when he smiled. So he figured that canceled out the gap.

The crewmates sat around the table, dressed in rough jersey shirts and faded trousers. Their ship was immaculate and strong, built to haul virgin ore to processing plants, and he hoped it could impress her. A truck in space. Later they would show her the barge section, where the raw ore was loaded and unloaded, and how they moved it in and out, and he would spend time telling her about the interstellar mining industry.

Yup, they'd have lots of hours together, and he'd enjoy every minute.

The mood in the galley mess area changed, if subtly, when Nancy Ransom herself shuffled in and scowled at the steaming breakfast buffet laid out over there by the wall. She had her jacket on, the one that made her look short and stocky, and her brown hair was pulled back so tight that she looked like a seal sunning on a rock.

It was a nice breakfast—Louise had outdone herself back there over the hot stove—but Nancy still wasn't mustering so much as an approving nod.

Mike went a little cold, worried that Nancy might make fools of them all in front of Turry.

"Should I say hello to her?" Turry asked, almost whispering.

Mike shrugged. "Maybe later."

"She's a little touchy," one of the load operators said.

"Mind your meal, Stevens," Mike ordered.

"Okay, okay."

Turry kept her voice low. "Is something wrong? Is it me?"

"Naw, naw, nothing to do with you. Couldn't be you, hon."

"Marry her, Mike," the engineer popped from down the galley's old trestle table where they and four others were gathered. "She's pretty."

"Like them big eyes," deckhand Harry Stevens commented.

"We'll talk about it when you aren't around," Mike said, but he blushed in the cheeks a little.

And even more when young stockman Sam Oats roared back, flapped his elbows, and crowed like a barnyard redcrest.

The laughter of his shipmates was a blend of humiliation and sustaining joy for Mike Frarey. He smiled, inched his big form a little closer to the best thing that had happened to him in ten years, and offered her some more coffee.

Reaching for another couple of slices of sourdough, Mike was doing what he always did when there was a visitor or an ore company rep on board. Entertain them as best he could and keep a buffer zone between them and Nancy.

And there was sure no trouble entertaining this sweet thing from the host planet. He couldn't remember when he'd been so puffed up with good old-fashioned billy goat, turkey cock, tomcat feelings sitting next to a lady. And he liked it.

He liked *her*.

Not that Nancy Ransom wouldn't be civil to Turry, but that was the best she'd be. For someone who came from a long spacefaring heritage, right out of one of those small spaceports where shuttling cargo or space taxiing were just about the only ways to make a living, Nancy never had much confidence in herself. She always *thought* she had confidence, so she always blamed somebody else when she faltered. She was naturally suspicious and refractory and would instantly resist whatever was pushed her way.

There was something pioneer about her, though, that made others continue to sign on her ship and work for her in spite of the odds they'd be blamed for something.

And she was the hardest worker Mike had ever known. She managed to keep her parents' marginal ore shipping business in the black. Barely, but always. Her draft-horse work ethic was the most infectious trait about her. Add that she was one of their own kind, flew the Stars and Bars on her ship, and wasn't quite convinced the Confederacy lost the American Civil War, that was enough to keep down-homers like Mike signing on season after season.

"You know anything about the Old South?" he asked spontaneously.

"Oh, yes I do," Turry said. "Earth studies are their own experience. I took as many as I could at our university. I'd like to live there someday."

"Like to do that myself, all of a sudden," Mike muttered.

He expected a crack from his shipmates, but nobody said anything. There was nothing but the clinking of forks on plates and the slurp of coffee. That meant they could tell he was serious and wasn't just teasing. He could barely pull his eyes off Turry as he shoveled the gray-white gravy onto his bread.

"If you want to get to know Nance," he went on, "best you can do is ask her about her family history. She's got this rebel way about her. Comes from one of those families who can name the company, brigade, regiment, and major battles of all their ancestors who fought in the war. Fact is, we'all a little like that."

Turry worked to swallow a forgiving mouthful of eggs and grits. "Are you all from the same colony?"

"Yeah, we're all from Port Apt. Most of us, anyway."

"Where's that?"

"Near Alpha Centauri. Ask me how it got its name."

"All right . . . what kind of name is Port Apt?"

"Colonized by an Arkansas family."

"The United States."

"That's right as rain. We'all second and third and ninth and tenth cousins and like."

Andy O'Boyle choked down a spoonful of grits in time to belch, "Couldn't tell that."

Turry grinned and everybody else chortled.

Encouraged as the mood got better and better in spite of Nancy Ransom's presence down the table, Mike went on.

"Most of us had relatives in the group of original settlers. They come from Jonesboro, Harrisburg—that side of Arkansas. Over there was a road sign with some houses around it, and on this road sign was the name of the place—Apt. It was named that back in the 1920s, because folks said there was 'apt' to be a town there someday."

Turry covered her mouth and was trying to smile and chew at the same time, but Mike picked up the satisfying delight in her great big brown eyes. Just like a doe's eyes . . .

"Anyway," he continued, "our great-grands, they named their colony Port Apt 'cause they figured it was an optimistic name for a place where there was apt to be a big mining port some day. Now Port Apt is about two hundred times the size of the place it was named after. Done real well. Lots of good free industry and entrepreneurship. Never lost our heritage. Kept the Confederacy's idea of small government. They keep the roads clean and the space lanes clear, and the people do the rest. Love to show it to you."

Turry gazed at his big round face, and Mike felt that he was nothing but a canvas of lines and scratches and scars, but her voice was like a song when she said to him, "I would love to see it, Mike. What about Arkansas?"

He blinked. "Pardon?"

"Is there a town at the road sign yet?"

Sam interrupted, "Not yet."

Mike pitched half a piece of sourdough at him, got him square in the face, then turned back to the lady. "Things move kinda slow down in those parts. You can't force a city to grow. Never quite developed the way some folks said it would. Prosperity pretty much followed the railroads in those days. There's no city there yet."

From down the table, the voice of their captain surprised them with a glint of humor as Nancy Ransom insisted, "Apt to be, though."

A pause—then the mess hall broke out in laughter.

Mike Frarey almost rolled backward off the bench, almost choking as he laughed. Must be something about Turry that just lightened their load some. Even Nancy was loosening up.

He hadn't expected that to happen, given that she wasn't too pumped up about running this race. She just couldn't stand to let it go on without her. Had a little problem that way.

Only when he realized he was laughing with his mouth open and a half-chewed display of food showing itself to the ceiling did he clamp down and grab hold of the edge of the big table. Down at the end, Nancy was eating, but she was eyeing them mischievously and her lips were drawn long in a grin.

"How we doin', Nance?" Joe Sibley asked from Mike's left.

"Marilyn's got the watch," their captain said, her concentration again on her breakfast. She ate with both elbows on the table, her shoulders up, and her head hunkered down. "We running behind *Blackjacket,* don' know how far, but we're gaining. Thought we saw *Alexandria* go by, but the sensor shadows were awfully big for a trader."

"Was it *Alexandria* or wasn't it?" Sam Oats asked.

"Just told you, we're not sure. All we know is something big circled around in front of us. You want to come up to the bridge and try to identify ships by silhouette, thrust, and size? Sure as hell let you have a try. We're coming up on a marker for a gravity well of some sort, so Marilyn's got us slowed down and on visuals. We got ahold of two beacons, but I think it's got to be some kind of lensing effect."

"Which one you gonna follow?" Mike asked.

"Haven't decided."

So Mike shrugged at Turry, who was watching the captain hopefully, and gave her a reassuring wink.

"After I get done eating," Nancy said, "I'm going up there and speed us up again. If it's a gravity hook, I can spin around it with enough speed."

"Or get caught in it," Louise Clark called from the galley cooking area, where she was shoveling hotcakes onto a communal serving dish.

"Don't drive, woman," Nancy called back. "Just cook."

Everybody laughed again, including Louise, and even Nancy this time.

Mike looked past Turry and Sam, and said, "Hey, Nancy, maybe you can catch up with *Blackjacket* and run him down. You know, impress Ian enough to bring you on board and make you the only woman ever in *Blackjacket's* crew."

Without looking up, Nancy snapped, "Who wants to be? That slippery carrot-top can have his all-male paradise if he wants. His loss. Besides," she said, leaning forward to leer at Mike, "if I was in his crew, I wouldn't have my *own* ship."

A stadium howl of approval jumbled through the crew as they shook their fists and pounded the table for her. And something unexpected happened—Nancy's cheeks rounded up with pride, and she must have felt real good because she reached past Sam and offered a hand to Turry.

"Hey," she said. "How are you?"

Turry caught the hand and responded, "I'm so completely delighted to be on *Ransom Castle,* Captain. You should be proud of all that you have."

"I'm proud," Nancy said. "Welcome aboard."

Mike and the others worked hard to avoid falling dead silent with shock. They forced themselves to keep chuckling, keep eating, and keep up the small talk, even if it was just "pass the coffee, will you" or "here, have a hotcake." A sense of conviviality skittered through the galley mess area.

Maybe this wouldn't be bad at all! Maybe they'd all have a fine ole time. Maybe at the end of the race they could get out their pickin' gear and make some music.

And maybe there was something tickling the wind for himself, Mike realized as he put his enormous hand between Turry's shoulder blades and gave her a little congratulatory pat. Felt just right—

Until the ship suddenly whined and cranked three-quarters onto its side.

As the hull pounded around them, they clung to the table and to each other as the lights crackled and thunderbolted, and their Ozark breakfasts and all the fixins came slamming into their laps. Mike managed to catch Turry on his left and two others on his right, but it didn't last.

Alarms blasted through the erupting darkness. The artificial gravity surged, twisted, sent them all careening against the port bulkhead, and tales of the new South died in their minds.

YELLOW
ALERT

Chapter Nine

Ransom Castle

"WE'RE OUT OF WARP, down to one-eighth impulse."

"Get the backup lights on. What hit us?"

"Something we hit. Looks like some kind of dark residual cloud. We didn't see it."

"Damage?"

"Well . . . I'm not sure about that yet."

"Get sure!"

"Okay, okay, don't yell—"

"I'm yelling at you, and I'm gonna yell at you because you're in charge of the bridge, and you're supposed to know what's in front of you, Marilyn!"

"You back off me, Nancy."

"I'm not backing off you, even if it's only a race. What if we had a shipment on board?"

"Then we'd have a plotted course and we wouldn't be running into clouds nobody can see, all right?"

"Uh, Nancy? 'Scuse me." Mike Frarey moved between the two women as half a dozen others scrambled around them. Behind him, Second Mate Marilyn Betts escaped around the pilot station and moved out of the line of fire.

"Looks like a puff of ionized gases and spinning dust left over from something that exploded maybe a million years ago. There's still reaction going on in there. It's off our sensors, so it's damn big."

Nancy fell silent for a count, squinting into the forward screen at a swimming smoke gray gauze that was almost invisible against the blackness of space. Even bumping up against it, they could barely see it. The only clue to its existence were faint bluish crackles of electrical activity and the fact that they couldn't see anything through it.

She scratched the side of her face distractedly and asked, "Where are the other ships?"

"The ones we can see are turning to go around it. We sent out a warning, so everybody knows about it now. I don't know for sure how this thing will affect our maneuvering ability."

"Who's in the area?"

"We saw the Tholian ship ahead of us, and *New Pride of Baltimore* right behind them, a couple others I can't tell who they are, *Blackjacket,* maybe, and we caught a glimpse of a Starfleet ship, but we couldn't tell what direction it was going."

"Starfleet ship? Which one?"

When Nancy's face turned gray with the reference, Mike realized he'd made a mistake. He should've just told her he didn't know what those ships were. Could've been anybody. Impossible to tell.

"Well . . ."

"It's Jim Kirk, isn't it?" She turned from gray to red even in the dimness. "Damn him, I can't get away from him even out in the middle of nothin'. Okay, let me think. And where the hell are my backup lights!"

Around, below, and above, they could hear the ship pound with wild activity, people doing their jobs and their best not to panic and not to have to bother Nancy. Like a gaggle of snake handlers, they'd learned that. Stay off the bridge unless there was really something to say. Then stay off anyway.

Everyone hung on with one hand and worked with the other as the ship was sledgehammered with blow after blow of force from the ancient furnace they'd stumbled into.

"Reverse the loading tractors," Nancy decided. "Give me some room to turn around."

"Got nothing to push against," Mike said.

"If they whine, we'll stop."

Mike twisted around as best his bulk could manage with the ship shuddering under him, and called down the engineering crawlway. "Tractors on full reverse, Sam."

"No—" Nancy grabbed his arm. "Wait a minute . . ."

Watching Nancy's small eyes get even smaller as she looked at the screen, then the readouts, then back at the screen, Frarey got one of those funny feelings down his spine. He waited what he thought was long enough, then prodded, "What're you thinking?"

"If everybody else is bothering to go around it . . ."

"Yeah?"

"Then we'll gain five hundred light-years on him if we cut right through it."

Mike kept his voice low. "On him, huh?"

"Yeah, on him!" Nancy erupted. "Shielding's full-up, isn't it?"

"Aw, Nancy . . . we're up in the front end of the field . . . we could put ourselves back God knows how far—"

"Or we could jump all the way ahead. Let's do what we do best and beat a bastard at the same time."

"Aw, boy . . ."

"Get the crew to put up the lead sheets on the interior bulkheads. Wake up the off-duty watch. Extend the stabilizers to maximum. Get the old pulse jets out in case we need them. We're gonna cut right through this thing."

"Nancy, I don't know . . ."

"All right, maggots, hang on and listen here!"

Red Talon

"The cloud is the remnant of an explosion when a neutron star collided with a class-C red giant. The result is highly ionized particles, hard radiation, dust, debris, and an above normal content of residual antimatter. There is also a great deal of momentum in the interior of the cloud, where the spinning has not yet completely dissipated."

"How old is this soup?"

"I would appraise . . . five to eight million years."

"Then we can expect it to spin one more day?"

The ship's science specialist turned his face up from the monitor to respond to his leader's peculiar question —or to see if a response was a mistake. "Yes, Commander . . . of course."

Valdus nearly smiled, but such a slip could in the long run prove damaging to any commander. He did, though, enjoy the look on the specialist's face when he asked his question. Apparently, he'd succeeded in convincing the poor fellow that he actually wanted an answer.

Perhaps he hadn't lost his touch yet.

The bridge crew wasn't used to dealing with him directly. Usually he told Romar what was to be done, and Romar dealt with them. They were confused why a simple race would not only draw his interest but his *direct* attention.

He enjoyed their confusion. He hoped also that he could commit his purpose without cost of their lives, but he wouldn't admit that to them either. A commander was better off all around letting his crew guess and suspect and being less sure of any conclusion they may make independently of their leader.

"Romar, where are you?"

"Here, Commander."

Of course. Never more than two steps out of sight, especially when he was measuring Valdus against every passing moment.

"Your orders, Commander?" Romar asked. "You wish to avoid the cloud, certainly."

"What are the other vessels doing?"

"All are piloting to avoid it."

"Not correct, Subcommander," the helmsman said. He spoke to Romar, but couldn't help glancing every other word or so at Valdus. "One vessel is nosing into the cloud. I believe they are playing to gain space by going through it."

"If this race was my only care," Valdus said, "I would do so also."

Romar moved a step closer and, judging from his drawn brows, didn't like having to probe the next steps. "Standard elliptical course around the cloud?"

"Yes."

Ah, the gift of a simple answer. Valdus enjoyed giving one today. Romar obviously found succor in it. One clear thing to understand and execute.

So much more the fracture when Valdus clutched Romar's wrist and held him back from approaching the helm. "A moment," he said. "The construction of this vessel going into the cloud?"

Romar stared at him, suddenly crisp again. He pushed the science specialist aside, waved him away, then hunched over the monitors and manipulated the controls until there was focus.

"Industrial merchant loader-transporter . . . cruising speed, hyperlight three . . . capable of five in short bursts. Heavy dragging engines, propulsional unit length overall—"

"That's enough."

Almost choking as he tried to keep the numbers from slipping through his lips, Romar made a tight sound in his throat, and drew himself straight again. He looked exhausted. The effort his patience was costing him was clear.

Patience.

Valdus silently offered his sympathy, but provided

141

no explanations. He was thinking about that ship and watching as it pressed into the gas cloud.

"And in a cloud of that type," he began, "a ship could pull abeam of another . . . and never be noticed. Yes?"

Enterprise

"A caustic brew. Very dangerous."

Spock cupped his readout monitor with both hands and peered in as the black cloud's facts piled up on the screen before him.

"Sweeping electrical activity," he went on, "turbulence in the high nineties . . . gravitational congestion toward the center, caused by residual spinning from the original collision . . . no plottable pattern to the spin."

Beside him, Jim Kirk glowered at the same power figures and chemical breakdown numbers and didn't like a single one of them. "What can happen to the *Castle* if she keeps going in?"

Spock came up from the screen and for a moment gazed at nothing as the numbers turned into pictures in his mind. "Ionization of her warp core, greatly compromising motive power, possibly stopping it altogether . . . sensor blindness . . . shield collapse, causing the crew to retreat to the interior of the ship, cutting off access to the engines and compromising their control over life support and hull integrity. They may not be able to extricate themselves."

His arms stiff, Kirk turned and looked at the forward screen. In the distance, on maximum magnification, a purple-black cloud with shaggy blue hairs of electricity was eating the *Ransom Castle*, and the *Castle* wasn't pulling out, and he knew why.

"Ship to ship, Lieutenant," he said. "Audio."

Behind him, Uhura's panel chirped in compliance.

"The *Ransom Castle*, sir," Uhura said steadily. "First Mate Mike Frarey on audio."

"Mr. Frarey, this is Jim Kirk. Put me through to Captain Ransom."

"She's here," the mate's voice crackled over the comm system, already affected by the cloud sucking on the *Castle's* power. *"Go right ahead."*

"Nancy," Kirk said, fighting not to sound patronizing, "don't go in there."

"Thanks for the advice."

Nancy's voice was composed—a scary sound from Nancy.

Kirk shifted a little and wondered about the sound of his own voice. Did he sound arrogant?

"Captain," Chekov interrupted.

"Go ahead, Mr. Chekov," Kirk said, trying not to communicate that he might as well talk to anybody other than Nancy Ransom, especially since he hadn't thought of anything to say to her yet.

Chekov was at his navigation station, but he was looking up at the science station on the starboard side, forward of Spock, as though to confirm what he had just seen.

"Sir . . . the beacon just faded!"

Kirk shifted and said, "Spock, confirm that. Did we guess wrong?"

Spock took the seconds he needed as everyone on the bridge watched him, and even Nancy Ransom had to listen to the silence on the open communication net as the *Enterprise* found out whether or not it had made a big blunder.

"No sign of the beacon, Captain," he said. "Evidently we have been following the sensor echo from the lensing effect instead of the actual beacon."

"You're lost," Nancy's voice concluded for them. *"After I'm inside the cloud, you'll have to follow somebody else, won't you?"*

"It's just a race, Captain," Kirk told her. "It's not worth risking your ship."

When she didn't respond, he got worried.

How could he talk to a woman who held him as her personal evil spirit? Would it be better to just tell her to go on in, try to cut across the course by swimming the quicksand, and hope she would do the opposite of anything he said?

Even Nancy Ransom wasn't that much of a child. Nobody could run a mining company transport and be a child for very long.

He wondered if she knew that he understood that, and that he'd learned things over the past ten years, whether she had or not.

"My science officer suggests that going into that thing isn't a good idea," he tried again. "We read red-lined turbulence in there."

"Yeah, and I don't have a fancy Vulcan to run my fancy computer. So if I dig my way through there and cut a couple hundred light-years off the course and blow you away, then I guess I'll just have seat-of-the-pants flying to blame. It's a trick I learned while I was still in Starfleet."

"Look," Kirk said, "you can insult me all you want, but don't degrade yourself by insulting my staff. I've given you my recommendation. You're welcome to take it, along with my assurance that no one else will hear about it. If you don't care about your crew, think about mine. I don't want to have to go in there after you."

Even as the words bolted out, he knew they were the wrong ones. She wouldn't let go of the past, and now he'd as much as laid a challenge at her feet.

"Then I won't call for you. Castle *out."*

The click of the channel closing was like a crack over the head.

"Not the reaction I was fishing for," Kirk said. "I made a mistake. I should've contacted Ken Dodge or somebody else to warn her off. Anyone's voice but mine should've been coming over the channels at Nancy Ransom, and I'm the one who should know that first."

"Is the *Ransom Castle* going in there?" Royenne asked from behind the action.

"Seems so." Kirk fought not to sigh. He'd forgotten

144

they were there. He had a certain appearance to uphold here—usually not the case on his own bridge.

Then again, they were here as observers, so they might as well observe the captain admitting he wasn't perfect.

"Captain Kirk," Tom added, "are you going to let them go into that thing?"

Kirk shrugged and gave them the awful truth. "There's nothing I can do if she doesn't want help."

"But isn't there an interstellar law you can quote or something?"

"A ship in space is an autonomous entity, Mister . . . Tom. That *is* interstellar law. Mr. Spock, Mr. Sulu, let's get back to the race."

As the crew frowned and tried to concentrate on a race that suddenly lost a bit of its imperative in lieu of something more precious, Kirk stepped back toward Spock.

"She's got guts," he said, "but I doubt she'll come out more than six or seven minutes ahead, and it might even slow her down. If she comes out at all—it's my fault if she doesn't come out," he murmured, still looking at the screen, at the dot of *Ransom Castle* against the monstrous crackling cloud. "Will the transporters work inside that mess if a rescue unit has to be sent in after them?"

"Unlikely," Spock said, "though I can't be sure."

"I should never have hailed her, Spock. I pushed her over the edge."

"I disagree, sir." Spock's tone was almost gentle as he turned to face him. "Captain Ransom displays an admirable willingness to take risks, but not the ability to weigh risk against gain. That . . . is what makes a commander of note."

This was his first officer's way of telling Kirk to go easy on himself.

"I guess you're right," the captain sighed. "That imbalance is what kept her out of Starfleet."

"Captain?"

Kirk turned to the aft deck. "Yes, Tom?"

The Rey man actually left the sanctuary of the turbolift apron and moved across the bridge toward them.

"Are you leaving that ship behind?" he asked.

They all watched the forward screen as it battled to magnify the great distance between the starship and the *Ransom Castle*. In those seconds, the last hint of the merchant ship—one glint of a tail fin—was consumed by the mindless mass of garbage left over from a cataclysm millions of years ago. Now, by any definition, the *Castle* was on its own.

Kirk didn't like the sound of his own voice or the idea of leaving a ship behind in potential danger in the name of sportsmanship.

Tom didn't seem like the type to face the bulls, but he wasn't going to let go until he got the honesty they were all holding away from him at arm's length.

He stepped between Kirk and Spock—something even the crew knew better than to try—and he pointed at the gaudy mass on the forward screen, and his voice carried a crack of insistence.

"But what if they don't come out again?"

Ransom Castle

"It's all right! Don't panic! It's just a little shakin' here and there!"

Ship's cook Louise Clark put her hand out on the shuddering metal sink, glared into the mirror she had mounted five years ago, and absorbed the shock on her own face. There was a tightness around her eyes and little lines that looked like the ones on her mother's eyes. Her face was flushed, hot.

"You been through this a hundred times," she told that face. "What are you doing shaking like a chicken?"

She pulled at her collar. Sweat drained down her neck.

"God, what's the matter with you?" she murmured at the face shriveling with fear before her.

She turned away from it and swore not to look again.

"It's all right—I been through all this before—we've got pounded before, plenty—"

Over the serving shelf of her galley she looked into the mess area, along the endless wooden trestle table, at another face. She grasped the edge of the serving shelf.

"Don't fret," she said. "No need to panic . . ."

The ship slammed sideways a few inches, enough to throw her down onto the slanted deck. She rolled against the bulkhead, then out the doorway and into the mess hall. A long-forgotten reflex let her catch the point of the table and keep herself from sliding underneath—a meeting place that was already occupied by the ship's guest.

The alien girl—what was her name?—had fallen underneath and was clinging to a table leg.

Louise concentrated on trying to remember the girl's name, just to give her brain something to do besides give in to the frantic feelings that seemed to be taking over. Why was she feeling this way? She hadn't lied to her own face in the mirror—most of those worry lines had come from sitting down in the galley and trying to prepare the next meal while the ship took some kind of pounding. Making food was her therapy. She had ignored orders to make fast and had peeled carrots and stirred hot chili in the middle of awful storms and even a couple of hostile pirate attacks. What was wrong with her today?

It wasn't even all that bad yet.

"Coming down with something," she muttered. "Got a crick in my neck. Just coming down with a bug, is all. How are you doing over there, hon? Scared as I look?"

Under the table, the alien girl's huge brown eyes were sallow with fear, but she was clinging as much to a vestige of common sense as to the table's leg. That showed in her face. With those milky bangs hanging over her face, the girl looked like a sheepdog who had been smacked with a glove and found a place to hide.

Louise summoned everything she possessed to overcome the fear strapping her chest. There was nothing she could do about her trembling hands—she could barely control her fingers. Only by using her fingernails could she get a grip on the tabletop and pull herself to her feet as the ship pounded and slipped.

"What's the *matter* with me?" she asked the air as her feet squared under her own weight. "I gotta think, gotta think, think, gotta *think*—"

But she couldn't. A blinding screen as wide as a shower curtain hung between her and rationality. She was furious at herself and frustrated at not being able to think. The air was shimmering, flashing, and turning hot.

Louise cast an arm over her eyes and staggered. Felt like the ovens were all turned on. Heat . . .

"Can't think in the heat—a cook that can't think in the heat—"

She laughed at this new disability, her lips quivering. Fear quickly swallowed any humor she managed to drum up. Only bigger was her need to get ahold of herself.

Reaching upward, she grasped one wrist with the other hand and pulled her arm away from her eyes, and she blinked until her eyes began to clear.

There was someone else in the galley. Not the girl. Someone different. Two of them. Not *Castle* crew, no one she knew—

Two men, soldiers of some kind, in tough uniforms that had metal fibers knitted into the fabric. With helmets! Helmets that looked like bird heads.

Why would anyone be wearing helmets?

"It's only a race!" Louise said out loud, choking on her own bile.

And this wasn't the transporter area. Wasn't the loading dock, wasn't the fantail where guests were brought on board?

"You're in the wrong place," she told the two stern-looking men. "You got in the galley somehow. This is the galley!"

The soldiers ignored what she was saying. One of them approached her with some kind of data-reading device. The other hunted down the Rey girl and went under the table to sniff her out with that thing.

A couple seconds, and the soldier under the table

pulled out what looked like a phaser, but longer and bigger.

Louise stumbled back. A surge of raw terror filled her mind, and she suddenly couldn't hold a thought, not even a word, not an idea. The motions around turned to fuzzy streaks. Her eyes watered until she could barely see.

A strident whine erupted under the table. The heavy table itself jolted just enough to notice, and the soldier under there drew back and straightened. At his feet, the Rey girl collapsed into imposed sleep.

Louise felt her debilitating terror suddenly drop off and good backwoods anger blast up inside her. She was drenched in sweat, but that didn't matter anymore. Her lungs pumped so hard she thought she was having a heart attack—but it was her galley, and she was part of the *Castle*'s working crew, and all of a sudden she knew what to do.

An instant later, the soldier coming at her had the pointy end of a can opener buried in his thigh.

As he choked in shock and pain, Louise shouted. "Don't you poker-faced nightcrawlers speak English? You are *in* the wrong *place!*"

Iron made good punctuation, and two skillets slammed into the two men's chests as they closed in on her, quick as bats.

The two devils didn't say anything, in fact even communicated through glances and motions as though cautious that their voices might be heard. They let the skillets clatter to the grease-soaked old deck and closed in. One on each arm, they dragged her into the cooking area and pressed her against the refrigeration units and the freezer.

"What do you want?" she croaked, struggling. "What do you want! There's nothing here!"

One of them held her down while the other reset his weapon—down or up, she couldn't tell—and aimed it at the sides of her secondary oven, the one mounted on the wall above the stove top.

"Are you stealing my oven?" Louise gasped. "That's crazy—you don't even have the same electrical systems on your ship . . . but take it if that's what you want . . ."

They ignored her. One held her back, one worked on the oven until the heavy unit shivered in its place, then nodded at his cohort.

Louise wiggled her shoulders and balled her fists, shook them and jabbed at the wide metallic chest before her, tried to kick and failed, but kept struggling.

"Your mothers ought to be ashamed!" she squawked as they bent her backward over the stove top. Her spine grated against the edge of the stove.

The smell of a thousand stews, chili pots, sloppy joes, egg dumplings, hush puppies, corn chowder, chicken puffs—all clinging somehow to the air of her galley—reminded her suddenly of a thousand meals, one at a time. A thousand, maybe two thousand, maybe ten. Most served in the midst of boredom. Her meals, one after the other, day after day, watch after watch, had been the only respite from drudgery for the crew, so she'd made 'em good.

She focused on the bottom of her old blackened oven as it shuddered above her head. A grim laugh jumped up in her throat and vibrated against her teeth, and suddenly she felt almost giddy. Something was wrong, but what?

How could they do her harm with her own oven? They didn't even figure that her oven wouldn't hurt her.

Almost a generation of cramming overstuffed turkeys into that oven, of casseroles tilted up on one end so they'd fit, of crews sparse and crowded, bulky with layered clothes and steaming with sweat, surviving off the fare of that long-suffering oven. Seasoned crewmen expected heavy chow to see them through a cold, long watch; young and confused deckhands wondered if this was what they wanted to do with their lives—how many of those young ones had she warmed with a hot home-cooked meal to help those confusions sizzle away?

Plenty.

On its inside walls, cooked hard beyond any hope of

scrubbing, was evidence of those ten thousand meals. Her knuckles were brown with old burns, each toting a memory.

The oven shivered on its housing and came loose on one side. Louise saw a knot of cooked-on white gravy somehow splattered on the underside of the unit. She wondered if she took a knife to it could she maybe just chisel it off, maybe get one more inch of the galley put away right—

She was thinking about getting out her scrub bucket and borrowing a common iron from the engineers when the oven suddenly caterwauled like a pig, tore off its broken housing and fell, and drove one pointed corner through Louise's left eye and into her brain.

Chapter Ten

"TIME FOR a calculated risk."

Good bait.

Everybody—Spock, Sulu, Uhura, Chekov, the bridge duty engineers, Tom, Royenne—turned to look at him. He was sure that down on the engineering level, Chief Engineer Scott was looking at the ceiling.

It was that now-we're-in-trouble look.

Now that he had their attention, he fixed his gaze on the forward screen and made sure his voice was just loud enough to make it to all points on the bridge.

"The best way to keep ahead of them," he said, "is to keep ahead of them."

He knew Spock was staring at him, understanding that he was talking about the Romulans. If the others understood that—fine. If not, then they thought he was just talking about the other race contestants and no harm done.

His own crew knew what he meant, but Tom and Royenne—how would they react, as representatives of Gullrey, to see that a Starfleet captain was preoccupied by what to them was just another contestant? Would he lose the edge that the Federation might someday need in this sector?

"Who cares," he muttered. "Mr. Chekov, plot a course z-plus ninety degrees to the galactic plane. Let me hear the course when you get it."

Silence fell, except for the sound of Chekov's sweating.

By the time he spoke again, his dark hair was plastered to his forehead like a line of belaying pins against a painted gunwale.

"Bearing, one five, mark zero . . . range, twelve parsecs," Chekov offered. He turned to Kirk, his terse accent clipping the words. "Will that be sufficient, sir?"

"If not, we'll go out farther. Mr. Sulu, implement at warp factor three."

Sulu didn't make any comment, but his voice was a rasp as he said, "Z-plus one five to the galactic plane, sir . . . warp factor three."

On the forward viewer, the growling dark cloud of residue from a millions-year-old explosion suddenly fell away to the bottom of the screen as the ship turned upward and vaulted for the galaxy's sky.

Kirk counted off the seconds, hoping that—

"Captain?"

Somebody would give him a chance to explain it out loud.

"Yes, Tom? Something I can do for you?"

"Would you mind . . . should I ask Mr. Spock?"

"No, no. I'd be happy to tell you. You see, most of the interference is in line with the racecourse, moving with the galaxy's natural spiral flow. We're going to rise above all that, go at a z-plus angle away from the course, 'up' in the common idea of up and down from where you're standing. By going above the sweep of the distortions thrown off by that cloud, we might be able to find a frequency window."

For what seemed like a shy and enthusiastic breed of people, the Rey would stomp right over their shyness for a thimbleful of new information.

Kirk figured that out when Tom appeared at his side,

right next to the command chair, as if he'd been invited down there and had been there before. *Nobody* did *that*.

Well, nobody but McCoy, but that was different.

And Spock, but that was really different.

"How far 'above' will we go?" Tom asked.

"You're watching, but you're not paying attention," Kirk told him gently. "Do you remember the range when Chekov stated the course?"

"He said . . . twelve."

"Twelve parsecs. That's twelve parsecs up from the standard zero—reference, an imaginary plane going through the center of the galaxy like an arrow. It's a navigational reference."

"What can go wrong?" Tom pressed. "You're not saying it, but I see in your face that you're worried about something."

With tempered irritation and even a touch of amusement, Kirk glanced at him then pushed out of his chair to put some distance between him and the persistent Peter Pan. Something funny about getting too close.

"You'll see when we get there," he said.

He moved toward the helm and stood behind Chekov.

Tom put both hands on the command chair and took a step back. "You mean I'll see when something goes wrong."

Couldn't fool him.

Maybe Tom was nervous. Or maybe he just saw through the knight-in-armor appearance Kirk tried to keep up for company, and realized that the wild maneuver could also make them fall irrevocably behind in the race. With every light-year they pierced as the minutes went by, they could be losing ground.

Correction—they *were* losing ground. There was no doubt of that.

But they were doing it on the chance of gaining sight.

"Chekov," he said, and poked his thumb toward the starboard science console, "up there. Start looking. Ensign Antonoff, take navigation."

"Aye, sir," Chekov said, and Antonoff dropped from the engineering station, echoing the "aye, sir," to the tone, and skidded into the vacant seat as Chekov jumped to the upper deck to look for a clear view below.

Down there other ships were having the same problem. The cloud was throwing the beacons all over the place. The field was scattered. They were risen above the course now. If they could go far enough, fast enough . . .

The forward screen gave them a vision of the galaxy below, the sweeping, thick spray of white dust most people still called the Milky Way.

"Are we above the galaxy?" Tom asked.

"We aren't really above the galactic arm so much as we're on the upper swell of it," Kirk told him.

He tried to sound calm, but he was tense, awed by what he saw, and nagged by the sensation that they were falling behind with every second that slogged by.

"I'm betting we can beat the *Ransom Castle* to the other side of that cloud," he uttered. He was speaking to himself. If anyone else wanted to listen, fine.

He knew Tom did, that was for sure. He could feel those big brown golf-ball eyes right now.

Spock stepped down to stand beside him, and let his hands fall behind his back and clasp in that casual manner of his, a signal that the seas were green, the sky was blue, the desert was dusty, the race was being run, and all was well with the world, whichever world that might be.

Too well.

Kirk lowered his voice—again. Not used to doing that on his own bridge. Why didn't he just buckle down and send those two below?

Nah . . . let 'em stay.

He leaned toward Spock. "What's the matter with you?"

Spock looked at him. "The matter with me, sir?"

"Even you should be a little on edge with a Romulan in the sector. What's wrong?"

"Nothing at all," Spock said, and he sounded perplexed, as though he felt obligated to provide something wrong to serve the captain's intuition.

"You're too calm, Spock," Kirk insisted. "We all are. I can't put my finger on it . . . and it's not exactly calm. Complacent might be more accurate. I can feel myself fighting it."

As his nominal obligation turned to concern, Spock faced him. His voice became quiet and his gaze was anything but cold. "I do not understand."

"You don't believe in luck, do you Mr. Spock?"

"No, sir."

Kirk shook his head. "Well, the only problem with not believing in luck is that you don't believe in bad luck either."

"Got it!" Chekov gasped. "Sir! A frequency window!" He twisted around, his face shining. "You were right! I have the beacon!"

"Plot it," Kirk told him quickly. "Ignore any further signals. This is the only one we'll follow. As soon as we start to move, it'll distort."

"Aye, sir, plotting."

While Chekov worked, Spock gestured up to his upper console monitor. He must have set it on automatic, because it was pouring out a graphic picture of the now distant cloud and the racecourse.

"Now that we can see the beacon," he said, "we can also see sketchy readings of several vessels within five hundred light-years of the cloud, moving in several directions at various levels. Your trick worked. There may be a few ships ahead of us, but we have quite a jump on the main body."

"But look at the configuration of that cloud, Spock, now that we can see the whole thing," Kirk pointed out. "Nancy's instincts were right."

"Yes," Spock agreed. "She'll come out right on top of the beacon."

"If she comes out. Chekov, get that fix. Let's not hover up here forever."

"I have it, sir."

"Locate ships in the immediate vicinity so that we can plot a safe course, Ensign."

"Aye, sir . . . two merchant transports . . . the museum ship, I think . . . the hospital ship . . . another merchant . . . the Starfleet Frigate *Great Lakes* on the perimeter . . . and one smaller emission, probably a private ship."

Suddenly the feeling of calm satisfaction was driven down. Kirk bolted past Spock so hard that the Vulcan was bumped back. "No one else?" he cracked.

"No one else, Captain," Chekov said.

"Confirm that, Ensign."

Chekov looked down at him and frowned. "Sir?"

"Spock, get up there!"

Too close to call whether Kirk's words or Spock's heel hit the upper deck first.

Spock's sallow complexion was sapphired by the sensor hood's light, his expression harsh and dissatisfied.

"Confirmed," he said. "There are no other vessels of cruiser thrust capacity within five hundred twenty light-years in any direction."

Together they turned to the big forward screen.

Kirk felt his throat go dry.

"Where's the Romulan?"

Red Talon

"This? This is your fear? *This?* For this we risk our ship, our lives, intrusion into another ship? For this, all the lies, all the trickery? Standing off a Starfleet captain? Valdus! Turn to me and say something! I want to know why I die!"

Romar held out both hands in a furious encompassment of the form lying crumpled on their deck.

"A *girl?*" he gasped.

His tone collected all the implications of girlness and girlhood and everything an innocent could be, including the silky complexion turned to paste by a disruptor stun.

"What are you thinking!"

Nothing he did succeeded in raising a response from his commander. Not his tone, not his expression, not even the threatening points and flashing hands meant as near slaps.

"You won't die," Valdus said, his voice calm but chapped. He stood as a man in the sun. Eyes squinted, face kinked, lips pursed. "You must trust me. If she is what I think she is, then she and her kind are dangerous to us."

"Dangerous! Again you toss these words over me! How are they dangerous? Tell me what they have!"

Romar tried to ignore his own fury and read his commander's eyes. Valdus looked different somehow. His normal air of complaisance was gone.

Romar put his fingertips to his temples. His head hurt, and his eyes throbbed. He wanted to understand, but had no idea where to begin. He threw his hands to his sides, and spat out with as much venom as he could muster.

"Valdus!"

Chapter Eleven

Enterprise

"EMERGENCY ALERT, all hands. Sensors full capacity. Helm, come about."

"Coming about, sir. Course, minus nine five on the descent plane. Sensors eighty-one percent. Best we can do on the sensors, sir."

"Get us between the beacon and that cloud. Skirt the turbulence as tightly as possible. Scan for other vessels."

"Mr. Scott reports ready for z-minus dive, sir. Helm is answering."

"Implement."

Jim Kirk turned to the back of the bridge as he felt the artificial gravity fight to keep his feet on the floor, and he looked at the two Rey guests.

As the guests sat side by side in chairs that weren't supposed to be there, skin tightened around their huge eyes, lips parted to draw in the breath of the moment. Tom sat forward on his chair, incongruous in his plaid and denim logging duds, his long fingers spread out over his knees. Royenne was hunched back and down, gripping the edges of his seat in a manner that didn't serve the Starfleet uniform. Both manners of attention were flattering for the crew around them.

"Might get dangerous, gentlemen," Kirk said to them. "You may want to consider leaving the bridge."

They looked at him as though he'd slapped them.

Royenne nearly whispered, "Are we in the way?"

All the captain's training and experience and instinct and all that stuff embroidered into his personality told him to take the opportunity to boot them below. Clear the deck. Give them a nice teacherly yes and that would be that. They'd be gone, below decks, nice and safe, relatively speaking.

"No, not really in the way," he found himself saying. Social convention or something had him by the throat. Was he enjoying showing off *that* much?

"Then we wish to stay," Tom said. "It's our race, sir."

"Your race, but if the situation develops into a crisis, you might not like what you see."

Tom cleared his throat. "We want to be part of this. You have come here for us and our people . . . we want to really *be* in the Federation. All your benefits will be ours, and we want to share your dangers. We trust you, and we're not afraid."

"Well, you ought to be," the captain said. He didn't feel like absorbing any compliments, or mollycoddling misplaced bravery, but something kept him from ordering them to join their friend on the observation deck.

Just when he had almost worked himself up to ordering them below, Tom smiled and said, "I have never learned so much in my whole life. Do you think I can steer a ship someday?"

"Probably," Kirk said, "but not this ship."

Well, at least he'd dug up enough authenticity to say that. Tom seemed to take it as a compliment.

Good enough. Kirk turned back to the screen, now providing them a bird's-eye view of the galactic arm and the spread puff of residual cloud, and instantly forgot the Rey guests. Something else took him over.

No trail of engine exhaust, no warning signals from

anybody else . . . what was it he'd heard about silence being deafening?

"Get us back down there, Mr. Sulu," he said. "I don't like not knowing where he is."

Red Talon

"The cloaking operation is a strain in the midst of this discharge, Commander. Shall we veer out and relax the cloak?"

"No, Centurion. Maintain cloaked status."

"Very well, Commander. Maintaining status."

Simple answers, simple orders, this was Valdus. The crew was used to him, but they were burdened today. Was this a suicide mission or not? If not, why couldn't he tell them his plans?

If so, why couldn't they be allowed to take part in the glory by knowing that they were to die in action?

Why wouldn't he tell them?

He himself did not know that answer.

Even here, secluded in the transporter chamber, speaking through the ship's crackling internal communications system distorted by the storm outside, Valdus could sense the burden of his crew.

Alone now in the chamber—at least, the only one awake—he turned from the communication panel, pressed a shoulder against the wall for balance, and looked at the unconscious Rey girl.

She had such a simple appearance. Narrow features, long limbs, a quiet face troubled from within. Large closed eyes branched with brown and red lashes.

As the turbulent cloud shook *Red Talon* around him, Valdus wrapped the ship's cloak around himself, around his purpose, and forced himself to be nefarious, though it wasn't his nature. He had always been an officer of open cause, who obeyed orders to the extreme, whose personal skills had never shown themselves above those of his fellows. From the beginning he had been an obedient, governable tool of the Empire, never questioning, never straying from the noted course, long ago yanked off the course set for his life by one incident and the deaths of all in a crew but himself, and somehow made a hero. His own tractability all those years ago had put him in command of this ship now, a destiny never set for him by nature, and had placed this moment at his feet.

If he did only one truly independent action in his life, this would be that one.

"Commander!"

He jumped with surprise as the panel blurted beside him.

Sharply he answered, "Yes, what is it, Centurion?"

"The Federation starship! It returns, sir!"

"Are you sure?" Valdus demanded. "It's not a distortion you're reading?"

"Absolutely not."

Rage filled his chest as Valdus glared into the immediate future and kept having his vision blocked by that ship and that captain.

His hand was being forced. There was nothing he could do about this but act as proscribed.

"Then we act," he said. "Bring tractor systems to bear. Prepare to turn them on, effect a hard pull, then turn them off quickly. Stealth is the key, Centurion. Let us move on that starship as animals move on each other."

Enterprise

"Arm phasers."

"Phasers armed . . . ready, sir. Leveling to angle with the racecourse. Approaching the cloud."

Sulu was keeping his voice a lot steadier than anybody felt. He was the best liar on the bridge.

The skin prickled on the outsides of Kirk's arms. His muscles pulled inward all over, every sinew experiencing his emotions full-out, and he couldn't stop it.

He didn't care if anybody saw.

"Skirt the cloud, Mr. Sulu. Mr. Spock, Mr. Chekov,

scan for *Ransom Castle.* I want to know if they've gotten themselves out of that thing."

"No sign as yet, sir," Spock said.

"I don't like this."

"Agreed."

"Captain," Tom asked, "by arming your weapons, aren't you inviting battle?"

Kirk glanced back at him, but his attention never really left the forward screen.

"Just being ready for battle never causes it," he said. "Sometimes, that's the very force that deflects it. Complacency is what sucks the unready into war."

If Gullrey was coming into the Federation, putting two of their representatives on the bridge of a Starfleet ship, advertising themselves to all the civilizations around, peaceful and hostile, better they know the galaxy as it really was, and know what they were getting into.

One hard lesson Kirk had learned early in his career in space—the innocent were rarely treated innocently.

"Skirting the cloud, Captain," Spock said. "Picking up some readings inside that might be engine exhaust."

"Can you confirm?"

"Endeavoring to do so. Bursts of discharge are refracting our sensors as before."

"I'd go on running the race," Kirk said, "but I don't like leaving until I know what happened to the *Castle,* and what happened to—"

The deck pushed up under him and drove him to his knees. The starship bolted forward and down several degrees on her descent plane, and suddenly they were tumbling down what might as well have been a spaceport grain-loading ramp.

Kirk ended up on one knee, hanging onto his command chair with one hand and the bridge rail with the other. Bodies spilled by all around him. He caught a glimpse of Tom rolling along the upper deck when, in a sickening motion, the deck surged until he couldn't see Tom or anybody else anymore.

His senses winked out, and the next few seconds were a provoked fight to get them back.

Red Talon

"Take cover quickly! Duck back into the cloud. Condition of maneuver?"

"It worked, Commander! The Federation ship is inside the cloud's perimeter . . . being drawn deeper toward the magnetic center. Shall I continue tractor maneuvers?"

"Can they see us?"

Valdus put his lips close to the communication panel, breathing against his vessel's wall as he might the warm shoulder of a woman. The surprise had drained him and he took the wall's support for what it was.

A starship—probably the *Enterprise*, the ship that had been haunting them since the beginning of the race—dropping at them out of the great vacuum, vectoring back toward the cloud and standing guard in their line of escape.

Not a good time to attempt taking over another vessel.

And now the *Red Talon* and its secrets were dipping back into the depths of the residual cloud, letting their prize slip farther away.

Deprived. Because of that man.

Reduced to lashing out like some kind of snake trying to protect its meter of ground, Valdus had struck. Now he would have to recoil or be detected.

"We are maintaining our cloak, sir," came the tentative answer from his bridge. *"I do not believe we have been seen."*

His command bridge. He saw it in his mind. He should be there. Not down here, guarding his crew from an unconscious alien girl.

Only a girl, Romar had told him. Only a girl.

The imperilment of his ship . . . even his civilization . . . was it from outside or from within? What would it be today? Was it his choice?

"Has Subcommander Romar reported to the bridge yet?" he asked abruptly.

"Not yet, Commander." The centurion's voice was laced with frustration about all the things he had not been told.

Valdus almost smiled. He'd heard the same tone from Romar only minutes ago. The *tell me* tone.

"Release the Federation ship from our tractor beams at one point of drag per second. Make it gradual, uneven. Then retreat slowly. Take care not to stir up the cloud or make any alerting of our presence here. Let the internal turbulence draw the starship in now."

"Shall I continue conquest maneuvers upon the merchant ship?"

"Not yet. Another chance will come. Retreat, and we will leave the cloud at another angle. Make all maneuvers subtle ones, Centurion . . . let us not be seen."

Enterprise

"Free drift! No steering capacity at all!"

The sheer power it takes to slam a Starfleet heavy cruiser forty feet sideways in open space is enough to break legs and spines and get anyone's attention, including the ship's computer.

Yellow alert, yellow alert . . . all hands, brace for turbulence . . . brace for tur—"

And even Uhura's silky voice was choked away as she was thrown from her chair when the ship pitched forward and to port.

Lights popped before the captain's eyes. White ones, yellow ones, the occasional little red or blue one. All he saw was Uhura and a few moving forms, then only the lights.

"Don't try to get up, sir—"

Whose voice was that?

There were hands holding him down. He fought to climb back up through the corridor of lights by counting how many hands were holding him down. One on his right shoulder, one on his elbow, one on the other elbow . . . who on the bridge had three hands?

His head pounded, drowning out all other noises, hammering down a retching nausea. He clawed feebly at the arms extending from those hands. Fabric—

"Medical emergency! Dr. McCoy to the bridge. The captain is down!"

"Graphic visual, Mr. Chekov." Spock's voice. "Engineering, report!"

"Scott here. There's a pocket of gravitons caught in the flow of that cloud, sir. It's taking every pellet of IPS to hold our position and not be drawn deeper inside. Reaction exhaust is pushing tolerance, thermal stresses are above critical per unit, and field polarity is unstable. I'll have numbers for you in two minutes."

"Valve off a portion of our reactants if you can't stabilize them."

"It'll cost us thrust, Mr. Spock."

"We'll have to manage."

"Right away, sir. Scott out."

"Shields up, fifty percent."

"Shields, fifty percent, sir."

That was Chekov, and Spock was running things. Kirk could see the lean blue and black form above him, floating against the lights. Spock's voice sounded shaky.

No, not shaky. Tentative . . . forced. There was a difference. As though Spock was fighting for stability. Was he hurt too?

"No, I'm not down," Kirk choked. His chest curved as he tried to force himself to a sitting position using just his diaphragm muscles.

Slamming aside the hands that held him down, he rolled to his knees, fighting against the centrifugal forces pulling him toward the port deck. He fixed his eyes on Chekov, clinging to the science subsystems monitor, hammering controls to bring automatic compensators back on line, which at the moment weren't operating automatically enough, and Uhura was crawling to help him. All around, others struggled back to their posts. The yellow alert Klaxon howled in his ears and told him they were stabilizing, or the ship would've automatically gone to red alert.

Well, it wasn't much, but it was something. With his mind he clung to that flashing yellow gash on the wall and used it to drag himself to his feet.

"But the doctor's coming, sir—"

Kirk shoved Sulu off. "It's just my head, Lieutenant."

"But sir!"

"I'll think with my ears if necessary. Get your hands off me."

"Aye, s—"

"Condition, Mr. Spock. What hit us?"

Spock stepped across the lower deck, reached for him, and helped him get to his feet.

"A gravity well," the Vulcan said.

Kirk frowned. "Which is?"

"We produce gravity without mass by artificial high speed spinning of gravitons," Spock told him. "However, such conditions can be created in nature if enough free-floating gravitons are caught in a spinning phenomenon. This residual cloud is still spinning with momentum from its original collision and has collected a large number of gravitons over the millions of years. They spool down into a drain, are rejected at the bottom, and pulled back in. Gravitons, combined with the energy of the spin, are creating a gravity well. Like the energy of warm water creating a typhoon, this well is self-perpetuating as long as it has the energy to spin."

"Are you telling me we're caught in the remains of a collision that happened six million years ago?"

"Yes. Residual momentum." Spock pointed to the small visual readout on Sulu's console. It showed a serrated blue tornado of corrugated space—the computer's enhanced idea of what it was reading out there. "The current is funnel-shaped and rifled, creating a washboard effect, which is responsible for the turbulence we're experiencing. We're caught in the spooling action, near the top."

Kirk squinted at the picture until his eyes hurt. "If the gravitons are being drawn down and spat out the bottom, can we go down and get spat out too?"

Spock glanced at him. "Not without being crushed. The power down there is enormous."

"How big is it, Spock?"

Spock pushed the captain to his command chair so he could lean on it, then crossed to Sulu's console and tapped into the science readouts. He fell suddenly silent.

Kirk clamped his lips. He knew what Spock was doing—he'd have to give him the time to do it. By measuring areas of stress on the ship's primary hull, the computer could project upon that and come up with a figure. That figure would show them the size of the trap they were caught in.

It could be a light-year across and ten thick in a cloud this size. Like a tree, growth depended upon a thousand conditions in the galactic garden.

Briefly subjugated by his pounding head, Kirk resisted the urge to go over there and pound an answer out of the computer. Spock would do that. It was afraid of him.

Suddenly the ship heaved and the deck dropped out from under them again. Kirk ended up bent in two over the helm, with Spock and Sulu clinging to the console at his sides.

He let his chest take his weight, reached down with both hands, floundered until he found cloth, clawed on, and started to haul.

At his sides, Sulu fumbled for his chair, and Spock levered to his feet and at the same time kept the captain from slipping to his knees again.

Sulu gulped, "Thank you, sir," probably just to get Kirk to let go of him.

So he did, and pushed himself off the helm and back toward his chair, pulling Spock up with him.

The turbolift hissed open and McCoy appeared, white as frost and staggering. His eyes were wide as he made his way down the tilted deck between the stunned Rey guests to the rail.

"Jim, sit down!"

"I can't right now," Kirk snapped. "Lieutenant, patch me through to engineering."

"Aye, sir—Mr. Scott, sir."

Kirk slid sideways into his seat and held on. "Scotty, can't we get control over this?"

"This is the control, sir." Scott's voice sounded strained and annoyed, but not worried. A good sign.

"Suggestions?"

"It's a storm, sir. We've got to put our nose to it and plow against the wind until we're clear."

"Not sideways under these conditions?"

"Not recommended."

"Noted. Keep on top of it. We'll do it your way."

"Aye, sir. Engine room out."

The intercom clicked almost imperceptibly against the howls and bleeping of other emergency systems. Kirk straightened, pressing a shoulder against the back cushion of his chair, and raised an arm to intercept McCoy's hand as the doctor tried to bring a medical scanner toward his head.

"I said not now, Doctor. Mr. Sulu, one quarter impulse. Any sign of the *Ransom Castle?* It could be caught in this thing too."

"Why can't we move sideways against this thing, Jim?" McCoy asked.

"The ship's designed to move forward primarily and aft secondarily," Kirk told him, seeing the maneuvers in his aching head. "Moving abeam is the highest level of stress on both hull and engines."

"Captain," Uhura called, calmly but abruptly, "receiving a signal . . ." She paused to adjust her instruments and listen. A second ago she had been sure of something, and now she wasn't.

Kirk turned to her and did the thing he hated most. He waited. Giving orders instantly relegated him to an observer when he really wanted to do something with his hands. He should take up knitting. He could give orders and knit.

Finally impatience got the best of him. "Lieutenant, do you have a report?" he urged. "Is it the *Castle?*"

"One moment, please, sir."

Kirk made an ugly sound in the bottom of his throat and twisted around to McCoy, who was hanging on to the back of the command chair and forcing it against its tendency to swivel with the turbulence.

"All right, Doctor, hurry it up."

"You should report to sickbay, but I know I'm barking up a tree with that one."

"Have you got a prognosis or not?"

"Yes. You hit your head on the rail. Hold still for three seconds."

"You've got two."

"Jim," McCoy began, then he paused. He glanced behind them at Tom and Royenne, but the Rey guests were busy trying to stay on their feet. As he pressed a medicated pad to the bruise on the back of the captain's head, he leaned a little closer and lowered his voice. "There's something about these Rey people that I can't put my finger on. They read out as essentially humanoid, along the same lines of sensible evolution as you or I, or any mammal. Most things the same, a few things different, eyes, noses, mouths—my instruments don't tell me anything, but all my medical instincts tell me there's something."

Kirk jerked forward and snarled, "There's something on that pad is where there's something. What is that?"

"It's medicated."

"It hurts. Back it off."

McCoy scowled with grim disapproval. "You're a bad boy, Captain."

"Sir," Uhura called, "receiving contact with the Lightship *Hiawatha*, sir. Apparently she was placed here to mark this well of turbulence."

"Little late."

"Aye, sir."

"Mark the contact, Lieutenant." Kirk eyed the swarming blue mess on the forward screen and wanted to rub his eyes and wave a magic wand so he could see through it. The churning blue-black garble made him feel like a drunk on wood alcohol.

As he felt McCoy's hand on his arm, steadying him in the chair and keeping him down, he focused his vigilance at the screen and the undissipated energy that held the starship in check. And he knew that thing out there wasn't his real menace.

"It was him," he said.

The doctor leaned forward to see if there was anything he could do.

Jim Kirk stared relentlessly at the screen.

"He's out there, Bones . . . I can hear his heart beating."

RED
ALERT

Chapter Twelve

Red Talon

HANDS COULD BE EYES. Romar knew.

Through half his childhood he had been blind.

When science gave him back the eyes nature had taken, he had vowed never to abandon the credit of having once been blind. He kept his senses sharp, paid attention to other than the obvious, remembered to listen. The breathing of another person could reveal that person's thoughts. One who was once blind, if he didn't forget, could move in places where others would only stumble.

Such places were many on a converted Klingon star cruiser. Many hidden and dark places.

Here, in the thorny electrical bowels of a captured alien vessel from the wars of another lifetime, Romar closed his eyes and followed his hands and his ears. His finely tuned hearing could perceive tiny crackles, faults in the power flows. Harmless faults, but as good as a map for such as he, the crackles led him through the innards of *Red Talon*.

When he got to an appropriate place, a cross section of electronics, he moved his legs up underneath him and sat down in the cramped space with his head hunched down and the back of his neck scraping the top of the crawlway. It wasn't even meant to be a crawlway—that's how small it was.

Power flow valves. Very simple, basic, no secret technology. All over the ship. He felt them under his palms. Blood in a body. Like any blood, it could be made to clot. The clot would cause backups, until the body cried out in agony and exploded.

If Valdus was going against the Empire, there would have to be that explosion. A fairly simple idea, not particularly clever.

But it was all Romar could think to do.

The first thing he could do would be to kill Valdus, and he would do that if Valdus had somehow lost his mind, but Romar knew such an act wouldn't be easy and probably couldn't be done honorably. He would rather blow up the ship.

He sat in the cramped huddle until his legs were numb and his feet tingling.

When he was finished, he was ready to incinerate the *Red Talon*. He felt a twinge of sorrow, but none of regret. He was the ship's subcommander. If the commander was mad, it befell the subcommander to destroy him or destroy the ship, or both, in order to protect the Empire.

With a muttered explanation to the walls, he began his long crawl back through the blackness, listening to the unremitting crackles fade behind him.

If we live, he thought, *I shall have someone open the bulkhead and effect repairs on the crackles. If Valdus fails to tell me the truth* . . .

A different ending to the venture.

He broke through the slice he'd taken out of the wall and into the lighted corridor and held a hand over his eyes until they became adjusted. Still sensitive, all these years later. These corridors always hurt a little. Had he gotten himself promoted time after time in order to serve on the dim and quiet bridge? Perhaps.

No one would notice the gash in the wall. *Red Talon*

had many gashes in her old hull, inside and out. When the smoke from the cutting torch was drawn out by the ventilation system and the wall cooled, this would be just another gash.

He dusted his jacket free of lingering dirt from inside the walls, ignored a passing crewman who took care to glance only shortly at him, then strode down the corridor.

The ship was large and imposing, yes, but from the inside there seemed to be too much space. Romar preferred the tight quarters of smaller, quicker vessels. Larger ships made larger targets.

Usually larger problems.

He went directly to the transporter area, through the door opening without breaking stride—luckily the door panel slid open just right for him to make such an entrance—and ended up standing between the two guards who had been posted inside the door.

On the edge of the transporter platform, Valdus sat with his knees up and his shoulders slumped, staring in mute contemplation at the Rey girl they had captured. She lay now on the deck between the control console and the platform, still insensible from disruptor sting.

Romar chewed on his lip. He had hoped things would have improved, changed.

He accepted that, reviewed in his mind his own movements in the veins of the ship, and went to sit down on the edge of the platform beside his commander.

The two of them sat there for a pitifully long time.

Silence ate at them.

Valdus never looked at anything but the girl.

"Send the guards out," he said finally.

Blinking, Romar glanced at him, then turned to the guards and called, "Wait in the corridor."

"Yes, Subcommander," the senior of them said, and they both went outside.

Now there was silence and loneliness, too. Romar looked absurdly at the starch white door panel and suddenly missed even the company of low level guards.

"Where were you?" Valdus asked him. "I needed you on the bridge."

"I was occupied."

"We had an action while you were occupied. I ordered an assault upon the merchant vessel, but as we moved, a Starfleet ship appeared suddenly. I was forced to abandon the merchant conquest and throw tractor beams on the starship to yank them off course and into the cloud. Now we linger in the periphery of the storm."

"They didn't see us?"

"No," Valdus said, "but he feels us." Wariness nearly approaching superstition showed in his face. "Let nature have them. We will slip out of the cloud at another point, pretend to continue the race, and pursue my target."

Romar squeezed his eyes shut. They ached now. "Commander, *why* do you want that ship? You have this . . . person . . . you have looked at her, and now you want the ship she was on?"

"I wanted to look at a Rey," Valdus said, "to hear my memory speak more loudly, to see if it lied. But it doesn't lie. Now that I see her, I remember everything."

Nauseated, Romar hunched forward until his chin almost touched his knees, and moaned, "And now you tell me we must conquer a merchant ship . . ."

"You know, Romar," Valdus said quietly, gazing at the girl on the deck, "expansionism is part of our evolution. Not only socially, but physically, too . . . it keeps us strong. If someone were to conquer us, we'd consider it perfectly normal. We know that eventually one race will dominate the galaxy. It's our duty to be sure it is our race that dominates. There's nothing wrong with conquest. It's been normal for eons . . . until the Federation came along to act as a stopgap against us. They've taken away our ability to expand. Therefore, they prevent us from evolving. They protect weak races who would otherwise be absorbed by a larger power."

He paused and changed the position of his legs, taking the time to think. Without blinking he looked at the unconscious Rey girl.

"By protecting weaker races," he mused, "the Federation is diluting their own strength and guaranteeing that they themselves will eventually be conquered. To put more and more people on the cart, with fewer and fewer drawing the cart . . . a civilization puts the blade to its own throat this way."

He kept staring at the girl, at her silvery hair and large closed eyes, at her simple shirt and wrap skirt.

Romar stared at the girl, too.

"I've put a bomb on the ship," he said.

Valdus looked for a moment as though he'd been struck in the chest, then actually smiled and looked disapprovingly at his subcommander.

"You have no faith in me," he said.

"I have tremendous faith in you," Romar admitted. "But presently I am confused. When I'm confused, I pick one thing to do and I do it."

They sat together in a longer silence, not looking at each other, but only surveying their captive.

"I would hate you for this," Valdus said finally, "if I did not understand."

Pricked by the idea of having to ask another question, Romar gritted his teeth to do it. "*What* do you understand?"

"That she is doing something to us."

Romar wiped his brow and felt suddenly hot. "She," he said, "is unconscious, Commander."

"But she is doing something. Can't you feel it?"

"I don't feel anything from her, Commander."

"You're hot, aren't you?"

"Yes, I am warm, but I've been working."

"Planting your bomb."

"Yes."

With a subdued nod, Valdus drew a long breath, as though searching for the right words.

"You see the movement in her legs and arms. Her body knows it has been stunned. She's doing something to us. Making us warm and uneasy."

"Commander . . ."

"Look at her. Look, Romar." He clasped Romar's elbow and squeezed it until the other man winced and did as he said. "Her body moves. Her face is disturbed. That tension is coming to us. Through the air, to us!"

Romar shook the hand away and stood up. "Yes, I am fatigued, of course, and this is what I feel."

"Because you have been stunned," Valdus insisted.

Romar pointed at the Rey girl as she lay twitching on the deck and irritably said, *"She* has been stunned!"

"And she is giving it to you. If you strike me—" Valdus held up a warning finger even as Romar pulled back to smash his own knuckles into Valdus's face. "I will have to restrain you. Or kill you. So lower that hand."

Breathing heavily for some reason, Romar willed himself to stop, his hand still drawn back, ready to strike. Knotting his fingers, he glared down at his commander and held still to hear what Valdus would say at such a moment.

"And I have spent my life practicing for this moment," Valdus said. "To resist this moment. I will stay sane one minute longer than you will, my friend, and the last gesture will be mine. So sit down."

"I can't sit down," Romar choked. He clutched one wrist with the other hand as though to hold his limbs in place. "I'm distressed."

"The ghastliness of what I know," Valdus told him, "distresses me too."

Romar paced away.

Being near to his commander was confusing. His purpose had seemed so clear earlier. Now, as he looked at Valdus, at those eyes he had read so often, the steadiness he had served for years, he couldn't think.

"I can trigger the explosion from any console on the ship," he said.

Valdus looked up at him. "Why didn't you arrange a hand remote? That's what I would've done."

Romar sank on a shoulder against the bulkhead. He stared at his commander until his eyes ached.

"After all," Valdus commented, "I could knock you down." He leaned back a little, shifted his feet again in their heavy boots, and added casually, "I'll help you do one. Then I'll have to be very sure of myself. Is it a chain reaction trigger?"

"Stop! Stop talking."

Romar paced the transporter area twice, three times, four, trying to come up with an explanation. Something about the Rey girl. Something about the Rey *people*. Something from the deep past in Valdus's life, something Valdus was very sure about, enough that he didn't even raise his voice when he talked about this fundamental, irreversible threat.

Whatever it was.

Valdus just let him pace.

Suddenly Romar made his decision and turned, pointing at the Rey girl on the floor. "Wake her up."

Valdus came alive and rose to his feet. "No! I'm not—ready!"

"Ready for what? What happens when she awakens?" Letting his question ring, Romar moved to the transporter control panel and fingered the communications grid. "Medical section!"

"No!"

Valdus snatched him by the arm, but Romar was young and could stand the pressure of his Commander's grip. He let his arm ache and shouted into Valdus's face.

"Why not! Awaken her and face her! Are you a coward?"

Pushing away with both hands, Valdus suddenly went stiff as a log and backed off the length of the girl on the deck.

His brows lowered and drew tight. His eyes were heavy—laden with undefined torment. His chest contracted as his respiration grew shallow and he battled his own apprehension.

He stared at Romar, his lower lip pressed upward and breath coming in shots.

Romar forced himself to be silent as his commander

struggled with past and present and some undeclared ugliness that could mysteriously endanger the Empire.

An otherwise calm leader turned before Romar's eyes into a gargoyle, an image of disfigurement and gracelessness. Valdus's battle with himself was a sight to behold. After a few seconds, Romar didn't have any more trouble remaining quiet for he himself had said something to cause this volcano to shudder. And he wasn't even sure what that something had been.

When Romar thought his back would break from the tension, Valdus suddenly drew a single sharp breath.

"All right," he choked. "Awaken her."

Chapter Thirteen

Enterprise

"Go to red alert. Emergency status, all decks. Excessive turbulence."

James Kirk's voice was all steel and firm resolve as it echoed through his ship. It sounded a lot steadier than his stomach.

Luckily, his stomach was private and he didn't have to tell anybody about it if he didn't want to. He'd rather face a dozen Romulan ships than that raw force of nature swirling on the viewscreen. Enemies could be outsmarted, outgunned.

Everyone would be awake and working now, most of the positions double-manned, crew teaming up.

On the bridge, the Klaxon was turned off so the bridge officers could work without shouting. Kirk was sure he heard the red alert horns throbbing below him, even though the designers insisted the starship's bulkheads were soundproof.

The ship bucked and dropped again. Half his mind went to Spock, the other half to Scott in the engineering section.

He resisted an urge to smack the comm unit. Calling

down there wouldn't do any good. Scott would be distracted from his work, and all he'd be able to report was that he was doing his best.

The ship slipped sideways and threw everybody to port. Kirk lost his grip on his command chair and ended up bent forward over the rail. Like a treadle the bridge heaved and dropped several times before he could even look up. Knowing the crew would be watching him, glancing at him to see how hurt they should be, he pressed both palms against the rail and shoved himself up against the pressure and back into his chair.

Pressing an aching shoulder against the chair for balance as the deck dropped another ten degrees on one side, Kirk barked, "Forward thrust one-third sublight."

Standing—not sitting—at the helm with his feet spread apart and his body hunched over his console, Sulu nodded. "Forward thrust, sir. One-third sublight."

"Keep fighting it, gentlemen," Kirk encouraged them. "Give engineering a chance to get its bearings."

He eyed Spock, who was working hard at the computer controls, getting hyperaccurate measurements of the well and its pulse spikes to see if they couldn't find a pattern to push against.

Working was an added complication to just hanging on. One hand for yourself and one for the ship. Old adages came back to life at these times, and screamed for attention.

The artificial gravity system whined as the ship pivoted against it, a gyroscope forced to turn its axis in another direction. If space had an "up", the ship was turning upward, and twisting to one side, being dragged down into the churning mouth of the gravity well. The crew was being heaved like bugs on a boomerang.

"One step at a time, gentlemen," he warned, keeping his voice a link between his mind and his bridge crew. "Handle each stress as it presents itself. Spock—"

"Vector force at right angles, sir," the first officer anticipated. "Attempting to compensate."

"Ship's power? Can we crank out of it?"

"Possibly."

"Lieutenant Uhura, try to release a recorder marker. If it has high enough thrust, it may shoot free of the well and make way into the race lanes. Specify location of this anomaly and that any markers stationed here have drifted and are no longer viable for safety."

"Aye, sir, recording—"

Kirk wanted to put his hands on something, steer something, *do* something—

Then Uhura's voice broke into his thoughts. "Contact, Captain—*Ransom Castle*."

"Put her on."

"This is Nancy. What are you doing inside there? Did you follow us through?"

Her voice was crackling, distorted.

Kirk straightened in his chair. Too late he realized he had just failed to read her tone, her inflections, measure the words she had chosen to use—these measurements were trained into him, but he hadn't done it. Maybe McCoy was right and he needed treatment.

"No, we didn't follow you. We were sucked in. Some kind of gravitational spin force. You must have just missed it. Are you clear of the cloud?"

"I told you I'd get through, didn't I?"

"Have you seen the Romulan vessel? We've lost contact with them and believe they might be in the cloud."

"Yeah, they were going to pirate my ship and take my hold full of nothing. Or maybe it's my ship they want, the whole forty-year-old patched-up bundle of her."

Kirk glanced at McCoy, just to make sure he wasn't crazy and she really was galled at having to talk to him.

The doctor could offer only a one-shouldered shrug as he clung to the command chair.

"I'll take that as a no," Kirk said.

Though he too was hanging on to the chair to keep from slipping down the bucking deck, he almost smiled. Damned if she hadn't gotten her ship in and out of that cloud after all. She'd been right about her crew and her vessel.

Jim Kirk had heard all the superlatives applied to himself, wonderful words he had inherited from the *Enterprise* captains who came before him, whom he didn't dare let down. And his own reputation—the most rash, the bravest, the most confident, the most brazen, the one who had gone farther than anyone else and somehow come back. While those words were compliments and epithets all rolled into a package any wild dog would be proud of, he found himself bolstered by finding out that he wasn't the only one of a breed—even if he found that out from Nancy Ransom.

Nobody with any sense really wanted to be the only one.

"Do you want help getting out?"

"Negative," Kirk quickly told her. "Under no circumstances approach us. Continue on the racecourse and notify one of the other Starfleet entrants to remain alert on the Starfleet channel. If we need assistance, we'll broadcast an SOS. *Enterprise* out."

"Uh . . . wait a minute."

His body aching, Kirk shifted in his seat, felt the weight of McCoy leaning against the chair back to keep from falling, and watched his crew try to keep the bucking ship from twisting apart inside the cloud. The gravitational currents had a grip on the primary hull, the secondary hull, and both nacelles and their struts, all at different tolerances. This was the kind of thing that could rip a ship apart like a piece of paper.

They had to use the ship's deflectors and internal artifical gravity to keep those tolerances near equal, or they were scrap metal.

All he needed was more of Nancy Ransom.

"Go ahead," he said, and forced himself not to slap a *hurry up* on the bottom of that.

It was five seconds before Nancy responded.

"We had kind of a rough ride."

Kirk leaned forward. "You need assistance?"

"No . . . I'm just constrained by Federation Interstellar Maritime Collision Regulations, according to Rule 38,

paragraph 2, to report the following to the nearest Starfleet vessel of Scout Class or above. We've had one death aboard, apparently accidental. Okay, I've done it. Ransom out."

"Wait a minute!" McCoy shouted.

"Ransom!" Kirk pushed out of his chair. "State the nature of your casualty."

"It was an accident. Turbulence, I guess. I've reported it. That's all I have to do."

"Read the rest of the order, Captain," Kirk insisted. "I have requirements here too. I'm obligated to conduct a Level Three investigation."

"I don't want you here."

"I'll go," McCoy interrupted.

"Maybe you don't," Kirk said. "But at least let me send a team to investigate."

Behind him, McCoy said, "I should go."

"Keep your details to yourself, Kirk. I don't need any Starfleet interference on board my ship, least of all be beholdin' to you."

The doctor pulled himself along the arm of the command chair. "I want to go."

Kirk stepped forward between Sulu and the ensign at navigation.

"Nancy, listen to me. It doesn't matter what you think of me. I admit you were right. There was something to be gained by going through the cloud. And you knew your ship, your crew, and you made it through. That's the sign of a good captain. A little faith, a little knowledge, a little risk. But there's more for a good captain to do." He paused, and wished he could do the listening for her. "You owe this to the crewman you lost."

McCoy sidled up beside him. "I think I ought to go."

Not five seconds went by before the unexpected, unlikely, and certainly unpredictable answer bunched through the channel, so sharply that it sounded like just another electrical crackle.

"All right."

* * *

"Stand by, *Castle*."

The situation went ticklish as Uhura tapped off the vocal connections and held the channel open. Kirk didn't look around. He knew she'd done it.

"What just happened?" he murmured. He gazed into the forward screen's vision of the purple-blue cloud, with its electrical charges cricketing everywhere, and at the grave, ghostly figure of *Ransom Castle* turning on the screen's sensor periphery. If not for the form of running lights outlining the ship, he would never have even noticed that she was out there.

"Did Nancy Ransom just agree to Starfleet intervention? Without an argument?"

"There's been a death on her ship," McCoy simply said. "I know how you would be feeling."

Kirk turned to him. "And when's the last time I heard you begging to have your atoms scrambled?"

"Now, don't hold that over my head."

"Then explain it."

McCoy paused, realizing his joke had fizzled under the stress of the moment and the captain wasn't in a mood for quips.

"Merchant ships don't carry medical officers, and I don't want those people setting broken legs with soup spoons."

But Kirk didn't turn away. "What else?"

The doctor fidgeted, his ice blue eyes moving with self-consciousness. "Well . . . you have a feeling there's more going on than a race," he said, "and I trust your impulses."

Kirk gazed at him a moment. "Mr. Spock, stability of transporter under these conditions?"

Spock turned from what he was doing to another secondary console and tapped in. "Transporter conduits read stable . . . matter stream transmission on line, buffer operating . . . however, target scanners are fluctuating nominally due to ionization within the cloud."

"Thank you. It'll have to wait, Bones."

"Jim—"

Kirk shook his hand off, and a jolt nearly threw McCoy to the deck. "You're dismissed, doctor. This isn't the time."

"Jim, how many times have you and Spock insisted on beaming into dangerous situations to come to somebody else's aid? Why would you deny me the chance to do that when I'm the one who swore the oath to do it?"

"It isn't safe. You could materialize two feet outside the *Castle*'s hull."

Spock heard them and as he leaned on the console, he twisted around enough to say, "Unlikely, Captain, if we use the *Castle*'s transporter instead of ours, using our transporter pads as homing points."

"That's right!" McCoy said. "Receiving is a lot easier for those popcorn machines than sending. Scotty told me that."

Kirk glowered. "I'll have a word with him later."

McCoy pushed off the command chair's back and made his way past Tom and Royenne to the upper deck. "I'll get my pack and be waiting in the transporter room. As soon as that thing can be aimed and fired, beam me over there so I can do my job."

Red Talon

The mania seized him like poison advancing through his system.

Romar's eyes hurt and his arms and legs twitched. How had he lived so long among deceivers?

Insane mutineers—how had he survived here? Every voice was threatening, every sound shrill, jarring. He smelled the noxious stench of his own terror, felt his brain shattering—the nightmare sensation of a brittle body, as though a movement would crack him in half, but failing to move would melt him.

He wanted to look away, but he could only stare at the Rey girl, and she stared back at him.

She was pressed against the wall of the transporter chamber, a cave into which there was no more retreat. She could only stare in her horror at them.

Romar's hand trembled, tightened around the hypodermic that had brought the girl back from her stirring unconsciousness. He was standing alone in front of her where a moment ago there had been two interns from the medical team, but they had fled.

Madness . . . they were all consumed by a mania and he was the only one on the ship who hadn't been caught in the web of treason. They were patently psychotic! The entire crew, all this time! How could he have been ignorant to it?

A clapper was ringing in his mind, maddening him, but he fought it. How were they doing this?

Hadn't he planted a bomb? He should go to it! He should ignite it—

A movement in his periphery snatched his attention from the Rey girl—she was nothing, just a blemish— and what he saw was his commander's jacket flashing by, and he lunged.

Romar caught the hem of Valdus's sleeve as Valdus dodged for the entranceway, but tripped. As their bodies fell in a staggering heap at the door, the panel slid open, and out in the corridor crewmen were running frantically and at least two others were coiled in a personal battle on the corridor deck.

Escaping!

Romar vowed not to let them go.

"No! Coward!" He clawed at the leg of the man whose orders he once cherished and defended. "Animal!"

Valdus didn't say anything, but fought him with impunity, boxing his face until Romar was beaten back.

Dizzy, his face bruised, his head spinning, Romar found himself on his knees, staring at the floor. A puddle of lime blood spread there—his nose was bleeding.

He pressed a sleeve to it, snorted so violently that he almost passed out, and staggered to his feet.

With a passing glance at the Rey girl, hiding in the

transporter chamber racked with terror, he stumbled toward the transporter console.

He could do it from here. He could incinerate the ship and its poison with it. If he could just find the key pattern . . . foolish console! Built an age ago, never brought up to date! Traitors had been at work here—that was it!

"Treason, treason," he hissed, teeth grinding as though he had a traitor by the jugular between them.

The Rey girl whimpered, her brow drawn tight, her cheeks pasty, legs throttling and failing to keep up her meager weight. Her arms were spread out at her sides against the back wall of the transporter chamber. Nowhere to run.

Romar almost had it. He knew the orders to tap into the computer, how to make it go through the ship's walls and find his trick and set it afire. Almost there. Almost there—

—when the door panel flushed open and the buzz of a disruptor filled the air.

A chrome orange beam shot into the room, and it made a hungry sound.

Chapter Fourteen

Red Talon

THE HANDS BEFORE HIM were clay white. He stared down at the creased knuckles, the bleached fingernails, the swollen veins like winter ivy. Eyes were burning . . .

Against every impulse he had been following, he raised one of those hands and pressed the back of it to his eyes.

He staggered back until the bulkhead stopped him. His head began to clear slowly. Madness peeled back in thin strips, one at a time.

In the haze of immediate memory, a buzzing flash . . . the sizzling shape of the Rey girl, caught in an instant of horror, a glowing mass that expanded, then dissipated. Her expression somehow lasted much longer than her death.

Perhaps it only seemed so . . .

Romar sagged against the wall, one knee bent almost to the floor. Waves of his own paranoia flooded through him, each less than the one before, and the pounding of his heart in his throat started to lessen enough for him to notice.

He flattened a hand against the wall to steady himself, and drew breath after breath.

Movement in the room . . . he wasn't alone.

Valdus hovered nearby.

Too near—Romar wanted to strike out, drive him away, pierce him through the eyes, kill him.

But . . . why?

Strike his commander? The idea retreated, became more foreign, with every breath Romar drew.

Valdus approached slowly from the entranceway, still holding his disruptor pistol upward as though somehow the Rey witch would return and weave her intangible web around them again, to strangle them again. He reached out and took Romar's arm, and in the residue of madness, Romar yanked away from him.

The air was still crackling. They still felt on their skin the remnants of disruptor fire. Romar stared at Valdus, battling within himself to decide whether he should submit or strike out. For an instant longer he truly didn't know what to do or who was enemy and who friend.

Then Valdus sighed and lowered his weapon, but made no more attempts to touch Romar or help in any way. He seemed willing to wait.

"You resisted well," he said, "considering."

Feeling burned and short-winded, hollow-eyed as he stared across the short space at Valdus, Romar rolled against the wall until both shoulders were pressed back against it and he could straighten his legs.

When he found his breath—or some of it, he gasped, "Why did you . . . keep this secret to yourself!"

Valdus let the echo fade, then quietly answered, "Would you believe me had you not felt it for yourself?"

Simple truth.

Romar's shudders of rage left him weak. He didn't argue. He watched as his commander looked away.

"Even I wasn't sure," Valdus murmured, gazing at the empty transporter cubicle. "I had to convince myself as much as you. Memory is a trick, Romar. I couldn't trust it. When I felt it again, the unsureness of the years peeled away. All the doubts I have harbored for decades suddenly cracked. I *wasn't* imagining or remembering incorrectly."

He left Romar to his recovery and paced toward the empty chamber where minutes ago the great threat of his life had shriveled before his weapon.

"I knew they could do something," he said. "Emit a smell, cause a thought, put something into our atmosphere . . . something that made us go mad. But I didn't know who they were or where they were from. There was no planet nearby . . . I thought perhaps I was mistaken. Until the Federation found them for us. As the galaxy unfolded and the Empire was held in tighter and tighter check, I realized what a weapon this could be against us if the Federation were to discover it."

Stumbling, Romar caught himself on the transporter control unit and pulled himself around to the front of it. "I almost . . . I almost . . ."

"Yes," Valdus said. "You almost did . . . what I did."

They stood together side by side, both nearly exhausted from this bizarre experience, each trying to piece together the past and finding it most unsatisfying.

"The attack upon the *Scorah?*" Romar rasped. "All the legends—"

"Are half true." Holding a palm up at the transporter chamber, Valdus said, "That . . . was the attack. They came aboard, as subtle as that girl. As their fear spread among us, we saw each other as enemies and were killing each other. Except for me. I turned and ran."

Romar looked at him. How could a statement like that be made so easily? He knew if he tried to say such a thing, his tongue would freeze in his mouth. Had Valdus lived with this so long?

"It has haunted me my whole life. I spent my life trying to prove my worth to myself," Valdus went on, "but in my soul I was deathly afraid. I only survived . . ."

This time his strength gave way. Shame flushed his face and he lowered his eyes. His shoulders sagged. He turned from the chamber and from Romar.

"I only survived because I was more afraid than angry."

The room seemed unduly cold.

They were both shivering, but for different reasons.

Valdus sat down on the edge of the platform and sighed.

"I couldn't return with the truth . . . that we all went insane and I destroyed the ship and murdered my crewmates, my commanders. Even if I had said it, who would have believed? So I invented a tale. An attack of which I was the only survivor. I shunned celebration. I despised myself for not having the will to think my way through what happened. Weakness . . . I don't know, Romar. This time, I killed the Rey instead of my own crew. Experience, most likely. I have taught myself to focus on the enemy . . . determined such a mistake would never come at my hand again."

"How can the humans deal with them?" Romar coughed.

"I've pondered that. Two possibilities. Either the humans have simply never been in a threat situation with these fear-projectors yet or . . ."

"Or this only affects those of our descent! Commander—" Romar almost gagged on his own words, but forced them out. "A weapon against us!"

"Yes." Valdus said, staring at the floor between his boots. "This event, this race will bring commerce and colonization to these creatures. They will never be contained again. They are just another weak culture the Federation will have to protect, but also they are a ruthless weapon against the Empire. This is more dangerous to us than losing a war. These people's very existence strips away control and turns our civilization into a weapon against ourselves. Losing a war only means occupation for a few generations until the yoke of failure can be thrown off. But this—these people can turn back our evolution a million years. Turn us into elemental survival instincts with arms and legs. We must not have that, Romar . . . we can't have it."

Horrified, his face still white with realization, Romar also sank to the platform and stared. Seconds ticked by. Truths compounded until the two officers felt the weight of all their kind upon their shoulders.

Finally, when Romar thought his throat had opened and perhaps he could find a breath, could speak without a creak in his voice, he parted his lips and pushed out a question.

"What is your plan?" he asked.

Ransom Castle

"A dozen injuries of various severity, the worst being a dislocated knee and two concussions, and I've made a preliminary postmortem on your cook, Captain Ransom."

"Keep your voice down, will you? And don't call me Captain Ransom. My crew acts like farty schoolboys if they hear that too often."

"Oh—sorry. The incident seems to be as you reported. A tragic accident when the old auxiliary oven came off its anchors. Fatal cranial implosion. You might be comforted to know . . . it was quick."

Leonard McCoy was used to Jim Kirk's face, a passionate verdict of anything that was happening at a given moment, good, bad, or otherwise. Nancy Ransom was stoic as a Vulcan, but in a constantly off-putting manner.

It made him want to check her blood pressure just to see if it could possibly be as low as Spock's.

"I'm still confused by the cook's body position when the oven came down," he finished. "Judging by the injuries, it seems she must have been leaning backward over the top of the stove. Is there any reason she would be in a position like that?"

"Probably fixing something."

"Under the auxiliary oven?"

"Look, she could'a been tripped and been knocked under there by the turbulence. You can't figure that out?"

"It's my job to ask, Captain," McCoy said saucily,

forcing himself to keep the peace, even if that meant getting technical. "There's one other thing I can't account for, however," he plowed on. "I've checked your personnel rosters and everybody is accounted for, except one person. Your guest from the planet of Gullrey. Turrice Roon. She's nowhere to be found."

From the bottom of the access wiring trunks, a big man with a mustache popped up—the first mate, if memory served—his wide face suddenly mottled with concern, distorted by trails of electrical smoke from the damaged underworks. The whole bridge smelled like burned wiring and plastic.

"You mean Turry?" he asked.

McCoy spun around. "Do you know where she is?"

The big man's eyes narrowed. "I left her in the galley. You telling me you can't find her?"

"The galley," McCoy said, and turned back to Nancy Ransom. "The site of the only fatality on board. In my book that's cause for suspicion, Captain."

Nancy shook her head and winced. "Suspicion of just what?"

Feeling his skin prickle, McCoy leaned forward. "There are Romulans in the sector. As chief surgeon aboard the nearest Starfleet vessel, I have an official duty to suspect foul play. It's in the rules, and it's in my nerves right now, and I'm not going to ignore either of those things."

"What do you take me for?" she said bluntly. "You're just scared of answering to that captain of yours, and you know what he'll do to you if you don't bring him back some fancy-pants report of trouble on my ship. Jim Kirk watched me get drummed out of Starfleet ten years ago, but he can't instruct me what to do on my own ship, and neither can any of his stooges. My crew expects to run a race. That's what we're going to do, Romulans or no Romulans. I don't care about those stick-eared bastards."

"But they may have kidnapped a member of your ship!"

"Kidnapped?" Nancy blurted. "Hell! That hen-hearted insect's just holed up under a mattress or something. You're making up stories in your head."

McCoy felt a rasp of frustration in his throat as he raised his voice, widened his eyes, and tapped a forefinger on the pilot station. "The Romulan ship was last seen in this immediate area, and now it's gone and so is a member of this ship's complement. I'm not doing a very good job if I don't suspect a connection. I'm going to conduct a full investigation down there. I want one officer to help me."

"I'll do it!" the mate said, pushing to his feet.

"You stay where you are, Frarey!" Nancy snapped. Her shoulders came up so tightly that they almost covered her ears. "Doctor, don't make me sorrier than I already am that I let you come over here."

Straightening his shoulders under the flashing damage-control lights, McCoy hammered his words at her, matching her ill humor with his own.

"Captain, I don't know what your story is, but apparently you had to blame somebody other than yourself for it. One innocent person is dead and another is unaccounted for. I'm beginning to see why Starfleet didn't want you, and in my estimation it didn't have a damned thing to do with James Kirk. Now, do the right thing and declare that galley off-limits. You—let's go. I'm worried our 'accident' just turned into a murder."

McCoy envied these small private ships, like the *Ransom* with their non-processed food that didn't come out of a replicator. Sometimes, on the *Enterprise,* he felt like he was eating diodes instead of fried chicken.

The galley on a ship like this held true magic. The poets might think it was the masts or the sails, the engines or the shape of a hull, but the crew knew differently.

The galley was the place where they could walk in, get warm, and catch a whiff of home.

And "home" could be plenty of places in these times. Maybe there was only chicken stew cooking, but it might be stewed with potatoes grown on a planet from the Aldebaran system, or laced with illegally traded spices washed through the black market from Orion. Those illegal chickens . . . they tasted best somehow.

Didn't matter. Once the cook cooked it, it was legal.

McCoy only cared about allergic reactions. As long as most of the *Enterprise*'s crew was human, there weren't too many problems. Eventually there'd be more and more aliens threaded through Starfleet. Then he'd have his hands full.

On the *Castle*, the crew was all human. Nancy Ransom was too much of a stuck pig to have it any other way.

That made McCoy's job easier today.

This time, as Mike Frarey locked the galley hatch after them, McCoy wasn't doing a medical inspection or looking for injuries. He was looking for clues. He had locked everybody else out, all the people they'd met in the narrow corridors on the way down here, all nervous and sag-eyed with grief. No matter how they'd plied him with questions, he couldn't tell them their surrogate mother was anything but dead. And they had their own job to do—searching the ship for the Rey girl named Turrice, who, so far, hadn't been accounted for.

"That captain of yours is a brat," he said as he glanced around the mess area with a different purpose than when he'd been here before.

"Nancy?" Frarey said. "Everybody's got a style, is all. That's hers."

"Why do you people stay with her?"

Frarey faced him, mantled by the dark-painted door. "Steady job, Doc. Nancy's the dues. She's tough, but she'll get every order and there's never been a lean season for any of us. And all of us came here 'cuz we know what lean is like."

McCoy swaggered and said, "Son, you haven't seen lean since your mama fed you bacon."

The big man allowed himself a chuckle. "Got that right." Then he sadly commented, "We're pretty sure it was an accident, Doc, what happened to Louise."

McCoy screwed a glare at him. "What makes you sure?"

His brow furrowed, Frarey shrugged, opened his mouth, closed it, then shrugged again.

"That's what I thought," McCoy said. "Don't touch anything unless I tell you. Don't walk unless I tell you. Try not to breathe."

"I'll do that, sir."

Then the doctor started asking himself questions. He moved into the cooking area, using as few steps as possible.

"I find it much too coincidental," he said, "that the woman ended up wrenched over on her back on top of a stove at the same instant the auxiliary stove came dancing down from its hooks." He leaned downward and peered up at the blackened oven housing, then straightened, bent sideways, and peered between the oven housing and the wall.

"Scraped," he barked. "Not broken. Somebody put weight on this. A lot of it. You can see the raw metal where the soot couldn't get to . . . and here the metal anchors are twisted, not just broken. The oven's weight alone couldn't do that. Somebody came in here and brought this oven down on that lady while somebody else held her over the stove top."

In the mess area, Mike Frarey's wide face crumpled. "Jesus, poor Louise . . ."

McCoy came to the doorway. "Pretty gruesome. And damn heartless."

Frarey nodded, sniffed, tried to get over it, then said, "You sound like you belong on this ship instead of that fancy job. I can barely hear it."

"What you barely hear," McCoy said, "is Atlanta, Georgia."

"Thought so."

"Let's see what's in here, now that I know what to look for."

Frarey got a confused expression on his face and asked, "Now that you know what to look for? I don't know what you mean."

"You don't have to. Where's my medical pack?"

"Right here you go."

"Thanks. Let's set the tricorder for atmospheric analysis."

"Atmosphere? The air's the same all over the ship."

"Let's see if it is."

The tricorder worked silently in his hand, no vibrations, no hints of the great auxiliary computer power in its small casing, and he watched the tiny screen.

"Mmm," he grunted. "Not much there. Not conclusive, anyway. Could be some traces of unlikely gases, but I can't hand traces that small to the captain. My captain, I mean. All right, we'll try something else. You go over to that bulkhead and break open the vent. Pull out the filter and bring it to me."

"Well . . . okay, sir."

With Frarey occupied, McCoy put his own creaky knees on the floor and his nose almost that low. He lay the tricorder down and used his hands as brooms to gather up a tiny pile of dust. There wasn't much. He hoped the floor hadn't been swept since the incident happened. Sometimes cleanliness could be an annoyance.

This from a surgeon? He scolded himself and muttered under his breath, then stopped because he was huffing his little dust pile away.

He scooped a square centimeter of it into the top of his hand-size mass analyzer and was suddenly glad he'd brought it along. The little machine blipped anxiously, and he decided it was confused because he'd given it something other than a bone fragment, but after a few moments it fed him back a readout of the DNA.

"Got it!" he snapped.

"Pardon?"

Taking only two steps as he was told, Frarey appeared beside him with the drumhead-size air filter.

"Hair particles," McCoy said as he allowed Frarey to hoist him back to his feet. "No wonder mankind evolved into a biped. We weren't meant for knee work."

"I got your filter here."

"Put it on the table."

They both leaned over the circle of meshed dust, hair, and lord-knew-what else, and McCoy turned his tricorder on it. He had to readjust twice before it understood what he wanted it to do.

"There it is," he uttered. "Right here. Look at the screen. Hair particles, epidermal flakes . . . airborne aerosol of fatty acids. Here's the DNA analysis, and here . . . is the separation of DNA. Human . . . and Vulcanoid."

"Huh?" Frarey straightened up so sharply that his spine cracked.

"Romulans, my lumberjack friend," McCoy said knottily. "That's 'huh.'"

"There's never been a Romulan in here, not ever!"

"There've been Romulans in here within the past ten hours."

"Aw, Doc, that's nuts! How can you know that? From some dust and crud?"

"No, son, from what's caught in the dust and crud, and what makes up the dust and crud. Skin flakes, fatty acids in moisture," he finished, tapping his tricorder, "that is nonhuman."

"Are you saying they came in here for some reason and scratched themselves?"

"I'm saying they left some sweat behind. Sweat, hair, skin, all living things do it just by walking through the air. Air isn't a vacuum. We're not walking through nothing. There's friction, however diaphanous."

"But I thought those buggers didn't sweat."

"Everybody sweats. Just at different levels. I'd call this conclusive. Somebody beamed into this section, killed that poor woman, and either killed the Rey visitor with a phaser or they took her with them. One of the two women was the target, and the other was the witness. I'm betting the cook was the witness and got killed for it. The other girl . . . they wanted to have one of her kind to look at for some reason." He ran a finger along his lip and squinted at the table. *"Some* reason."

"They won't keep her . . . alive for long, will they?"

"I doubt it."

Sore emotion twisted Mike Frarey's big friendly face. He lowered his eyes and turned away, still careful not to take a step.

Pausing, McCoy watched him and read the set of the wide shoulders.

"Oh," he said. "I'm sorry. I didn't realize."

Frarey's throat knotted and he blinked. He stuck his thumbs in his belt and tried to look casual. "S'okay."

"No, it's not," McCoy said firmly. "It's not okay at all. We've got to get a message back to the *Enterprise* somehow. The Romulans have turned this race into a blood sport."

Chapter Fifteen

The *Castle*

"WE HAVE TO SEND a message to the *Enterprise*."

"I doubt you can."

Nancy Ransom sat on the cooler and peeled a banana with more care than McCoy had ever witnessed. She gazed at it, not at him, not at their small main screen, but at her banana, peeling and peeling, very slowly.

McCoy almost stopped to watch. A banana could only last so long.

"Why can't you?" he asked. "Is there a legitimate reason or is it just you?"

She made him wait until she was almost through peeling.

"Since you're convinced it's just me, there's not much I can say, is there?"

The doctor glanced to his side at Mike Frarey, who thumbed his belt and fought a shrug.

"Captain," McCoy attempted, "I may owe you an apology. That doesn't change the fact that in my opinion a murder has been committed and the perpetrators are still in the race. If they've got what they wanted, why are they staying here?"

"If they're staying in the race, what makes you think your theory's not all wet?"

"I only have the facts I've gathered. I admit there's margin for error, but we can't afford to assume error. If the Romulans are responsible for your missing guest, then they still think they have something to do here."

"When we find 'em, you can dinghy over and ask 'em."

McCoy felt his eyes start to crawl out of his head. He decided he'd better go ahead and raise his voice before somebody called a team with a butterfly net.

"I am answerable to the *Enterprise,*" he said, "and I'm compelled to relate this information. I've already reported to you. It's now incumbent upon you to make sure I fulfill the next stratum of my duty. Don't make me quote the paragraph, will you?"

Nancy broke off the top of her banana and said, "Communication panel's right over there. Have yourself a roundup."

As she savored the first piece of her treat, McCoy stepped past Frarey, ignored the two other people manning their posts, and bent over the panels.

"*Enterprise* from *Ransom Castle* . . . *Enterprise,* this is McCoy. Come in."

He opened the reception grid more and more, and kept trying.

"*Enterprise, Enterprise,* McCoy here . . ."

Two minutes later, he glanced at Mike Frarey, then turned to Nancy.

"It's broken."

She shook her head. "Nothing wrong with my subspace. Some hotshot swamped the subspace nets. Probably full-blasted their emitters. Somebody's idea of a race trick."

"That shouldn't be allowed! It's dangerous!"

"Anything that gets you ahead is allowed. You were sitting next to Mr. Epaulets at the Captains' Meeting, weren't you? Just wish I'd thought of it."

"Who would do that?"

She raised and lowered one billiard-ball shoulder.

"Helmut Appenfeller might do it, maybe Ian Blackington. Could be Pete Hall. He's around here someplace. We'll come out of it in an hour or two."

"Then you'll have to turn around and go back to the *Enterprise.*"

She shot him a black-browed glare. "Like hell! Even your captain told me to move on, and I'm moving on."

"Can you contact any of the other Starfleet vessels in the race? *Great Lakes* or *Hood* or the other one?"

"Intrepid, and no I can't contact them any better than I can send a message back. You just tried to get through, didn't you?"

"Captain Ransom, aren't you affected at all by the murder of your cook?"

From behind McCoy, Mike Frarey caught the doctor's shoulder and drew him back from saying anything else, but it was too late.

Nancy didn't look up anymore, but her posture showed what must have been in her eyes. She shifted away, then farther away, brought her knees tight to her body, and stared at the deck.

McCoy slumped mentally, and even a little bit physically.

"All right, I'm sorry," he said. "I'm just afraid of what can happen if we don't act right away. Whatever we think of each other, I don't think either one of us wants the death count to go up."

"Louise wouldn't want it, Nance," Frarey said, almost too softly to be heard.

But Nancy did hear.

She drew a long breath, picked a piece of banana fiber from her teeth, wiped her hand on her shirt, and rubbed the back of her neck.

"If you can conjure a way to send a message back to Captain Hog Wild and his Vulcan sidekick," she said, "we'll transmit it."

Red Talon

"Our vessel is secure, Commander."

The bridge was too spacious for comfort. Romar found himself still beating down shivers, still wishing for privacy, wishing for a time of cloistered safety in a defensible place.

Valdus met him near the weapons station. "Report."

"Skirmishes were less violent as distance from the transporter room increased. There must be some range limit on this sorcery. Six injuries, five minor. One guard is dead. We were most fortunate."

"Fortunate that no one did what I once did," Valdus elaborated for him.

Romar averted his gaze. "Yes. You foresaw what would happen and destroyed the witch before she could overwhelm us. You saved us, Commander."

"Don't stress yourself, Romar," Valdus grumbled. "Damage?"

"Several blades in several walls, some circuitry cut, currently being mended. The crew is confused, somewhat shame-faced, but I have neglected to explain to them."

"Better they remain confused. Their duty is only to man their posts."

"In their inner minds," Romar said, "they understand why we must do this. They are asking no questions. They only look at each other. No one speaks."

"All the better. You have isolated the target vessel again?"

"Yes, they moved out of the cloud while we were involved with the starship. We lost a prime opportunity. Now we must follow them in the open and hope for another chance."

"You see?" Valdus told him solemnly. "It is that man."

Romar paused. "Their captain? But he didn't see us."

"Yet his senses brought him to us. He forced me to take action without even realizing what he was doing. I have witnessed such instincts before . . . but never used so forcefully."

Valdus moved to the bulkhead, and he touched the wall. His finger ran from the wall at his waist to the wall at his cheek.

"You know, Romar," he went on, "I had this ship refitted before we came here."

"Yes," Romar said. "I know."

"These bulkhead frames, these wall forms . . . are specially ordered. You see the graininess of them? They were created by my own scientists and laborers. I had them built, and I replaced the walls in six major sections with them."

A few hours ago, Romar would have taken this as the signal of insanity in his commander. Walls? What matter could walls possibly be?

But he had felt the effect of the Rey and he no longer trusted anything, including his own arbitrary judgment. After all, Valdus had been right.

He remained silent. He didn't even ask the obvious question. When Valdus was ready, he would tell him the significance of the wall material. He studied Valdus's face. So little age showed, despite the decades of service. There were some lines, if he looked closely as Valdus blinked, swallowed, breathed, and there were circles under the experienced eyes today. Perhaps they had always been there, but Romar had never looked.

Fatigue? Regret? Commitment? Yes, all this knitted into the years. Valdus wasn't having any second thoughts. This was a man who had slaughtered everyone around him once before and knew the taste of mass murder for a purpose.

Romar moved to him, his own sense of purpose boiling in his chest.

"Your order, Commander," he prodded.

"I want you to arm a boarding party," Valdus said.

"Provision them for siege. Bring all weapons to bear. Angle gradually toward the target vessel."

The commander's face released its surly edge. Unlikely peace came into his eyes, as though speaking orders that released his burden finally . . . finally.

"Overtake it," he said. "We will turn that planet to glass."

Chapter Sixteen

"Captain, I'm picking up a recorder marker signal. Extreme range . . . closing slowly at warp one. I think I can pull the message in through the cloud's interference."

"Do it, Lieutenant. It's somebody trying to communicate through the washed-out subspace nets."

"One moment, sir . . . message relaying. It's Dr. McCoy, sir. I'll draw the message in."

Jim Kirk, his bridge crew, and the two Rey guests clinging to the back of the bridge had to wait another ten seconds before Uhura could pull the crackling, choked message through the ionization they were caught in.

"Dr. McCoy on audio, recorded, sir," she said finally.

They all hung on to the tilted deck and listened.

"Enterprise *from McCoy. In my estimation, there has been a murder and a likely kidnapping committed on* Ransom Castle. *My complete report, along with tricorder readings, follows this message. Spock can confirm the tracings from the galley on his library computer. I believe the ship's cook was killed to prevent her from reporting the kidnapping of the Rey host, whose name is Turrice Roon."*

No one reacted overtly, but attention stirred toward Tom and Royenne.

Kirk knew what it was like to lose one of his crew, even a finger off the hand of one of his crew. He saw that digging shock in the faces of the two Rey men as the doctor's message went on.

"My evidence is circumstantial, of course—it could be that somebody just rubbed up against a Romulan before coming aboard this ship, except that this woman was alive and accounted for only three hours ago. I can only speculate that the Romulans are conducting some sort of experimentation or analysis on the Rey and are using this poor girl as a guinea pig. It's crucial that you handle those people before they head back to their home space, or we may never know what happened to her. I don't think she'll be kept alive for very long. McCoy, medical pro-tem, Ransom Castle, out."

Silence fell under the hideous whine of the ship's impulse engines grinding in their effort to hold position.

Kirk yanked himself around and looked aft. There were two completely innocent people whose culture had done nothing to provoke anybody and, according to all reports, couldn't if they wanted to. The two large-eyed visitors were horrified. Grief ruddied their faces, and if he'd ever seen innocence ruined, there it was.

Tom looked shattered beyond thought, and could barely keep his legs under him. He seemed to be withering before the captain's eyes.

Grief plied Kirk too as he watched them. He felt his own body grow tighter around his bones, and he thought of the two women who were sacrificed, one dead, the other likely so.

Hopefully so. Experimentation by the Romulans was a mind-choking possibility.

Suddenly he could only think of those two women.

In an era when women served equally with men and wanted it that way, for James Kirk there was still something about the death of a woman. Women were still special and somehow instinctively precious to him, no matter that they often chided him for thinking that way. He couldn't help it. In spite of the pressures of expanding society, he was a 19th Century man in those ways, and to him every woman looked like a work of art. He wanted to protect them all. Women were the charm of the open galaxy, and their needless death shredded his heart.

He forced himself to look away from Tom and Royenne, forced his feelings down before he became too angry. What would the Romulans want with a Rey captive?

"We've got to get out of here," he said, suddenly breathless. "It just became a matter of life and death. Spock—hypotheses?"

There was no answer.

Kirk pulled himself to the rail, battling the deck as it pitched another degree in the wrong direction.

"Spock?"

On the upper deck Spock caught the back of his chair and barely kept himself on his feet. He kinked forward as though he'd been punched in the chest. For anyone else, it might've only been a cough, but for Spock, whose reactions were so subtle, so reserved—

The captain collected his strength and was there in four steps.

Spock didn't look at him. "I'm sorry, Captain—"

Kirk caught his arm and kept him from slipping sideways onto his computer panel. "You all right?"

With a pale hand clutching the neck of his monitor hood, Spock battled for control over a creeping misery. "One moment," he rasped. "Fighting it."

"Fighting what?"

"I don't know."

If anyone else felt nauseated at what they were going through and what they'd just heard from McCoy, Kirk wouldn't have been surprised. He saw it in all their faces and felt it pull at his own features like weights attached to his muscles and bones.

The burden in Spock's eyes was suddenly contagious —Kirk could feel it.

They'd shared empathy before, but this kind? As though they could reach down and pick it up?

"Never known you to be space sick before," the captain said quietly.

"I never have been . . ."

"Are you dizzy?

"Not . . . yes, somewhat."

The mid-answer change was tantamount to a cry for help from anyone else.

"Sit down." Kirk drew him to his chair and he didn't resist.

He *didn't* resist.

And now, as Kirk saw the effort there . . .

"Fine time for McCoy to be off board," he muttered. "Can you hang on?"

Spock turned the chair and pulled himself back to his feet. A knotted shudder wracked his arms. He held his breath, stiffened, and fought for control. When he looked up, his black eyes were resolute through a glaze.

"Yes, Captain," he said. "A few moments to process McCoy's forensics . . ."

He was asking to be left alone. Kirk balled his fists and forced himself to walk away, all the way to port, to draw attention away from Spock.

"Uhura, call Mr. Scott to the bridge."

"Yes, sir," she said. There was strain in her voice too, as though a plague were sweeping the bridge.

Clinging to his panel, Spock turned. "I'm all right, Captain."

"Precaution, Mr. Spock," Kirk insisted, in a tone that wouldn't take backtalk.

For a second time, Spock didn't resist. His face was crumpled with stress. Weakness dragged at his elbows. He forced himself back to his work, obviously disturbed that he might need relief just when the ship was in trouble.

Scott was on the bridge two minutes later, scowling

and shaking his head, and without waiting to be asked he said, "Intermix levels still jumping, sir. Very bad exertion. She's huffin' and puffin', but we're holding her down from red-line and managing to keep from slipping deeper into this hole."

"Understood," Kirk said. "Stand by, Scotty."

"Better I get back to my engine room, sir—"

"I need you here."

Scott dropped to his side on the lower deck. Tied into the engine's heart, soul, and sinew though Montgomery Scott might have been, there was enough of the pub bartender in him that he was hard to fool and quick to pick up on what he saw in the captain's gaze as Kirk watched the upper starboard deck.

Scott leaned in and asked, "Something wrong, sir?"

Allowing himself a custodial glance to starboard, Kirk muttered, "Well, he's not tearing his hair . . ."

"Think he's ill?"

"Give him a minute."

Scouring his mind for crazy ideas, the last refuge of the desperate, he wiped his face with a hot palm and paced around the helm—if he could only *think*.

"Captain," Spock said, fighting for every breath, "molecular examination of the data Dr. McCoy's tricorder picked up in the galley . . . no longer any doubt—there were Romulans on board *Ransom Castle* within the past twenty hours. In my opinion, this shores up the doctor's hypothesis . . . I must agree that the Rey girl was kidnapped by Romulan intruders."

Kirk stepped toward him, prepared to ask the ugliest question, but Tom arose from his silence, moved to where Uhura sat clinging to her console, and beat them all to the awful question.

"Mr. Spock?" he began. He was clearly forcing himself just to get the words out. "Would they keep her alive?"

"She is a witness to her own victimization, sir." Spock lowered his voice, but everybody heard him, and there was heavy sympathy in his inflection. "It is unlikely she would be kept alive."

Tom's face crumpled as grief gathered with shock. He pressed a palm to the back of Uhura's chair, and he slipped to his knees. He held himself there, in misery, though he made no noise, and with the other hand he covered his face.

Kirk started toward him—only now pierced by the common sense that should've hit him hours ago. He should get these people off the bridge. All this was too much for them. Tom was folding. Royenne wasn't much better, over there huddled against the wall in the turbolift vestibule, watching Tom's breakdown.

As his feet thumped up the short steps to the upper deck and he found himself standing over Tom, about to reach down, Kirk got a truncated, dreamlike view of Tom here, gutted by grief, and Spock over there—the same.

Suddenly Spock could barely stand, leaning almost his entire weight on the heels of his hands, pressed to the control panel, no longer even pretending to try to work. His vandalized senses were battling in his face.

Vandalized . . .

From between the shreds of thought in a mind that had gone blank, something clicked.

He reached down, put his palm on Tom's shoulder, dug his fingers into the red-and-black flannel shirt, caught a strand of Tom's fair hair between his fingers, and pulled the Rey man halfway around.

And way over there, Spock flinched—and turned.

"So that's it," Kirk breathed.

Instinct boiled up and he moved protectively between Spock and Tom, backed off a step, and looked down at the young Rey man. Royenne stumbled toward them, and the two guests stared at him like stranded calves.

"It's you, isn't it?" Kirk said bluntly. "Somehow it's you."

They didn't say anything. They didn't really have to. Unlike Vulcans, those faces didn't hide much.

"Where's Osso?" the captain demanded.

"In our quarters," Royenne said. "He didn't want to . . ."

"Overwhelm us?"

Royenne lowered his sorrow-laden eyes. Sadly he admitted, "Yes."

The bridge crew watched. Kirk felt their attention like needles in his skin.

"Tom," he said, "you got anything to say?"

Still on his knees, his face glossed with sweat, Tom struggled to gain control over his own emotions—and obviously just tried to keep them to himself. His voice was a braid of grief and effort.

"Turrice was my sister," he said.

"It's not Tom's fault!"

Royenne suddenly towered over the captain, protecting his companion. Probably the first time any Rey had felt inclined to defend his own against anyone from another world.

And it had to be on the bridge of Jim Kirk's *Enterprise*.

"Before the Federation came to our planet, we didn't think it would affect anyone else," Royenne said anxiously. "We never thought about it!"

Suddenly his shoulders slumped. His hands moved back and forth a few times as though someone was working him on strings, but after a moment he frowned and huddled near Tom.

Kirk knew without looking that Spock had come close behind him. The captain felt like a bulwark when Spock deliberately stayed back there. Kirk let himself be a barrier. Everyone, even Spock, was entitled to a twinge of childhood from time to time.

"Is it possible?" Kirk asked. "Can all this be because of them, Spock?"

"Vulcans are somewhat telepathic," Spock said, forcing past the strain. "Romulans may be also, instinctively, though they do not seem to have developed it as a discipline." He paused, his curiosity overcoming the Rey effect upon him, though he still stayed behind Kirk's shoulders. "There is no ruler by which to measure telepathy, Captain. I can't scientifically prove I am feeling what is on me now."

"That's why fake psychics have thrived through the age of science," Kirk agreed. "It can't be proven *not* to exist."

Spock's eyes were tight as he nodded. "I suspect this trait is of no more concern to the Rey than perspiration or hair color is to humans."

"And we don't suspect our own hair color to be driving somebody else mad." He looked at Tom and Royenne, felt his own inner empathies at work, and couldn't help but feel mellow toward a people who hadn't wanted to hurt anyone, but only wanted to talk to the outside galaxy, and not be left alone in the dark. "I can feel it, but I can push it down. Why?"

"Vulcan and Romulan instincts are much stronger than humans," Spock said, fighting to stay clinical. "And humans handle emotion daily. You . . . do it better."

Kirk avoided tossing him a thank-you. "We handle a hundred ups and downs every day. Their happiness was contagious, but the more violent emotions don't do much more than make us edgy. But to a Vulcan—"

"Or a Romulan . . ."

Kirk swung around and jabbed a finger at Tom, then at Royenne. "You knew about this, didn't you?"

Royenne's expression was layered with shame and apology. He looked past Kirk to talk to Spock.

"At first we never considered it. When we found out it affected others, we were afraid you wouldn't talk to us anymore."

"We thought you might turn away from us!" Tom blurted. "That you wouldn't want us in the Federation. We never thought it bothered anything but . . . but—"

"Lower life forms," Royenne finished.

They both seemed to think they were insulting Spock, and cutting off their chances for a future at the same time.

"Likely evolved as a way to cause predators to be

frightened," Spock said. "Vulcanoids are susceptible because at one time we were of high emotion. We developed our controls because our violent base emotions were destroying us. We did not slay the dragon," he added, "but we drove it back to its cave."

"And something about these people brings it back out," Kirk concluded. "And the Romulans stumbled on it. They must be afraid the Federation might use the Rey against them!"

He sucked a breath, cleared his head, and managed to throw off the creeping grief radiated from the two gentle, unusual beings with their faces grilled by the situation. He stalked the deck, past Spock, toward the bow, then back again, and his eyes took on a devilish gleam.

"Not a bad idea," he added.

"Captain!" Chekov gasped. He glared with unhappy horror.

Scott watched too, but his dark eyes carried a blunt comprehension that junior officers hadn't had beaten into them yet.

"What they don't understand is Federation ethics," Kirk allowed. "We wouldn't sacrifice any Rey by putting him—or her—in proximity with Romulans just to get the upper hand. They're not bait," he said, waving his hand at Tom and Royenne. "They're people."

"And this 'talent' isn't voluntary," Spock offered. "The Rey would have to be in a deadly situation to illicit this response, and that negates their value as weapons."

"I don't care if it does or doesn't. We wouldn't use them that way. But the Romulans think we would." The captain turned and glared with bare accusation at the forward screen. "So where is Valdus? He's got the girl . . . has he rushed out of the area? Or is he still here, pretending to run the race? What's his plan? Why would he want to involve himself in an event that culminates at a planet full of the people he *must* fear?"

Tom bolted to his feet and grabbed for the rail, his face worried as a rotten peach. "They can't hurt my planet, can they? They couldn't do that, could they?"

"It'd take days to cut up a planet," Scott said, "even if they had enough firepower."

"Firing on the planet gets them nothing but dead," Kirk interrupted. "Valdus is experienced enough to know that. He's not the suicide type. If he were, they'd have been at Gullrey long ago. And they wouldn't wait for a public event with four Starfleet vessels and a fleet of rugged independent merchants and excited weekend adventurers—"

Suddenly he stopped.

"Captain!" Sulu gasped.

Chekov blurted, "Another ship!"

"Sacrifice another vessel!" Sulu said. "Hyperlight engines—"

"Atmospheric corruption," Scott decided. "There's nothin' to it, sir!"

Kirk twisted toward Spock. "And with all these ships going to that planet, nobody would suspect anything was wrong. Spock, what would they need to corrupt an atmosphere?"

"A ship with . . ." Spock tried to think, but paused, still struggling. One hand was pressed on the buffer board along the communications panel. The other hovered in midair with nothing to lean on. His shoulder muscles worked for control. "A ship with irreversible warp field chain reaction capacity."

"Like a starship." Kirk used his own voice as a bridge. He stepped toward Spock.

"They might covet a starship, sir," Scott swaggered from the lower deck, "but woe's them if they tangle with a Starfleet crew. A smart tiger stalks the weak zebra first."

"Yes, he does. And Valdus struck me as a smart tiger, Mr. Scott. Assuming he's found out whatever he wanted to know from Tom's sister, he's moving to the second leg of his plan. He needs a ship that could corrupt a planet. That means ships the size of *Haunted Forest, Blackjacket, New Pride of Baltimore*—"

"*Ransom Castle* would serve, sir," the engineer added.

"Think so?"

Scott chuckled grimly. "Oh, aye."

The pieces clicked into place, and Kirk squinted sharply. He dropped to the lower deck and circled his chair along a well-worn path. "That's it! He's focused in on *Ransom Castle*. That's how he made his choice of which Rey guest to kidnap."

"But why kidnap anybody at all?" Sulu asked. "I don't understand, sir."

"I know why," Kirk said. "I saw it in his face."

"Why?" Tom begged. "Why would he take my sister?"

Kirk couldn't bear to look at him. "He wanted to be sure he was on the right track. That he wasn't about to attack a planet of the wrong people."

"A Romulan?" Chekov barked. "Why would a Romulan care?"

"Because he's a decent man, Mr. Chekov," Kirk said. "And Romulan or not, there's nothing more dangerous than a decent man who's convinced he's doing the right thing."

Chapter Seventeen

Red Talon

"THIS IS THE SUBCOMMANDER. Is the engine power up to full standard yet?"

"In a quarter hour, Subcommander."

"If it is one moment longer, you will be executed!"

The crew glanced up, but no one said anything. In fact, they began to work a degree faster, a degree harder.

"Romar . . . such flames," Valdus commented from his command center.

With his face flushed amber, his body a bundle of agitation, Romar pointed viciously at the communication unit. "I will *kill* him!"

"Oh, I understand," Valdus said, "but take care. Your enthusiasm may disarm you."

"Nothing will disarm me."

Valdus didn't argue. His command chair felt uncomfortable to him today. Behind him, Romar continued to pace. Valdus knew how he felt—the experience fresh in his system, the inability to accept the plundering of his mind. Poor Romar . . . not seventy years, but only seventy minutes to get used to what had happened to him.

Valdus forced himself to be tolerant, and allowed the

younger man to rumble back and forth across the bridge, his rank sash swaying so hard it wrapped across his torso. The bridge crew kept their eyes averted. They knew something was wrong—had felt the intrusion into their own minds—and now looked to their leaders to deal with the threat.

"Where are the other vessels in the race field?" Valdus asked. He twisted to look over a shoulder at the centurion.

The centurion flinched as though stricken, then went to a different monitor than the one he'd been hunched over. "Scattered, Commander," he said. "Many unaccounted for. I assume they have gone ahead while we were detained in the cloud. The race may be nearly won by now."

"Then we shall have an audience when we arrive at the finish line," Valdus commented. "We will use the *Ransom Castle* for what the humans call a Trojan horse. While the Federation ships attend *Red Talon* with their suspicions, we can approach that planet with our disguised conquest." He glanced back at Romar and lowered his voice. "Its contaminated warp core will do the rest—"

"And our agents will hunt down every last Rey who escapes the eradication—crush any chance that we could be surprised a hundred years from now!"

He wasn't trembling but heaving with each breath. There was less anger in his words than oath.

"Commander!" the centurion interrupted. "Aft sensors show the Federation starship is powering toward the opening of the gravity well. Attempting to extricate themselves."

As Romar suddenly stopped pacing and stood hideously still, Valdus pushed to his feet and crowded the monitor. "They are escaping? With their power reduced twenty percent? Unthinkable!"

The centurion moved aside. "You see for yourself."

"Confirm this immediately!"

"Yes, Commander!"

Valdus went to Romar's side and spoke quietly. "If they extricate themselves from the cloud, they can head us off."

"They must not!" Romar boiled. He closed his mouth, swept a hand across it, and fought to keep himself in check, but didn't do a very good job.

"Commander," the centurion said, "readings show the starship holding position, power levels slowly increasing. I must conclude they are building for a single surge out of the well."

"We should have killed them!" Romar roared. He threw his arms into the air and spun around pointlessly.

Valdus sighed. "My fault," he murmured. "I had the chance to sweep the field, and I failed to do it."

Romar fumed at him with a ferocious loyalty. "Commander—you lie to yourself! I will have no witnesses to such feelings you have about yourself! Centurion, turn the ship around. We will go back to the cloud and obliterate those we should have obliterated before!"

The centurion, and all who heard, suddenly stopped working and stared at their leaders. The order was violent, yes, but unexpected and unplanned, and Romar had made the order without waiting for Valdus to make it first. What should they do?

The bird-head helmets of the crewmen flashed with lights from the struggling of the ship as the engineers were bringing *Red Talon* back up to full power, and in their eyes Valdus read a certain confusion—but also anxious anticipation. They approved.

And then he looked at Romar. It was the look on his face that convinced him.

"Very well," Valdus said. "Turn the ship around. Bring weapons to bear. We will make our subcommander a satisfied man."

"Captain!"

Chekov swung around so hard she almost threw herself out of her chair, but she succeeded in getting the captain's attention.

223

"Contact, sir," he gasped. "The Romulan vessel!"

Everyone turned to the forward screen, squinting through the snapping cloudy electrical mess at the one shape they never in a thousand years expected to see here.

"Are they coming back to help us?" Chekov wondered, staring.

Kirk pulled himself forward to the helm. "I think we can rule that out, Mr. Chekov. All hands, red alert. Shields up."

"Shields are already at maximum under these conditions, Captain," Spock said, his voice still thready.

"Enhance screen to maximum, Mr. Sulu. I want to see that ship's movements."

"Aye, sir . . . maximum enhancement." The helmsman tampered with his panels, but the view on the screen remained foggy and glitterbound. "That's as clear as it'll get, sir—sir! They're powering up weapons!"

"Hail him!"

Uhura hesitated an instant, held briefly by the glow of the photon ports shining through the cloud from that Romulan ship's great extended neck.

"He's receiving us, sir."

Kirk held the helm with both hands as the ship grabbed for a place to hang on in the residual spin, and didn't even try to keep the anxiety out of his voice. "Put him on visual if you can. Hurry, Lieutenant."

"Aye, sir, attempting visual."

He tried not to be distracted from what was coming, but he was suddenly aware of their guests—the subtle cause of all this—sitting on the starboard steps between the upper deck and the command deck.

Tom sat huddled, his arms crossed at the wrists in his lap, his hands limp, and he stared at the screen. His large eyes were glazed with tears, but he was fighting to keep his emotions in control.

On the upper deck Spock was fighting, too, but his attention to the ship and the moment had a tighter grip on him than Tom did.

Uhura tapped and tapped on her console, pulling in every pixel, every sliver of visual science available to the struggling, incompatible systems, and when she got the picture, she didn't even announce it.

She just put it on.

Jim Kirk straightened his shoulders as much as he could and glared at the forward screen, at the calm face of the Romulan Commander. Valdus. The decent man.

"Captain," the Romulan said, *"apparently you are clawing your way out."*

"You don't have to do this," Kirk said to him.

Valdus showed no surprise, no attempt to appear vague. He seemed to know that Kirk had figured it all out.

"I do," Valdus said. *"I thought about killing you, Captain, a few times. I searched for a utilitarian hatred, but found it unworthy. Having met you in person, and having seen the light in your eyes . . . I resisted being the one who put out that light."*

Surprised by the intimacy, Kirk held silent a moment. He only watched, sought weakness, looked for lies.

He didn't see any.

Moving slowly forward around the helm, he kept both feet under him as much as possible.

"I have the same sensibilities about you," he admitted. "Fortunately, my phaser banks don't feel that way. I'll fight if you force me to."

Valdus nodded. *"You don't understand what I am attempting?"*

Kirk held out a hand, felt his blood rush hot in his fingers. He let his instincts draw the conclusions. "How can anyone think of killing an entire civilization?"

"The stripping of the mind, Captain Kirk," Valdus said, suddenly harsh, serious. *"There is nothing like it. If someone could control your mind, drive you to madness you couldn't even see coming, wouldn't you want to contain that person? Even if you had to kill him? If a predator gets in your house—"*

"They're not predators!" Kirk lashed out to his side,

got a fistful of flannel, and hauled Tom to the center of the bridge, presenting the baffled Rey man fiercely to those who feared him the most. "Look at him! These are innocent people! Possibly the most innocent the galaxy has! You know that!" He threw Tom to one side so hard that Tom ended up on one knee beside the steps. "I understand your fear, your concern, but there are other methods."

"Methods we would have to consult the Federation about, now that the witch planet is joining you," Valdus said. *"Because of what is done today, the temptation will never arrive years from now, a century from now, for you to use those people against us. I do not hate them, Captain, but if I don't kill them, they will eventually kill my people."*

"You're letting your fears rule you," Kirk insisted. "You should try something different."

Valdus's brow creased. *"This is not fear. You know us. We have no fear. We have fought you before and will fight again, in any contest, with anyone. But this—this is fundamental! This can destroy our minds—our minds!"*

"We haven't attacked you—we never will," Kirk roared. "You don't have any reason to act in self-defense!"

On the screen, a younger Romulan officer pushed into the screen so sharply that his face appeared twice the size of Valdus's, and the screen blurred as it tried to compensate for the distortion.

"You're right—this is *not self-defense!*" the young officer bolted at them. *"This is survival!"*

Valdus drove forward, grasped the officer by the shoulders, and pulled him back, but made no attempt to quiet him.

Kirk raised his voice. "If your empire would join us in a common purpose, you wouldn't have to worry about survival."

"If we join you," Valdus said, *"we become weak like you. Then someone else comes along and conquers us. If*

the weak survive, Captain Kirk, eventually all are weakened."

"How weak are we?" Kirk shot back, boiling mad and striking his words like matches. Down at his right, he caught a glimpse of Tom turning to watch him instead of the screen, but he didn't turn from his glare at the two Romulans. "Decades ago we beat you back. The Klingons haven't gained an inch either. Open your mind, man! Freedom is more potent than force!"

A portentous silence fell. The bridge of the *Enterprise* throbbed around him.

"You cannot turn me, Captain," Valdus said, and his voice confirmed his words. *"Be comforted. I know you would be willing to die to save a crewman. Instead, you will die to save a civilization. Your disappearance and the destruction of the Rey world will prevent war between our intergalactic peoples. There may be a chilling between us, but no war. All with the sacrifice of one ship and one world. I will forever speak of you with honor."*

The screen crackled, and the picture dissolved.

Before them, the Romulan ship hovered in her veil of static. Two fluorescent blue glows swelled upon her hull and spat two white hot lancets directly toward the engineering hull of the starship.

"Incoming!" Sulu shouted.

Chapter Eighteen

Enterprise

THE PHOTON TORPEDOES blazed a couple of paths through the ionization and hard radiation of the cloud, and the cloud argued. The telltale white lancets turned to bright sizzles, streaked under the viewscreen, and into the engineering hull.

The *Enterprise* cannonballed downward, impulse engines moaning as their strength drained away. The deck dropped out from under them as the crew grabbed for their controls and tried to hold her together. The red alert Klaxon sounded again as the ship plunged deep into the gravity well, caught in the inside of the natural tornado.

"Valdus!" Kirk shouted. "Get him back, Lieutenant!"

"Too late, sir," Uhura called back over the whine.

"Slipping into the well, Captain!" Spock rasped over the noise of the ship twisting under them. His voice was rough and taxed, his stone-cut features blanched. "Losing thrust against the current! Mark plus five! Plus seven! Plus nine!"

"They kicked us down into it." Kirk swung around,

pulled himself across the bridge—the longest distance in the universe, sometimes, especially at times like this, when he wished he didn't have to be the one in command, but couldn't have tolerated watching anyone else do it. His heart hammered against his breastbone. "Chekov, assist with helm control," he called. "Damage report!"

One of the junior engineers turned, clinging to his panel, his voice passionate with effort. "Impedance in the electropneumatics, sir. Voltage indicators falling out of sequence. I don't know which inputs to accept!"

They watched the starship begin to come apart around them. Warning bells peeled. The shriek of effort buzzed up through the internal structure as though the ship were caught in a drill press.

"Slipping, Captain!" Spock shouted. "We cannot push up against the flow pattern at this depth."

"They shoved us down—now we're stuck," Kirk grumbled, his teeth gritted. "Scott, we need power!"

The quickly sculpted confidence in his voice didn't fool Scott, who's ruddy complexion was almost as red as his division shirt. His piledriver accent put an extra sting on every syllable and a brutal immediacy to the next few seconds. "Those starbase stumblebums removed parts instead of just shutting them down, sir. We're manufacturing facsimiles. Trying to get power up to the nineties."

"How long?" Kirk demanded.

His engineer shrugged. "I can't say, sir." He paused, "Not soon enough, though."

"All right, if we can't get out the top, we're going to have to go out the bottom."

Spock turned again. "Impossible, Captain. We cannot break the laws of physics. The deeper we fall into the well, the greater the pressure."

Kirk slammed a hand down on the rail. "I don't want to break them, Spock. Just bend them for a minute. Come on—how can we do it? How can we introduce chaos into the system?"

Spock's face crumpled with the effort of thinking. "Magnetic field disruption . . . rupture of the current—"

"Breaking the flow pattern?"

"Very little chance—"

"But our only one. Sulu, arm photon torpedoes!"

Sulu looked baffled, but poked the weapons panel. "Armed . . . ready, sir."

"Prepare to fire down into the well. When the torpedo detonates, it might disrupt the well long enough for us to get out."

Sulu hesitated, worked his controls again, then croaked, "Ready, sir—"

"Captain," Spock called again, and somehow maneuvered toward him with the dark prediction it was his duty to provide. "Our hull will be crushed."

"Not if we break this thing open first," the captain said, his lips tight with determination. "Sulu, plot a course to follow the photon torpedo down into the well as close as possible. Try to find a path for the torpedoes that won't cough them right back up at us. Chekov, rig the photons for remote detonation, five hundred kilometers."

"Sir!" Scott thumped down from the engineering station, his face pasty, tension apparent in his voice. "A blast at that proximity could take our warp nacelles with it."

"You got an alternative, Mr. Scott? Now's the time."

"Uh . . . no, sir, I don't have one of those."

"Then prepare to stabilize all systems as they break down."

"Aye-aye, sir!"

"And Tom, get off the bridge."

"No! No!" Tom pulled to his feet and held onto the rail. "No—you're fighting for your lives and the lives of my people—I don't want to know for the rest of my life that I crawled away just when I should stay. Captain Kirk, I've learned so much from you—you wouldn't let them frighten you. I have to keep control and teach my people," he said, and stabbed a finger toward the forward screen, "or his fears will come true."

Kirk found five seconds to gaze at the cause of the trouble and saw in Tom's face the hope of a young civilization moving out of its own adolescence with every step toward Federation membership. Tom, and with him his culture, would have to learn the responsibility of being good neighbors.

Tom wanted to learn it, no matter how much it hurt.

Kirk looked past the gentle fair-haired man to his very antithesis, pleat-perfect Spock, there on the upper deck, his face drawn with tension. Even the colors they were wearing were opposites.

Spock gazed down, and he nodded at the captain. Not even for his own sake would he ask the Rey man to leave the bridge and remain a child.

"Captain!" Scott interrupted. "Red-line plus twenty on the external shields! Breakdown at any minute!"

"All right, Tom," Kirk said, "get ready to learn. And hold on." He slid partly onto the seat of his chair and hung on to the edge with one thigh. "Ready remote detonation."

"Ready, sir!" Chekov squawked, his throat sandpaper.

"Prepare to fire the salvo on my mark. Three . . . two . . . one . . . fire!"

The photon torpedo spun down into the well, and after it came the starship.

Starships were tough, but they weren't spandex. A ship that seemed impenetrable could suddenly tear itself inside out. What had been pliant safeties and springboards built into the beautiful systems were being pushed into brittleness and a good third of them were snapping as pressure increased.

James Kirk held onto his command chair and willed his ship to stay in one piece. His head started to ache, reacting to the change in pressure. Behind him, Uhura made an almost inaudible squeak, and before him Sulu and Chekov hunched their shoulders in pain.

The ship started sizzling around him. Hissing, snapping—

His stomach rattled like a sack of rocks. He resented the call echoing in his head and he resented himself for hearing it.

What the hell am I doing here?

One day nature would get him. Maybe that was why he wasn't afraid of enemies who could think.

As long as he didn't crack, as long as he didn't give the order too soon to do any good—the fight would go on until they won or broke in half.

On the forward screen, the glow of the photon torpedo's track blazed a path before them down into the gravity well.

"Pressure nine thousand PSI and increasing!" Scott reported.

"Captain!" Sulu called. "We're losing helm control!"

"Stay with her, Mr. Sulu!" Kirk's eyes were squinted and his face felt heavy. "Follow it down!"

His fingers dug hard into the arm of his chair, his starship.

"You're coming back," he gritted to her. Sweat drained down his face. He thought his skull was imploding. His voice hummed inside it.

He caught Sulu's pained glance and clamped his lips shut. The helmsman had heard something over the whine. The captain's voice? An order to detonate?

Not yet.

"Twelve thousand PSI!"

Scott's voice was a distorted boom over the scream of the ship.

Kirk tried to turn his head. The pressure pounded at him. Beyond Tom, who was huddled there on the deck, he could barely see Spock—just in the corner of his eye . . .

Spock looked at him, brow puckered, eyes tight. Another few seconds . . .

Kirk found one last breath in his collapsing chest. "Detonate!"

No one responded.

Chekov and Sulu both moved a little, but he had no idea which one of them detonated the torpedo.

The forward screen exploded into a nearly solid white flash that overtook its frame and seemed to fill the bridge, so bright that no one could see for several seconds.

If Sulu could keep control over the helm, he didn't need his eyes to pilot the ship clear—

The pressure fell off abruptly, fast enough to cause pain even in the relief. Kirk grabbed for his scattered senses. He tried to turn to Spock, moving one shoulder in that direction, but the deck fell away and he hurtled starboard, as though falling off a steeplechaser, and landed on top of Tom. Chekov landed on top of them, Spock beside them. Through the deck Kirk felt quakes as the other bridge crew hit bottom.

The ship convulsed—might as well have been Kirk's own body. He wanted to take hits for her, but he couldn't. Some things she had to take for herself. She was in a crash dive out of the well's axle. He tried to see it in his mind, but all he could do was cram his eyes shut and hold his breath.

Forward force held him to the deck. If he could only *think*—

He willed his eyes to open. Past Chekov's shoulder he saw Spock pressed to the upper deck, and the bridge rail over them all. One hand . . . just one hand . . .

He reached upward with his right hand, fingers spread toward the struts of that rail.

I just have to feel it in my hand . . .

His fingers bumped the strut, then clamped around it. Suddenly he felt like an acrobat with one hand on a trapeze, and he wasn't about to let go. Pain bit into his fingers.

He shoved Chekov an inch to one side and pulled against his own weight. The muscles in his shoulder and arm trembled for relief, but he kept pulling. He had to get up. He *had* to be on his feet! If nature was going to beat him, it was going to beat him standing up.

He was about halfway there when the ship roared suddenly and the pressure lifted. His head buzzed and turned light, and for an instant he couldn't see anything more than the upper deck and Spock's legs nightmarishly elongated in front of him, or hear past the ringing in his ears and the clacking of his sinuses.

"All stop!" he shouted. "Stabilize!"

Had they heard him? He couldn't hear his own voice. Was there an echo? Or was it—

"All stop, aye!"

That was Sulu. Good.

Kirk reached over the rail and grasped Spock's arm and pulled him to his feet. Then he looked around, checking on the bridge crew. Uhura was at her station, wobbling but working. Sulu was crawling back into his chair, though somehow in spite of the kicking, he hadn't let his hand be pulled from the controls. Magic, probably. Scott was working with one arm—the other was numb at his side, but he was on his feet.

"Scotty, report!" Kirk demanded.

"Clear of the well, sir," the engineer gasped. "Not as bad as I expected."

"It wasn't?"

Only now realizing he'd bumped his head on something, Kirk made the mistake of shaking it.

"Secure from red alert. Go to yellow alert . . ." He paused as the blur in front of his eyes recoagulated into a bridge. "Maintain general quarters. Damage control parties report to—to Mr. Scott."

"Aye, sir."

"Sickbay," Kirk said.

"Sickbay here. Dr. Rothbaum."

"Report, doctor."

"No deaths, sir. Sixty-two injuries, mostly in the propulsion and magnatomics areas. Twenty of those are down

for the count. I can have the others back on duty within ten minutes."

"Acknowledged, Doctor, bridge out. Lieutenant Uhura, reposition standby crew to those twenty stations."

"Redistributing assignments, Captain. Having some trouble staffing the reactor loop."

"Put earth science staff up there if necessary. Those positions have to be manned."

"Yes, sir."

Still holding the rail as his legs rattled under him, Kirk turned to Spock. "Condition of the vessel?"

"Intact," Spock said, then paused for breath. "Some . . . exterior structural damage . . ."

Though Spock was trying not to breathe as heavily as he needed to, his hands were twitching.

"Are you hurt?" Kirk asked him.

"I don't believe so," Spock answered. "Are you?"

"My head feels as if it's been sledgehammered. We've got to get McCoy back on board so he can tell us we're all imagining it."

Spock only nodded, but seemed relieved.

"Captain," Uhura said, her voice weak and fighting upward, "Process Control Chief Edwards insists those positions in the loop can't be manned by anyone other than systems interns or supervisors."

Scott snapped up and thundered, "Strangle him and step over the body! Get those panels green-lighted. And put one of 'em on spectroanalysis and the feedbacks."

"Yes, Mr. Scott."

Kirk offered him an approving nod, but Scott hadn't waited for it. He was already back at his station, tending to the ship.

The captain reached down to the deck and caught Tom's elbow, bringing him to a standing position. Tom pressed back the hair that had fallen into his eyes. Kirk saw him beat down the fear he'd been trying to control—for everyone's sake.

"Thank you," he said. And he pulled his arm away. "I can stand alone."

"Keep to one side. This isn't over," Kirk said. "We've got to catch up to the Romulans and deal with them while they're still out in deep space. All hands . . . this is the captain. Report to battle stations. Screens at full magnification. All departments bring your systems back up to Starfleet regulation level as quickly as possible. Arm all weapons batteries. Shields up."

"Full magnification, sir."

"All phaser and photon systems ready and functioning, sir."

"Nine-three percent shields up, sir. All stations report battle ready."

"Very well. Brace yourselves. We've got a real race to run now. Mr. Sulu, full ahead, warp factor five."

"Warp five, aye!"

BLOOD
SPORT

Chapter Nineteen

Below Decks, *Ransom Castle*

"TAKE COVER!"

The hungry whine of phased light. The slash of knives. Wretched unforgiving violation of living bodies torn atom from atom. Primitive weapons given work in the modern age side by side with the hand tools of space conquest. Blood-spattered passageways.

No warnings. No questions. No prisoners. Only the efficiency of predators, unforgotten from eons past. Unforgotten . . . and refined.

An Imperial visitation.

Violence boiled through the ramshackle, weather-scarred tramp packet, bringing a crescendo of losses. A scorched, hacked, and pitilessly savaged crew of innocent men and women slammed through narrow companion-ways and hatches in many directions, moving on blind impulse, trusting to reflex, and losing.

Leonard McCoy had no idea how many he had been forced to leave behind in the disruptor-smashed corridors as he was shoved headfirst into *Ransom Castle*'s forward lazaret. Three people piled in after him, and all he heard for five seconds were screams and the ping of fire returned from a captured disruptor.

"Kill the crawlway lights!"

"Get in! All the way in!"

"Here they come!"

"Gimme room—back! Back! Okay, I'm in!"

"Shut it!"

The lazaret portcullis, two separate slabs of metal sandwiched between the bulkheads, rolled out and clanked shut—*slam . . . clack.*

"Oh . . . God."

McCoy knew the sound of injury when he heard it, and in the dimness he grabbed for it. "Set her down. Can we get any light in here?"

"Yeah." Mike Frarey's big bulk moved in the haze of disruptor smoke. "Marilyn, let me get past you. There's a utility worklight right . . . here someplace. There."

Three tiny pinkish lights popped on in a row along the far end of the ceiling, and McCoy forced his eyes to adjust.

He found both his hands on Nancy Ransom's bloody upper arm, and the irascible young captain pressed up against the portcullis, both knees bent, her face crushed with pain.

"Where's Mike?" she gasped.

"I'm right here," Frarey wheezed. "Big as life."

Nancy squinted at him. "I saw you go down."

"Yeah, well, I went down for a minute. My head's swimming some."

"Let the doctor look at you."

"Nah, forget about me."

"I'm busy looking at you right now, Captain Ransom," McCoy said.

"Mike! Quick, tell 'em what's going on. No surrender!" Nancy tossed something to Mike—a remote of some kind—and he plugged it into a little glowing access in the wall.

"Attention!" he rasped. "We're boarded! Take cover

and fight. It's Romulans! Our people are being killed. Take cover and double-lock yourselves in. Fight if you can!"

"Okay, okay," Nancy said, stopping before his warning started to sound like panic. "If they haven't got that, it's too late."

"You, come over here," McCoy said. He gestured to a goggle-eyed crewman about twenty years old. "What's your name, son?"

"I'm . . . Sam Oats."

"Come over here and see if you can't stop this bleeding. Just hold this chamois over it. Now, don't pretend to be an intern and make it too tight."

He left Oats to deal with Nancy's upper arm, and went after the pasty faces and shivers first. Burns, cuts, gashes, even stab wounds could wait. That cold sweaty shock had to be handled first.

Didn't seem to be any fractures. No one was collapsing. No spurting punctures. No breakdown. They were all drenched in sweat, beaten to shadows because they had protected him by pushing him out of harm's way and taken the brunt of the Romulan attack for him. He knew the signs of decency when he saw them.

"Are we safe in here?"

"I don't hear anybody trying to get in," Nancy muttered.

"Everybody stop moving around. There's a lot of blood and I can't tell where it's coming from. Calm down so you can feel where your pain is. Breathe and conserve strength."

He had his work cut out for him. There were four of them crammed into a six-by-six refuge, squeezed between winches, brackets, chain hoists, devil's claws, bumpers, fenders, double-fluked antiroll hooks, all equipment for maneuvering large cargo in space. There were also boxes of chamois cloths and dirty rags.

At the moment, the dangling ordnance looked a lot more alive than the poor wretches gasping between them.

Their faces were pasty or flushed, some looked queasy or faint, others sharply suffering. They looked like a club of longshoremen in their olive drab turtlenecks or black jerseys, less uniforms than just a shipment of factory seconds they'd stumbled onto.

"What the hell do they want?" Frarey choked. "Are they looking for cargo?"

"We aren't carrying anything," Nancy said heavily. "We had to leave it all at the starbase."

"Romulans aren't pirates, generally speaking." McCoy dabbed at Frarey's bleeding black eye. "Does the air circulate in here? Will we be able to breathe, trapped like this?"

"It circulates everywhere on board," Frarey said. "We don't take chances with each other."

Nancy forced herself to one knee. "Who'd we lose?"

"I saw Eric go down," Sam Oats said, his voice a pathetic shatter. "And Luke and Clancy. Dead or out, I don't know which."

"Marilyn and Mitch and a couple of others are trapped in the stacks, Nancy," Frarey said. "I saw the hatch close."

"How many raiders have—we got—" A wave of vertigo hit their struggling captain, and she thunked sideways against the portcullis.

McCoy caught her good arm. "Simmer down, will you? Panic won't serve us any."

"I'm not panicking," she insisted, flaring with insult.

"Don't get defensive. What's this ship built like? I might need to know."

Sam Oats and Mike Frarey blinked at him as though they'd never heard of such a thing, then Frarey shrugged. "Forward, the commons, where we eat and sleep, and the larder. In a square from there back to the engine room, there's a causeway we call the quadrangle. It's just a walkway along the ship's gunwales."

"I got it. Go on."

"Well . . . in the midship is the dry stores, then the lazaret, where we are now, the ore bunker, the wet stores—that's where we put barrels, casks, and tanks. Then the bunkers and the coops and stores are all divided up with reinforced airtight removable wall sections. Then there's the engine room, and that's about it."

"Solarium," Sam Oats gasped, licking a swollen lip.

"Oh, yeah, there's a solarium on top of the dry stores, where we can, y'know, get away from each other once in a while."

McCoy crawled a few inches deeper into the vault and went after Oats's bloody leg.

"I don't know what they want with my ship," Nancy growled, speaking out of her corner. "But I've got weapons on board and I'm going to start using them."

"Wait!" McCoy grabbed for her sleeve. "How many of these people do we have to kill?"

"All of 'em, Doc," she said.

"But why? There are ways to fight them without slaughter. They hear too well—we can bombard them with high-frequency sound. Or we can drop the temperature on the ship because we can maneuver in cold better than they can. They're used to breathing thinner air than we are. We can use that! Or we can make them itch, or any number of alternatives!"

"I don't want alternatives. I want dead."

"But the *Enterprise* will be coming! All we have to do is hold out until she gets here."

"Oh, get off it," Nancy spat. "You telling me you think the Romulans let that starship haul itself up out of that well without a fight? I'm not going to believe it."

"Believe what you want, Captain," McCoy told her sharply. "I've seen Jim Kirk throw off some mighty big chains in his time."

"He's dead. Give it up."

McCoy glared at her, anger swelling to sadness. He hadn't thought of it that way. Jim Kirk dead . . . the ship gone . . .

The death of one, the death of a hundred—he couldn't swallow it bluntly like that.

Nancy eyed him in the dim ugly light. "You some kind of pacifist?"

"I just don't like to kill when there's another way," he said. His voice gave away his emotions.

"Well, great," the quaking woman said. "You go out and pacify them. Maybe you keep some high-frequency noise in your pocket, I don't know. But I can't let 'em take my ship." She looked at him closely. "Have you ever had to fight for your life?"

The question was almost light, for Nancy. It told McCoy that they were in trouble. Sympathy growled in his conscience. How long had he grumbled about space travel, yet continued on, deeper and deeper into space, comforted by the fact that he had the bulldog James Kirk doing his talking and his fighting and his bloodsweating for him. How willing would he have been to do his part without Jim Kirk to lie down on the daggers first?

All I've done is shadowbox, he thought. *Maybe it's all we've all done, except for the few captains who dare put their necks on the line. All us crew people who just expect the answers to be there in that chair up on the bridge. I never saw so many captains in one place, and I never thought they might all be a little bit Jim Kirk . . . and it looks like I'm not giving Nancy her due. Seems to me she's willing to hold up her end against the galaxy's evil princes.*

Nancy suddenly sighed. "You really think that starship and Mr. Highpockets are going to get here?"

Her question was tinged with hope.

He could have given her an arrogant answer, a starship answer, but something told him not to.

"I think there's a good chance, Captain," he said.

"Okay," she said. "Then we'll assume that. Mike! Tie me into the sensors. I want the whole system crashed."

"Crash the sensors? On purpose?"

"The whole thing. If he's right and that starship can get here, then I don't want the Romulans on board here to see them coming. Come on, boys, let's hold up our end of the deal."

Red Talon

"The conquest is secure, Commander. We have their ship."

Romar's face was flecked with shaved metal dust from the fighting aboard the target ship, and there was a small gash on his right jaw, but otherwise he was in control of himself. His breath came with an effort. The metallic fibers in his uniform tunic were pulled in several places.

Allowing himself a moment to look carefully at his subcommander, Valdus viewed the results of hand-to-hand combat which so seldom presented itself to a spacebound crew.

"Are you all right?" he asked.

Romar halted suddenly, hesitating on one foot. "Am I?"

"Yes," Valdus said, and even allowed himself a moderate smile. "You."

Pressing a hand to his chest, Romar looked down at his tunic and his legs as though he might be doing something wrong or have forgotten something.

"It's a simple question, Subcommander," Valdus said. "Don't you know now it fits the mission?"

"I . . ."

"From infancy we have it drummed into our heads that we are tools of the Empire first and always. Too often we sacrifice our own personal value to this and we forget that we have any."

Taken more off guard than if he'd been struck from behind by stealth, Romar stammered, "Thank you . . ."

"You're welcome. Report."

"The . . . the vessel is under our influence. Its crew is locked away in various locations."

"Not taken prisoner?"

"Some, but most have locked themselves away. Shall I order they be drilled out and taken?"

After a pause for thought, a calculation of the time available to them, Valdus said, "Since they are contained, leave them where they are. There is little sense in expending energy to capture and hold them when they are holding themselves. You made a show of taking the vessel?"

"Yes, they all know they have been conquered. We were quite noisy."

"Then let them sit in their confinement. We must concentrate on our own crew's efforts."

"If I were in confinement," Romar said, "I would be trying to break out and sabotage the boarding party, Commander."

"If they show themselves," Valdus said, "kill them as they appear."

"Yes, Commander."

"Romar . . ."

"Yes, Commander?"

"Stop ending every response with 'Commander.' You're beginning to sound like a security beeper."

"Yes."

"Show me the graphic you developed."

"Oh, I had almost forgotten." Romar laughed nervously and led the way to one of the small computer access screens on the glossy, dark panels. He tapped at the controls. "A simulation. Fairly simple. The ship will be impregnated with the adulterant you so smoothly smuggled into this space . . . and it will slam at warp speed into the planet's surface."

On the screen a pretend ship bolted toward a green planet with a thread of mountain ranges and hammered into the planet's mantle, instantly blistering the surface.

"Because of the high velocity, the explosion actually occurs miles inside the planet. A huge fusion explosion ensues . . . the mantle cracks . . . there are massive earthquakes . . ."

The screen rippled with color as Romar's narration was given a disturbing illustration. The green planet swelled, cracked, was laced now with volcanic blight, then—very suddenly—swallowed by heat from its own core, first in a surge of red, then a gaudy purple. The color of plague.

"A supersonic fireball engulfs the planet along with a dense cloud of highly radioactive cobalt vapor. Everyone who is not a hundred meters below the surface is dead from the cobalt vapor. Anyone below is dead from earthquakes. It is very simple, Commander."

Valdus reached forward and turned off the screen. A whole planet. On his word alone.

"I value your work," he said.

They faced the forward screen, neither looking at each other. Instead they fixed their eyes on the main viewer's picture of the merchant workship they now possessed.

"Romar, I will transport aboard that ship and take responsibility. When I do, I want you to move off. We must have deniability. I don't want war with the Federation. I never did. Go back to Imperial space and forget me."

Distress creased Romar's dust-coated features.

"Commander . . . I assumed you would rig that vessel for high speed on automatic navigation and . . . that you would beam back."

"I never said such a thing."

"Please say it now."

Valdus started to respond but noted that Romar didn't want to follow his order to move off, didn't want to save his own skin and the *Red Talon*'s until he could be sure that Valdus wasn't sacrificing his life for nothing.

"Call a legion to the bridge," Valdus said.

"On their way—" Romar responded, and it was obvious that he had to choke down a "Commander."

Valdus glanced now at his second and tried to remember what it was like to be second in command. Since he was considered somehow special for surviving an attack and preventing the attackers from advancing, he hadn't been second for very long. The Praetor had personally ordered him a ship of his own.

He tried to remember those days, but all he could see in his mind was *Scorah*.

His eyes lowered. "I know you are . . . uneasy."

Wrenching suddenly to face him, Romar gulped, "But I am not unsure! I know we are doing the right thing. I *know* it. I have *felt* it for myself!"

"Then you have the advantage." Valdus inhaled deeply and sighed. "I have never been very sure of myself, Romar, not even in my most glorious moments. Even as I stood before the Praetor and received awards for my successes, I would think back and wonder if those successes were genuine, or if I had spun onto them through the misfortune of others or simply my own happenstance. I've never been completely convinced of my own worth."

Quaking, teetering on the edge of disillusionment—perhaps with everything but the person before him—Romar choked out a raw whisper.

"I believe in you," he vowed. "You told me the need of our Empire, then you showed me that you were right. What more could I ask? When has the galaxy been simpler for me?" He put his hands out, one, then the other. "I know what I must do."

Valdus rubbed his hot palms on his thighs and watched Romar for a few moments, only watched him. Leaders learned early in the Imperial fleet not to expect too much loyalty or stretch it too much.

And yet here it was, bending before him.

He wanted to pay Romar a compliment, and tried to do it with his expression, but to come out and say such a thing at this instant of conquest and question—he couldn't.

Always there had been awkwardness at such times for him. Not because he couldn't find it in himself to be benevolent, but because he had found too much of that in himself and had never polished the timing. Awkward, always awkward.

"I've never believed in myself as much as others have believed in me," he said. "You are fortunate."

Frustration colored Romar's face a mottled olive and even made the wound on his jaw bleed again.

"Commander—"

"Yes, I know," Valdus said, and smiled.

Nervous strain pulled at the corners of Romar's mouth. The bridge was empty, for they had sacrificed the bulk of their crew to board the other ship and man the transporters, but he spoke as though a crowd pressed at his shoulders.

"Shall we . . . turn back, sir?"

Dismay crossed both their faces in a single crawling shadow. They were sons of a culture whose millenarian demands made a cynical chime and allowed no quarter. Chances were few and irrecoverable. Would changing their minds be less vulgar than making a single savage attack without authorization?

"If we turn back now," Valdus said, "the Empire will have to answer for our actions. If we push forward, you and the ship are merely tools of a commander gone mad. No, we shall push forward with my insanity. And what happens will be our responsibility. Save yourself the distress I see in your eyes, Romar. The galaxy boils with crude reason."

As poor Romar stood in knee-high torment and stared at him, brow troughed and mouth open without any noise coming out of it, the aft doors opened and eight armored legionnaires thundered onto the bridge. The senior among them stomped toward his two senior officers and asked a question with his eyes.

Valdus held up a staying hand.

"One moment, Subcenturion," he said.

He offered Romar a grip on the shoulder that failed to comfort either of them.

"I treasure your confidence. I won't fail it. Once our plan is in motion, and before I board the acquisition, you and I must pause and talk. We have a pact to make."

While apprehension plagued Romar's face, he seemed willing nonetheless to tweeze his body hairs out one at a time if that was what was needed to push this ghastly situation from the doorstep of their homeworlds.

Valdus smiled a graveyard smile, shook his head, and

gave up for now. He offered the impatient subcenturion a nod.

"You may begin."

The subcenturion spun and gave a single motion to his squad. The others pulled tools from their belts, then broke into couples and dispersed around the bridge.

And they began to dismantle the walls.

Enterprise

"Contact, Captain."

At Uhura's announcement, James Kirk pushed out of his chair and flexed his hands, coiled with impatience and a frantic flush to grab for the controls himself. His voice was gravelly and chopped through the bridge clicks and blips.

"Sulu, identify it."

"Contact is . . . I believe it's the *Alexandria,* sir."

"Speed?"

"Warp three point five, sir."

"Scan for Romulan presence aboard."

It took a few damning minutes. Kirk damned every tick. Even then, he didn't get what he really wanted.

"Their shields are not up," Spock reported. He looked at the captain. "Scanning is erratic. I wouldn't trust it."

"All right. We'll do it the hard way. Reduce speed to match."

"Aye, sir," Sulu said, his voice tight. "Reducing speed . . . warp five . . . four . . . three point seven . . . point five, sir."

Kirk hammered his direct contact panel. "Bridge to security."

A few grueling seconds prickled his skin before an answer came up.

"Security here. Chief Hanashiro."

His blood boiling and his mind reeling with pictures of the dozens of possibilities, what could happen and what might not, which of his guesses would be wrong and which people would pay—Kirk forced himself to concentrate on one gram of information at a time.

"Prepare an armed boarding party. Heavy gear, combat conditions. All weapons on heavy stun setting. You're going to take over a vessel."

There was a distended pause on the other end, then Hanashiro's voice came back, a fifth higher. "Yes, sir! What's the mission?"

"Unannounced beam-in to the vessel *Alexandria,* assuming the ship has been overtaken by hostiles. Assume innocent crew are being held aboard and that Romulan antagonists are in charge of the vessel." Kirk leaned forward and started to talk through his teeth. "Go over there, and take it back."

"Yes, sir, I will! Any preliminary contact?"

"Negative. Contacts can be faked."

"Orders when we have possession?"

"If there aren't any Romulans on board, confiscate the ship under Starfleet authority. Establish a Section Three security blockade. Stop and check every vessel that passes you. If all's well, send them on their way with orders to be cautious for possible takeover."

"Aye-aye, Captain. Boarding detail will be in the transporter room in three minutes."

"I'll hold you to that. Kirk out."

He glanced at Spock, needing—and getting—that stable glance that was longer, calmer, more reassuring than any other he might have found.

Was he doing the right thing? Was he jumping to the right conclusions? Was fear, or maybe anger, clouding his experience?

Could he be as cold as he needed to be? Was he cold enough right now?

He'd been frightened before in his career, frightened for his own existence and those of others, prepossessed with the safety and sanctity of his starship, within whose walls ran his own blood, pumped from his own heart, but there were many kinds of fear and anyone who said anything else was lying. Fear for himself or his ship was one kind. Fear for another ship . . .

A panic at heart level, a kind in and of itself.

Especially when that ship had one of his two closest friends on board.

"Sir?" Engineer Scott tipped cautiously into the captain's periphery.

"Yes, Mr. Scott?"

"I thought we decided our course of action, sir."

Kirk kept his voice stable. "I've got the armed parties. I'm going to use them to secure this sector if I have to go down to the last man on this ship and drive her myself."

Scott's face took on a quirkish admiration and he rocked on a heel. "Very good, sir."

"Thank you, Mr. Scott," he said solemnly. "Authorize transporting of the assault team onto *Alexandria*. Then take us back to warp five."

Scott nodded, and there was almost a wink. "Aye, sir, will do."

The captain dropped his gaze, tightened his shoulders, then released them, and half expected his neck to snap. He heard Scott move away, back toward the engineering station to carry out the orders. In his bones he felt the transporter humming, and in his mind saw the beams carry his armed detail to another ship, there to draw arms and take over.

Half his blood curdled at the idea. The other half was still boiling. He scanned the flickering viewscreen as though searching for a beacon, though he knew helpless others were watching the night, waiting for him to be their beacon.

A second later, Commander Scott motioned to Sulu. The starship vibrated with summoned power. Warp four . . . Warp five . . .

Ransom Castle

The two Romulans never saw what hit them.

That was because Mike Frarey hit them. Frarey was a

big man, but he was quiet and fast. So he managed to knock the tails out from under the two invaders before they even realized the bulkhead had opened behind them.

"Get their weapon! Mike, pull them into the closet. Lock them in there."

Nancy kicked at the unconscious invaders as Mike got them both by the metallic collars and hauled them into the utility closet. Sam Oats slammed the hatch and locked it, then Nancy pulled out a lipstick dispenser and marked the wall with a Z.

"What's that supposed to mean?" McCoy asked, careful to keep his voice down in case there were more Romulans coming along the quadrangle.

"Zorro. What else?" Nancy popped off. "So we'll know where they are, and nobody'll just open the door without being ready to fight. My crew's trained, too, you know. Now, what's that thing?"

She limped down the passage, to a coffin-size piece of metal hanging from two antigravs. It kept hovering and waited to be pushed along.

"Why were they moving a hunk of metal through my ship?"

"It looks like a folded section of wall material," Frarey said. "See the bolt holes here? And down there—"

"That don't make no sense." Oats went to look. "Why would they invade us, then bring a piece of a wall?"

"Pardon the expression," McCoy interrupted, "but why don't you ask the logical questions? Ask yourself where they were heading with it. What's down that way?"

"Nothing, just the engine room," Oats supplied.

"The engine room's not nothing, boy," Nancy grimly told him. "It's a hell of a lot of power."

"But they got their own engine room!"

"Shut up. I'm trying to think."

McCoy stepped between them to the wall section. "Let's let the tricorder do our thinking. Hold that section up, Frarey."

Frarey lifted part of the folded wall section. One side

was white crystalline, the other side silver. McCoy ran the tricorder along both sides.

"The white side is lithium hydride . . . hydrogen gas bonded to lithium. Why would they do that?"

"So the gas could be molded, that's why," Nancy said. She was suddenly pale.

"And this silvery material . . . is cobalt." McCoy swiveled from face to face. "What's the significance of that?"

"I'll tell you what. They're taking this stuff down to our engine room in order to fuse it to our warp core, that's what. It means they've been planning this since they left their own space. It's not an arbitrary hit."

"What's that mean?" McCoy badgered. "Do I have to keep asking?"

Bending in a pool of regret and grief, Nancy looked as though she was ready to throw up. "It means we're part of a long-range plan of some kind. The only thing they can do with lithium hydride and cobalt is turn this ship into a real big, real filthy bomb."

Chapter Twenty

Bridge of *Ransom Castle*

TRANSPORTING HAD ALWAYS SEEMED to Valdus a necessary evil of modern technology.

He thought of this all the way through the conscious moments of the process, and through its stomach-turning aftermath, until he could move and speak again.

The instant he could see again, he remained unsure if the transportation process had truly finished. All he saw around him was a distortion of shadows and flat areas, indistinguishable as a ship's bridge or any other organized work area. Only as he focused in the dimness did he realize the bridge was made this way on purpose, painted with blacks and flat dull colors to confuse the eye, without consideration to beginnings or endings of panels and consoles, corners or intrusions.

His analysis was confirmed when one of his own soldiers came toward him, lips parted to make a report, and instantly tripped on a set of steps which were painted the opposite of how anyone in their right mind would paint steps. The ups appeared as downs. The poor lighting here perfectly complemented the illusion.

Valdus caught the poor stumbling sod's arm and hauled him to his knees.

"Forgive me, Commander!" the soldier begged as he staggered up.

"Keep your eyes open, Legionnaire. This is a ship patterned with unwelcoming. Report."

"The ship is ours, sir. Its crew is imprisoned or locked away. Transportation of the wall sections has commenced from *Red Talon*, and we are moving them one by one through the ship to the engine room."

"Moving them? You couldn't beam them directly to the engine room?"

"No, Commander," the legionnaire said. "This vessel has some kind of antidissolution shielding in its after third. We attempted to transport directly, but the best we could do was to transport the plates into a freight—"

Valdus slapped his hands against his legs and snapped, "Why did I fail to think! I should have chosen one of those pleasure vessels when I had a chance to do so!" He stalked the confusing bridge, and the only thing he did right was observe the deck and not trip in front of his minion. Finally he stopped his stormy circle and thumped the back of his hand on the helm. "Fool."

"Commander! The sensors! They're shutting down!"

The soldier plunged for the nearest panels as half the indicator lights suddenly flickered and died out.

Valdus swung to his side. "Damage?"

"No damage—power is cut! The power is cut! How can they cut the power! We have locked them all away!"

"They must have a remote access of some sort," Valdus grimly told him. "Likely they are familiar with being boarded and have prepared for this. Quickly—check communications."

They both grabbed for the afterdeck, where the ship-to-ship communications hid under a black hood, but after a moment's frantic attempts to tap into the system, Valdus felt his brow pucker and he turned to look at the whole bridge, to take in the appearance of the control systems as a unit—and realized what had happened.

"The computer system!" he said. "They've shut the entire ship down!"

Enterprise

"Contact, Captain—extreme distance. Two vessels."

"Identify them, Spock."

"Not possible at this distance, sir."

Jim Kirk drew in an uncomforting breath. "Moving? Are they race contestants?"

Spock squinted into his screens and sounded unsure when he reported. "Very little movement registering, sir."

"Two vessels, no movement . . . I have to assume it's them." He paced back and forth behind the helm. He saw the rigidity in Sulu's and Chekov's shoulders. Both men had their eyes fixed on the forward screen, but there was nothing to see but empty space, and it looked suspiciously innocent out there.

"Is long-range communication available yet, Lieutenant?"

Uhura obviously heard the compacted rage in his voice and lowered her own voice to compensate. "Long-range subspace is still flooded, sir. No chance of calling ahead."

Kirk ground his teeth at the high-reaching effects of somebody's racing trick and pounded the comm panel on the arm of the command chair. "Mr. Scott."

"Engineering. Scott here."

"Power situation?"

"She's up to ninety percent sensor capacity, eighty-three percent thrust and weapons, eighty percent maneuverability, seventy-nine percent shielding—"

"Make weapons and shields the priorities. We'll need them within ten minutes."

"Aye, sir, working."

"I want warp six as soon as you can get it, and full warp capacity immediately thereafter. Kirk out. All hands, red alert. Go to battle stations. Arm all weapons."

Uhura didn't acknowledge, but her voice instantly flowed through vessel's internal communications systems.

"Red alert. Battle stations . . . all hands to battle stations. This is not a drill. All hands report to battle stations . . ."

Realizing he'd just ordered Scott to wave a magic wand over the weapons, and no excuses allowed, Kirk paused to listen to Uhura's voice and think of what his four hundred plus crewmen were doing below decks—rushing to their stations, snapping all systems on line, double-manning critical positions, and he felt as though he'd been given a stimulant.

That made him think of McCoy.

"Mr. Spock," he said, but then he paused. He leaned in a tense manner on his command chair, but couldn't bring himself to sit down just when everyone else on board was up and operating. He was glad they'd put Tom updeck in the engineer's chair Scott had abandoned. He couldn't see Tom's face. He didn't want to look at that gentle expression of hope in the midst of all this and remember that an entire culture was sitting on his shoulders.

Spock had his hands on his controls, but he was watching Kirk. He'd been alerted, and now he was waiting for orders.

That means I have to come up with something, the captain thought. *Something Valdus won't expect. He thinks we're dead—we have to behave like a ghost.*

"We're going to do something we've never done before," he said. "Attention all decks . . . rig for silent running."

Everyone hesitated for just a moment, to absorb the words. They'd all heard about it, all been trained for it, but this procedure was one of those things that appears in an Academy class for two or three days, shows up on a test, and is almost immediately forgotten. Silent while the ship is shut down, waiting out a situation—that was

one thing. Silent at high speed and closing on an enemy
. . . that was something else.

"Turn off all running lights," Kirk said. "Shut down all
systems but thrust, weapons, and life-support, including
all automatic reaction controls and deflector shields. Mr.
Chekov, plot our course to the two ships we detected,
then shut down the long-range navigational guidance
systems."

Chekov glanced at him. "Navigate without the computer, sir?"

"Navigate with charts and your own hands and eyes,
Ensign. Navigate with a stick if you have to, but don't let
them see you coming. You've been trained to do it—
now's your chance."

Now Sulu twisted around to him, too. "Are we going
into a battle situation without shields up, sir?"

"Deflection energy can be detected," Kirk said. "The
Romulans will be looking for an active ship. We're going
to try to become part of the background, like a dead rock
in space. That's enough, gentlemen. I don't intend to
explain myself any further."

The two of them snapped forward, chimed a muddled,
"Yes, sir," and didn't glance anymore.

The bridge of the *Enterprise* was normally a fairly loud
place. Bleeps and hums, whirrs and clicks, machines and
people working, correlating information, logging new
things, revising old things. Suddenly the lights started to
shut down. The bleeps began to fall silent. Harmony and
countermelody began to fall off, drop away. The breath
went out from the starship like a body going to sleep.

The greatest fear of space travelers is that the kindly
shell of precious air and heat should cease to protect
them, and that was what this looked like.

As the lights on the panels shut down section by
section, and finally even the overhead lights went dim,
everyone paused instinctively to watch, to see how far
into blackness the bridge would retreat. In minutes there
were only a few amber lights left on the panels—no green

ones—and the milky glow of Chekov's navigation astrogator.

The *Enterprise* crept forward, shrouded in silence.

"Mr. Spock . . ."

"Sir?"

"Bring all personnel inward from the ship's outer areas, secure those areas, then turn off the heat. Bring the ship's outer shell down to four degrees Kelvin. Do your best to make sure there's no leaking heat, and disguise any exhaust to the extreme aft portion of the ship."

"Yes, sir."

Working under the lingering strains of the Rey presence on the ship, and in his own way engaged in a battle of will, Spock forced himself to concentrate as he fed the orders throughout the ship. There was strain in his face, tension in his arms.

And enough was enough.

Kirk turned to the port side. "Tom," he said. "It's time for you to go below."

Tom looked more afraid to leave than to stay. "Oh, please, Captain, I'm trying to be calm—"

"No arguments. You're affecting my crew." Kirk raised a sharp finger. "Off."

The Rey man stood up, unsteady, disappointed, blinked those big eyes, and went shame-faced to the turbolift.

As he turned back to the forward screen, Kirk heard the hiss of the lift doors and thought better of watching Tom actually leave.

Spock gazed at him briefly, and remained silent.

"Mr. Spock," Kirk said, "secure the ship, then shut off all sensor emissions."

Surprised, Spock drew his hands from his panel and straightened. Uhura spun around. The two engineers on the port deck popped up from their controls. Even Chekov turned. Sulu was the only person who didn't overtly react, and Kirk could see him fighting not to.

Spock stepped down to the command deck and came to the captain's side. "We will be flying blind," he said. "We may not be seen, but we will not be able to see."

"I know that. I'm going to assume Valdus put his power back up to one hundred percent almost immediately after leaving Starbase 16. I was running the race, and didn't. Now we're ten to eighteen percent below power, and if we don't get in the first kick, we're finished. I want you to shut the ship down completely except for the warp engines. All hands keep movement to a minimum. Stay calm. No unnecessary activity. Clear the corridors. Prevent any electronic leakage. I don't want anything but speed, Mr. Spock, speed and readiness. Hold the impulse drive in abeyance. As little active power as possible. Once silent running is in effect, I want you to emit a subspace signal of one watt."

Spock's dark eyes went narrow and he hesitated. *"One watt, sir?"*

"Yes, one watt. Only one."

"A very . . . small signal, sir."

"That's the idea. I want the Romulan to squint into the darkness because he thinks he's seeing something. We'll look like anything but a starship. I want all his sensors fixed on that one little watt as we approach. When we get up close, we broadcast everything we've got in one singular blast—blow out their sensors completely. He'll be squinting into the dark, and we'll shine a spotlight in his eyes. Get ready to do it."

He slid into his command chair, his thighs aching.

Unable to send or receive, without so much as a light on her hull, the starship didn't even hum around him today, but only streaked through the darkness of space, now dark herself and no more than a slice of the night.

"We're flying blind and we could pile into a star, but if that's the chance we have to take in order to save a planet of strangers, then that's what we'll do. They've killed people and they've ruined an event that was intended to generate nothing but goodwill. They've made me lose the race, and I've had enough. It's time for them to lose."

"Subcommander . . . a signal. Very faint."

"Where?"

"From the direction we came."

Romar crowded the subcenturion at the science panel and looked at the readouts. "Another racing vessel?"

"Not enough signal to be a vessel, sir," the subcenturion said. "Reads only point zero zero zero one."

"Moving?"

"I can't tell with something so small."

Frustration gnawing at him, Romar pushed in closer. "Can you tell if it is natural?"

"What else can it be?" The subcenturion leaned back and held a hand to the screen in a gesture of disgust. "Nothing can be so minuscule while representing manufactured power."

Still, Romar could not trust what he saw on the screen. "Heat readings? Energy emissions? Thrust trail? Nothing? Are you looking at your controls?"

"I read nothing, Subcommander. You see it for yourself."

"What can it be, then?"

"A probe perhaps? That drifted into the area on the currents of the race exhausts. So many ships in one area—"

"Space is vast, Subcenturion," Romar snapped. "Too vast to be stirred up. Turn all available sensors on that blip, high intensity. Pull in every emission it may put out. And put me in contact with Commander Valdus."

"Communications on the other ship have been debilitated—"

"Then use his hand-held communicator! Are you waiting for a night's rest?" Romar leaned past the subcenturion and struck the necessary pads. "Commander, this is Romar. Do you receive?"

Several seconds plodded past. The hand-held communicator took more power, and more time, to draw in the signal and notify the landing party of the hailing.

"This is Valdus."

"We have contacted a signal, Commander, but it is much too faint to be a ship."

"An emission? Is there power involved? Movement?"

"Impossible to tell at this distance. We're focusing all sensors at full intensity upon it, attempting to identify it. It may be a probe, or one of the Race Committee markers . . . but it seems too faint even for those."

"Romar . . . raise your shields."

Romar leaned closer—absurd, because the officers on the bridge could have heard a whisper, and he had no intent to whisper.

"My shields?"

"Yes."

"But we have taken and secured our target. No ship can possibly approach us without alerting our sensors and having the shields come on automatically. . . . I resist using the shields without reason. They could be detected from far off. Our plan could be foiled for our caution. And if our shields are up, we won't be able to contact you through the hand-held system."

Silence blended briefly with the tension that always came with a mission of conquest. If only those who were conquered could realize that fewer deaths would come with simple submission.

"I suppose you're right."

"Don't fear, Commander," Romar said. "I will keep sensors focused on the signal. If it increases or grows near, the shields will go up."

"Very well. Soon we will be finished altering this ship's warp core, and we shall send her on her way to the planet of witches. Nothing will stop it then—no one will think to stop it."

"Do you want more personnel there? Is the ship's crew still fighting back?"

"There is some sparse resistance. We can deal with

them. No matter, Romar, for in a few minutes the entire crew of this ship will be fused to the planet of Gullrey, and Gullrey will be melting before the eyes of the Federation."

Kirk could have picked up the tension on a knife and used it to butter bread.

"Approaching the Romulan ship's last known position, sir."

Chekov's voice cracked.

"All hands, stand by . . . sensor emitters on alert . . . prepare for amplification of all systems, maximum broadcast. All frequencies open . . . all lights on standby . . . heat emission control, prepare to flood the outer sections. Phasers, stand by to fire, tight beam, short range. Avoid hitting the *Castle* with heat wash."

"All systems on standby, sir. Ready to flood all emissions power grids."

"Position, Mr. Chekov!"

"Coming up to five-tenths light-years distant from last noted position—three-tenths . . . two . . . one . . . ten light-days . . ."

"Helm, reduce speed! Now, Mr. Spock—blow them away! All systems on! Phasers—fire!"

"Overload! Overload!"

The bridge of *Red Talon* erupted in sparks and smoke as their own power was fed back at them in a violent gush.

"Full shields! Return fire! All systems to battle condition!"

"It's the starship, Subcommander!" the weapons officer gasped. "How can they be here? We killed them!"

"Obviously we failed to kill them enough!" Romar snapped, and backhanded the shocked man across the cheek. "Fire at them! Fire!"

He thrashed across the bridge, pushing injured crewmen out of the way and shoving blinded and confused others into positions where they might be able to operate something. The putrid stink of burned circuits flushed up at them so thickly that they could barely breathe.

"We can't aim!" the subcenturion shouted across the flashing consoles.

Nearby, the centurion batted at a fire and gasped, "Contact the Commander! Warn him!"

"No! We need the shields!" Romar shouted back. "Return their fire!"

"I can't aim at them!" the weapons officer choked. "The targeting computer is backwashed! They're everywhere!"

"Then shoot at everything!" Romar brayed. "Shoot!"

The officer grabbed for his console with burned hands, and took potshots into the darkness.

Romar clung to the helm as the ship was struck from above and plunged on the descent, then almost immediately was struck from the side, and twisted backward, and was struck again as it turned.

A dozen times they aimed and missed until their weapons board was flashing with lights warning of depleted power. A dozen times the starship whipped at them out of patches of sensor blackness caused by the sudden sensor blinding. By the time Romar realized how deeply crippled his own ship was, there were six men lying dead on the bridge and warning buzzers driving him to madness, and there was only one more course.

"Veer off!"

The centurion spun around and staggered toward him. "We're abandoning the commander!"

"Then abandon him!" Romar grabbed the man by the collar and drew him close, then pitched him viciously across the deck. "It is his own order! Veer off! Veer toward Imperial space! High warp!"

"Yes, Subcommander . . ."

"Corus! Get someone up here to plot a path! Corus!"

"Corus is dead, Subcommander."

"Then get someone else!"

Romar faced the forward screen, its image of the starship looping toward them again with her phaser ports glowing, and the glowering image of the *Ransom Castle* in the background—

And in an instant that image was suddenly launched into the distance, falling farther and farther behind.

He fixed his glare on the two ships. Even in the thunderhead of battle, he found himself searching in his own soul for what he had seen in Valdus's eyes, to catch that fading memory from a generation ago, to wonder if he was making the right decision. He understood the latent content in those eyes . . . a man who thought he should have died years ago aboard an ill-starred ship.

Ghosts of *Scorah* were in Valdus's eyes. The commander was summoning the crypt of his fellows, that he too might crawl in.

Romar bit down on thoughts of turning back, to beg a change in what was happening. The course was set and would snap to bits if he tried to change it. The starship was there, and nothing could be done to drive it away.

He wiped a bleeding cut on his face with the back of his hand, and fought to get a whole breath of the contaminated air in his lungs. He felt his innards tighten. Waves of grief thrashed over him.

"I am your son now," he murmured, "and I will fulfill your purpose."

Chapter Twenty-one

Below Decks, *Ransom Castle*

A NAUSEATING shimmer and whine dispersed, and in its place were the bracketing walls of this ship's port quadrangle passageway.

James Kirk shook off the effects and gripped tightly the phaser in his hand. He glanced to one side, then the other, at his five security men.

"Disperse," he said.

Two men went forward, two aft, and one stayed with him.

"Let's go," he snapped to the man who would be his personal backup, and led the way laterally through the dark passages of *Ransom Castle*. Only now did he remember what an industrial ship looked like on the inside. Color-baffled shadows, unseen ledges, dark doorways, bolted hatches. The ship was built like a medieval castle, with double locks and iron hasps, back-to-back freight holds, cold crawlways, and spiral steps between decks.

As he moved, he whipped his communicator up in a single motion that opened the grid without having to use more than one hand.

"Kirk to *Enterprise*."

"*Spock here.*"

"Are the close-range sensors back on line yet?"

"*There is some frequency confusion after having the systems shut down, but we are clearing it. Mr. Chekov is endeavoring to pinpoint the Romulan anatomical readings aboard Ransom Castle. So far we have only three readings, all of those in the after sections near the engineering deck. Security Officer Brennan is on his way there with his squad. He already forced open two holds and found several members of the crew, injured but alive.*"

"Any sign of McCoy?"

The silence was suddenly heavy before Spock answered.

"*Still searching, sir,*" the Vulcan finally said. And another silence followed. "*Sir, are you using the transporter aboard that ship?*"

"Me? No, of course not. Why?"

"*We're picking up unauthorized transporter use and cannot isolate the source.*"

"Could it be a malfunction in your alert system?"

"*Very likely, given the shutdown. I will pursue it.*"

"What about the Romulan ship?"

"*Their course was directly back toward the Romulan Empire at substantial warp. They do not appear to have come about.*"

"We gave them a good hammering," Kirk said. "They deserved it—"

"Captain!" The security man grabbed him by the shoulder and the two of them hit the floor of the narrow passage just as a disruptor bolt sizzled over their heads.

Without asking for permission, the security man returned fire, leaning with an elbow between Kirk's shoulder blades.

Kirk tried to get up, wriggled backward, but the guard wasn't about to let him up when there was a chance to protect him.

"Back off, Ensign—"

"DeCamp, sir," the man said, and fired two more times before he dared let the captain up.

The two of them skirted under an open hatch in the ceiling, and ducked around a corner.

"Romulan disruptor, sir," DeCamp said. "I'd know that sound anywhere."

Kirk clipped, "How would you?"

"Heard it in my head a hundred times. Been waiting for this my whole life."

Kirk looked at the young man, and for all the enthusiasm, it was a sorry sight.

"Let's hope you have to keep waiting," he said, and pushed the guard back another step.

"Sir, let me go first. I'm expendable." For a nice down-home polite kind of kid who probably used that "sir" on his father as well as his commanding officer, DeCamp had a hell of a grip.

"Nobody's expendable in my crew, Ensign," Kirk said. "But thanks. I'll go low, you go high."

"Yes, sir, I'm ready." The boy grasped his phaser with both hands and pushed closer to the corner.

Kirk dropped to one knee, and the two of them came around the corner firing.

In the flash of their weapons two helmeted Romulans went down, and two more found an instant to dive for cover, shielded by their comrades' flailing bodies.

Kirk rolled to the other side of the passage, giving DeCamp a clear shot—but before they could aim again, the two remaining Romulans were dropped by shots from behind them—from the other end of the passage, around another corner.

The deck was littered with fallen Romulans now, and the passage fell ghostly silent.

Kirk stayed down, his phaser aimed.

DeCamp had his long arms straight out, holding his own phaser braced in his hands. He looked at Kirk, and the captain nodded.

"Attention!" DeCamp called. "This is Starfleet! Drop your weapons and come out of there right now!"

Nicely said. Not an expletive to be heard. A polite takeover.

I'd have had an expletive for them, Kirk thought.

The shadows moved at the end of the passageway. He braced his legs.

"This is Dr. McCoy! Are you from the *Enterprise?*"

Kirk stood up. "Bones, it's me. Are you secure?"

McCoy's flushed face popped out at the end of the passage, and an instant later came Nancy Ransom with her first mate and another crewman who was limping.

"Stand guard here," Kirk said to DeCamp, and jogged out to meet them. When McCoy got to him first, he asked, "Are you all right?"

"I'm fine, Jim. Boy, am I ever glad to see you!"

Nancy Ransom stepped over a tangle of two Romulans and said, "Yeah, *I'm* even a little bit glad to see you."

"All this ship's sensors and computers are down, Jim," McCoy said, "which gave us the chance to sneak up on them, section by section. It was Nancy's idea."

Kirk looked at her.

Nancy blushed and palmed back some of her scruffy brown hair and said, "A trick I learned at the Academy. You can kick the girl out of the Fleet—"

"But they sure didn't get the Fleet out of the girl," Kirk said mildly, and found a grin for her. "Congratulations. Your engine room is secure too. Have you got a report for me?"

"Yes," Nancy gasped, sucked breath. "The Romulans beamed over here and brought sections of wall plate with them and started moving them down to my engine room. We analyzed the plate and found out it's a lithium hydride and cobalt compound. There's only one thing they can use that for."

Kirk's heart hit his feet. "Fusion incendiary."

"And I think I know why," McCoy interrupted. "It's those Rey people. They—"

"They leak emotion, right?"

Astonished, the doctor glared at him. "How did you find out about it?"

"Spock's a sponge."

"Oh—that makes sense. Well, what do you know? Wish I'd been there . . . after talking to Mike here, and Nancy, and a couple others, I concluded that the Rey's emotional levels are contagious somehow."

"Yes," Kirk said. "They have a little control, but not much. After all, you can't will yourself to sweat. Or to stop sweating, for that matter. The Romulans are susceptible, and because of that, they're scared." He paced down the passageway, looking at broken railings and shattered remains of disruptor fire. "I'd be scared too, Bones."

"But what about the lithium hydride and cobalt?" Nancy persisted. "They bound it around my warp core."

The picture got uglier and uglier in his mind as Kirk sifted back through his education—the unspoken part of his education, the part with subtle killing and assault training, and how to make bombs out of toothpicks and saltine crackers.

"I see . . ." he murmured.

Mike Frarey shook his head. "What do you see? What were they going to do with our ship?"

He lowered his voice. "Early hydrogen bombs were actually fission bombs surrounded by fusion bombs. The fission bomb was the detonator. This time, the Romulans planned to use your warp engines as the detonator, so they surrounded your warp core with the fusion material. As the engines exploded, the heat would set off a fusion chain reaction in the hydrogen, and there would be an incredibly massive explosion."

Frarey stepped forward, his face reddened. "But what's the point of the cobalt?"

"After the ship punched a hole in the Rey's planet atmosphere," Kirk told him, "and drove through the mantle and ignited, the cobalt's purpose would be to salt the bomb. It would vaporize and release a cloud of intensely radioactive cobalt vapor into the jet stream. The Romulans would have eradicated what they must perceive as a potent weapon against them."

"Gives me the drains," Nancy said. "I'da killed 'em all if I'd known."

Kirk gestured down the passage at the lump of unconscious enemy bodies. "You'd have killed 'em all anyway, Nancy. DeCamp!"

"Sir!"

"Secure those Romulans."

"Aye, sir!"

Nancy snapped her fingers at her first mate and crewman. "You two, help him tie up those suckers." She waved her confiscated Romulan disruptor and said, "I'm going down to take charge of my engine room. You got any problems with that?"

"None at all," Kirk said. "Bones, you go with her and render medical assistance. Authorize to our boarding party that she has command. They're to assist in freeing any of her crew and securing any other hostiles on board."

"Right!"

As they flooded down the passage, Kirk snapped his communicator up again. "Kirk to *Enterprise*."

"Spock here, Captain."

"This ship is nearly secure, Mr. Spock. What are your sensor readings now?"

"I was about to notify you, sir. We have hazy readings of several low-level Romulan presences—"

"Probably the unconscious ones."

"Yes. And one additional reading that is relatively strong. Slightly agitated but regular lifesigns, and moving about."

"Moving where, Mr. Spock."

"The bridge, Captain."

"Take over the boarding operation. I'll notify you in a few minutes."

"Captain . . . you're not going alone."

"Yes, I am, Mr. Spock, I am. I'm going up there and box the ears of the individual who ruined our good time. Beam me directly from here to the bridge of this ship."

"Ready when you are, sir."

Kirk glanced at his phaser. Heavy stun. He squeezed the hand grip.

"Energize."

"Commander, stop where you are."

Valdus turned sharply. Why hadn't he heard the whine of transportation? Concentrating too hard? Too much excess noise from the crackling systems broken and burned when his boarding party took this ship?

No matter now. There stood the captain of the *Enterprise,* alone and armed. He hadn't come through the open hatchways, but beamed directly here, for he stood beside the viewscreen's vision of open space as a sentinel stands a post.

"Captain," Valdus said.

James Kirk pursed his lips in annoyance because now he had to be polite, even for a minute.

"Stop what you're doing."

Quiet, subdued, Valdus said, "Some things cannot be stopped."

Valdus didn't move or make any attempt to defend himself, reading that a Starfleet captain would talk to him before taking more primitive action.

Simply watching the *Enterprise*'s captain was an education, and he allowed himself that. A compact and muscular young man, James Kirk had an old man's eyes. Pouched with gamesmanship, strict, shaded, sparked from internal electricity, those eyes were angry magnets.

Unable to look away, Valdus wasn't sure he wanted to. He knew he had put those lines of anger there today, and somehow he was proud.

He leaned forward. "This is the warp core detonator. I'm sure you know all about that by now. The thoroughness of Starfleet boarding parties has a reputation."

"I know about it. Move away or I'll stun you."

"Look at the way I'm standing. If you stun me, I will fall forward onto the detonator."

Kirk glared. "Better that," he said, "than let you take this ship and poison a whole planet. I'm as ready to die as you are, as long as it's out here, in the middle of nowhere."

Valdus offered him a judicious nod. "You look furious, Captain Kirk."

Kirk's eyes flicked to the open hatches, then back to Valdus. Caution dominated every muscle in Kirk's body.

"It's fun to be furious," he said. "Until you push that thing down, you're under arrest. Charges range from barratry—fraud, smuggling, plundering and violation of treaty—to conspiracy to commit mass murder."

"A very big charge," Valdus said. He kept his palm on the detonator but remained motionless.

Kirk tried to despise him, but it wasn't easy. Soft-spoken, contemplative, not harsh, not cold, Valdus wasn't like other Romulans.

As if I've met that many . . .

Maybe it was only the reputation, or the rumors, that he was remembering. He felt the withering of an old habit—a human's peculiar tendency to think about Romulans as just Vulcans gone sour.

That wasn't what he was seeing right now.

What prodigal creatures they are. I wish we could get them to join the Federation.

With one eye on Valdus, Kirk scanned the helm with the other. Wouldn't do any good to stand here talking while some timer ticked away that he didn't know about.

"You can stop me, Captain," Valdus said. "I understand. But there are things that cannot be stopped. The flame is going out of Starfleet's adventure. Some day there will be no flame left. You will go from day to day and preen your feathers with nothing else really to do."

Kirk scowled at him.

"Not in my lifetime," he said.

Valdus paused, searching the captain's glare, and understood. James Kirk wasn't going to let the flame die, not as long as he was alive to pester questions out of the galaxy, then hammer the answers into place. What a unique young man . . . with such genuine electricity in his eyes. Valdus had expected arrogance. After all, Kirk had stopped him. With the wide switch cupped under his palm, Valdus could blow this ship to slivers and accomplish nothing.

But the Starfleet leader wasn't satisfied yet. He was still concerned about the other people in the lower decks. Anger was building in that face and in those eyes, fury was still rising.

Valdus felt a wash of confidence. The Empire would ultimately prevail because this captain was still concerned about a gaggle of the conquered.

"I can forgive your reasons, but not your actions," Kirk said. "It's not my job to decide what to do with you." He wagged his phaser toward one of the two large step-through passageways. "Either push the button now or I'm going to turn you over to my security squad and turn this ship back to its captain and crew."

He angled toward the step-through that led to the lower decks.

Valdus blinked at him. Nothing else. His lips were parted but there was no sound. The muscles of his throat shifted and pulsed. Breath was caught deep in his throat.

Kirk stepped toward him. "I said move."

There was a flash of movement behind Valdus.

"Tom, no!"

But the Rey had already moved.

Valdus collapsed forward, over the helm. His hand skidded across the three-inch diameter detonator switch, then his elbow, then his chest.

Kirk plunged forward, but the button was down. An instant later they were nothing but a giant ball of ignited incendiary glittering in some distance planet's midnight sky.

So why were they still looking at each other?

Kirk shoved Valdus off the button, then caught Valdus by both arms as the Romulan's legs buckled and he went down on his knees on the deck.

Unauthorized transporter use . . .

Tom stood on the ladder of the deck hatch, halfway up into the bridge, his hands still raised, still clutching his weapon by its neck.

An old glass whiskey bottle, the bottom smashed away to a jagged glass shard, was embedded deep under Valdus's right shoulder blade. The fabric of his command jacket puckered around the bottle's body, and there wasn't even any blood yet.

The Romulan canted forward over Kirk's arm, unable to take a whole breath because of the jagged glass buried in one lung. Against his arm Kirk felt the palsy of agony and astonishment. Enmity dissolved under Valdus's begging grip, so clear that Kirk put down his phaser and devoted attention where it was needed.

"Tom! Get your hands off him!"

He slapped Tom's hands away from the bottle, then suddenly didn't know what to do next. The incongruous formed glass shape protruded at a horrid angle from Valdus's back, brutally efficient in its unlikely purpose, and Kirk actually felt the pain spread deeper.

The Rey man turned loose of the bottle and recoiled. Valdus fell forward, rolled against Kirk's grip, and landed on a thigh on the deck.

Kirk held him up and stared at the big orange detonator button.

"A dummy!" he spat. "You were distracting me. Why?"

He shook Valdus.

The commander coughed, but it came out as a wheeze. Kirk took a step to keep his balance, tripped twice on the clunky deck structure, and somehow kept the Romulan from falling backward onto the thing protruding from his back. Underneath all his cautions and the strung-up tension of just getting here, there was a plain human being who couldn't help but react when he saw that look in somebody else's eyes—that helplessness, caught in the unkind grip of pain.

"Tom!" Kirk scathed. "Is this the way to stop anything they're doing? What's the matter with you!"

Blinking those big brown eyes from a shadow, Tom looked like a sad child. He wasn't proud of himself, even though there weren't any regrets in his face.

"We aren't very strong, Captain Kirk," he said, "but we're not idiots."

That seemed to be his whole story.

After saying it, the Rey man looked away, down.

"What about your sister?" Kirk demanded. "You haven't given us a chance to try to get her back."

Without looking up, Tom said, "I don't tease myself that my sister is still alive."

Exasperated, Kirk nodded toward the Romulan. "If you were here, why didn't he feel it?"

Tom glanced at the victim of his bottle and his determination and simply said, "I wasn't afraid anymore."

Kirk grabbed Valdus by the collar with one hand and used the other to snap his communicator up. "Kirk to *Enterprise*. Medical emergency. Three to beam over, immediately."

With Tom hovering on the other side of the hatch, Kirk only had Valdus to worry about. He did all he could to hold the gasping Romulan up, leaned against a deck box, and waited.

Nothing happened.

He brought the communicator to his lips again.

"Kirk to *Enterprise*! What's going on over there?"

"Contact, Captain," Scott broke through. *"Vessel passing at high speed! Identification—the Romulan ship!"*

"Evasive action," Kirk blurted. "Do whatever you have to."

"They're not closing on us, sir! Vectoring around us to a new course . . . powering for high warp speed. Bearing . . . right for the finish line!"

"Captain, that's it!" Tom gasped. He crawled toward them on his hands and knees, faultily pointing at the screen. "He was stalling for time so they could get past you! A few seconds at hyperlight speed—you'll never catch up!"

As the three of them stared at the streak on the forward screen, Valdus hung over Kirk's arm and felt his bones shake, found the strength to raise his head and seek the viewscreen.

Yes, there it was . . . his ship, his *Red Talon,* blazing past them at hyperlight speed. He pushed forward against the captain's arm, and the thing in his back bit him again.

He gagged on his own bile, but kept his eyes on the forward screen, on the rushing hope of his Empire.

"The beauty of light speed," he rasped. "You'll never catch him now . . . you can't stop a fully shielded battleship barreling in at high warp . . . Expand or die, Captain . . . my civilization must be the one to survive."

Kirk leaned him against the deck box and knelt to look at the Romulan at eye level.

"Why can't we *all* survive?"

Valdus choked as he tried to laugh. His vision was closing in on both sides, the curtain of his life closing on the image of his ship as it disappeared into its destiny.

As the curtain darkened, he managed to turn to Kirk.

"Because it never happens that way," he said.

Kirk looked at the forward screen, where seconds ago the Romulan ship had shot into high warp speed.

"If you want fair," he murmured, "don't enter races."

He brought the communicator up.

"Enterprise, beam us aboard!" he shouted. With his thumb he recalibrated his signal. "Spock, come in, quick."

"Spock here, Captain."

"Transport back to the ship right now. This race isn't over!"

THE
REAL
STARSHIP
RACE

Chapter Twenty-two

Enterprise

"FULL ABOUT, STARBOARD!"

"Full about, aye!"

"Mr. Scott, emergency warp speed!"

"Emergency warp, sir. Warp one . . . warp two . . ."

"Helm! Phasers, three points abaft starboard—fire!"

"Three points abaft starboard, aye . . . phasers firing! A miss, Captain. They're beyond range for—"

"Uhura, hail that ship. Warn them off their course."

"Trying, sir, but they've drenched the channels in high-frequency noise—"

"Go to Flags and Pennants Code. Semaphore N-F to all other vessels. Coming into danger. Try to flash X ray through to the Romulans. Stop intentions. If they don't understand that by now, they haven't been flying in the same galaxy we have."

"Trying, sir . . . sir, they don't accept X ray. I doubt the signal's flashing through the impedance they've put up."

"Keep trying. Scotty, I want more speed."

"Warp four, sir. Powering up for warp five. Maximum safe speed in . . . three minutes, sir."

"Uhura, try long-distance communications. Hail *Intrepid* and *Hood* at the Gullrey solar system. Warn them what's coming and not to let the Romulan ship through."

"Inhibitors still hampering the systems from the Starbase mechanics. I'm trying to clear it, but there's nothing I can do about the Romulans' high-frequency noise. Doubt I'll be able to pierce it."

"Try anyway. Send the warning. Somebody might pick it up and relay it."

"Aye, sir."

"Warp five, Captain," Scott said as the humming of the ship went from an easy harmony to a notable strain.

Kirk snapped, "Go to warp six."

Everybody tightened a little. They didn't look at him, but he felt the change.

He didn't need the glory. He would be thrilled, relieved to let Ken Dodge or T'Noy take the medals for destroying the big threat.

If only he could make that happen, he'd pin the medals on them himself.

If he could just *make* it happen. Wish it. Beg it. Whip it. Order it . . . his hands were shaking.

And his crew was sweating over their controls, snapping at their own departments, pounding on their equipment, but a starship against a warbird with plain raw speed—

There were a lot of people here. The bridge seemed crowded. Almost every station was manned. Scott had an assistant with him at Engineering, Chekov had a young lieutenant manning the upper deck Navigation station, and another ensign was at the Defense and Weapons subsystems monitor. Everyone was at battle stations.

Where was the battle?

He wanted one. He always preached against battle, but right now it was all he wanted. A chance to stop and square off and use cleverness and quickness, plunge this way and that, use his ship's defensives and offensives the way he was trained to and the way his experience had taught him, but he wasn't being given that chance. The Romulan was refusing to face off with him and let the best man, ship, crew, win.

This was just raw running, wide open, into a wire at throat level.

A big wire with a lot of innocent people standing on it.

"Captain," Spock said, as he leaned over his screen, "Romulan is at warp factor six."

Kirk snapped a glare at him, then at the forward screen.

"Go to warp seven."

Sulu turned and looked at him. They all did.

Then Sulu said, "Warp factor seven . . . aye."

The ship hummed and protested, but speed whacked into another dimension of warp. On the upper port side, Engineer Scott started sweating. Then everybody else started.

The indicator lights all over the bridge flickered for attention.

Kirk prowled again. If they could just get close enough for a phaser shot into the Romulan's propulsion system . . . one bolt without loss of speed . . . just enough to slow them down, overtake them . . .

Speed. It was all he could think about. Speed.

"Captain," Sulu said, his voice gargling, "he's pulling away from us . . . now at warp . . . eight."

Some of the crew looked at Kirk. Mostly the younger people. Then they looked at their immediate superiors.

Some of the superiors were looking at Kirk now, too. Scott, Chekov, Spock. Sulu wasn't looking at anything but the screen, his narrow shoulders hunched and his hands spread and poised over the controls, shaking a little. But he was listening.

Kirk swallowed once. Then again.

"Go to warp eight," he grated.

"Warp," Sulu began, then had to clear his throat. "Warp eight, sir."

From the bowels of the ship beneath them, a low

whistle came up. A painful sound of effort. A guttural buzz coming through the deck as system after system was sacrificed to the speed. The ship was going into automatic shutdown, conserving everything but life-support, and even some of that. They were all sheeted in sweat now, as air-conditioning systems were reduced to the bare minimum. Comfort was a privilege the ship couldn't afford right now. She'd keep them alive, but that was all.

He damned himself for letting the ship be hobbled for any reason. They'd be on that Romulan already if he hadn't agreed to run this race. He would never again ask his ship to be less than she could be. Now she was ripping herself apart because he asked her to. He turned to pace the command deck again, but this time, he stopped.

He found himself looking up at the science station. At Spock. Yet it was the face of Valdus haunting his thoughts. Honest, determined Valdus. And he wondered how the Romulan Empire could be made less afraid. He'd failed to convince Valdus that the Empire had nothing to fear from the Federation.

He'd failed, and he wanted somehow to unfail. He wanted to fly into Imperial space waving a big white starship and go stand before the High Supreme whatever and convince them.

If only he could do it in the next half hour.

Spock came to the rail.

"What do you think?" Kirk asked.

"He is on a suicide mission," the Vulcan said. "Burning his ship with excessive speed has no effect on him. I doubt he'll allow us to outrun him."

"What's his ultimate purpose? To just slam a fifty-thousand-ton projectile into that planet at high warp?"

"Possibly. Such an impact could conceivably do much damage. The ship would instantly disintegrate." Spock shifted his weight from one foot to the other as though discussing cabbage at a fruit stand. "However, I would suspect this is a more clearly calculated backup plan. They probably didn't off-load all of their lithium/cobalt compound, and have sufficient supplies left on *Red Talon* to—"

"To poison that planet, I know," Kirk snapped. "What are the chances that *Intrepid* and *Hood* could see him coming?"

"Under normal circumstances, fair, given that they were posted outside the solar system."

"But?"

"But at last report the two starships were intending to stand guard at the planet itself. Mr. Chekov's analysis of his trajectory implies the Romulan is screening himself with Gullrey's sun. At such high warp, there will be only instants between the sun and the planet. The vessels standing guard at the planet—"

"Won't even see him," Kirk interrupted again. "In fact, they'll become just part of the fireball. We're finding out what Allied ships found out during Earth's World War Two, Mr. Spock. It's almost impossible to stop a kamikaze. If we don't get him . . . nobody will."

Spock nodded. "Yes."

Kirk turned and raised his voice. It rasped anyway. "Scotty."

Looking up, brow drenched in sweat, Scott blinked. "Captain?"

On the command deck, James Kirk drew a breath.

"Go to warp factor nine."

The ship was tearing itself apart around them. Kirk could feel the shudder coming up through his soles. A grinding that wasn't supposed to be there. And it was getting worse by the second. He felt slightly nauseated and knew the inertial damping fields were being compromised.

Below decks, four hundred plus crewmen were sweating and dashing, lashing and bandaging, trying to keep the vessel in one piece.

"MIE shut down!"

"Leave it down."

"Structural integrity field's being compromised!"

"Then compromise it."

The upper deck might as well have been a ledge on a skyscraper. Passing the navigation main station, Kirk was walking the ledge and trying to decide whether or not to jump.

From across the bridge, Scott tried again with a shout. "Captain, severe risk of meltdown!"

"It'll have to melt," the captain spat, and turned his back on his engineer. "Lieutenant Boles, how long for the Romulan to get to Gullrey?"

At the upper deck navigation station, Boles didn't answer, but only bent forward and picked at the controls.

Ten seconds later, he was still picking.

Cranked up tight, Kirk asked, "What's your report, Lieutenant?"

The kid glanced up at him and made the mistake of explaining, "Just a little nervous, sir."

"You're relieved," Kirk said. He gestured to the ensign manning defense subsystems. "Ensign Michaelson, take over this position."

At the nav station, the lieutenant's face dropped all its color. Some of that might've been relief, but most of it was shock.

At least he had the sense not to argue as the captain walked away.

Kirk didn't glance back. Somebody else could do the coddling. That lieutenant would either never be nervous again or would never admit it. Either one was fine.

"Mr. Sulu," he said, "attempt long-range phaser fire. Try to knock him off course. Shave his speed down. Anything."

"Aye, sir," Sulu said, with a lot more stability in his voice than anyone felt.

The phasers fired, a sense of electrical power bolting through the ship and out into open space. On the forward screen, thick lances of energy went forward into infinity.

They were all thrown forward suddenly, as if somebody had hit the brakes just for an instant, then the speed fought to come back. Several people rolled onto the deck.

Kirk ignored them.

"Do it again, Sulu."

"Aye, sir, phasers firing."

Again the energy coughed from the ship, and again the ship balked under them.

"Loss of closing distance," Sulu reported, glaring into his screen. "Attempting to close, sir."

"Sir, every time we fire," Scott said, "we fall off our pace by a hundred thousand kilometers."

"I know," Kirk muttered, "I know. Cease firing."

The science didn't add up. A strong phaser bolt at superhyperlight speed gulped too much power from the engines, caused a speed fall-off that they couldn't afford. What could they afford? The ship was falling apart. The Romulan was falling apart too, but a kamikaze doesn't care if the dive rips his wings off.

Bitter fury scorched him until he felt his lips burn and his heart shrivel with the worst thing of all—impotence.

"We can't break his shields at this distance," he ground out. "Can't get in front of him, can't warn ahead . . . we're racing behind him so we can record the death of a civilization."

Impotence. Worse than dying, worse than killing, the utter helplessness to do anything. He hated it. The Enterprise was all that could possibly stop Red Talon now, and they couldn't do it.

"Spock," he barked, "give me an idea! Any idea. Any of you—I'll take anything!"

He dropped to the command deck and took the back of his chair in his hand and shook it, just as he had shaken Valdus by the shoulders and tried to make him understand.

"Give me a way to stop him!"

The silence was damning.

The cleverest, the brightest, the most daring, and nobody knew what to do. Nobody had a way. Nobody had a suggestion that would let him drill forward through the next few minutes and change the future.

"Drill," he murmured.

Spock looked up. He was the only one who noticed. "Captain?"

Kirk's eyes cut into the forward screen. "What's the extended range on a pinpoint phaser? The same energy ratio, but roll it all down to a stream a couple millimeters across?" He looked sharply at Spock. "Could it be done?"

Spock's expression turned suddenly vague, then sharp again. "Concentrate the energy?"

"A diamond-tipped drill, Spock! Can it be done? Would it punch through those shields at this distance?"

Sulu tilted his head toward them without taking his eyes off the screen. At this speed, he couldn't afford to.

"Their hull structure's all self-sealing. So's the warp core. It wouldn't do any more than poking a finger through."

On the upper deck to their left, Scott stomped to the rail.

"Even if it got through the shields," he said, "it wouldn't bore through the warp core containment. But with lithium hydride packed around it—he's carrying the dynamite. All we have to do is light the fuse."

"If that's what they've done," Sulu added.

"If not, sir," Scott said, "we'll have lost too much speed to catch up. A maintained phaser shot like that—"

But Spock interrupted, and a lilt of hope sparked his voice. "It *could* work."

"I'll take the bet," Kirk bolted. "Mr. Scott, you work on keeping our speed up while we fire. I don't care where you get the power. Just get it. Mr. Spock, adjust that phaser down to a pinpoint. We're going to get them with a needle instead of a club."

"Fire the phaser, Mr. Sulu."

"Firing phaser, sir."

The ship was rattling. Warning bells rang. The overhead lights were so dim that the monitor screens put out more glare. Conduits snapped, sizzled, sparked, but other than jumping to keep their hands from being burned, the crew was under orders to ignore almost everything but the needs of warp nine.

Jim Kirk battled down a need to wrinkle his nose at the smell of burning circuits. He didn't want anyone to see him do that.

On the forward screen, a long red streak fed out from the ship, thin as a fishing line, and reached into the impossible distance until it disappeared somewhere in the blackness.

"Phaser's causing an energy competition in the reaction chamber," Scott sighed from up there.

"More speed, Mr. Scott," Kirk asked. "Push harder."

"Already at warp nine point three, sir." The chief engineer sounded like a whipped slave. "Could blow up at any time."

No technical reports, no heat ratios, no reactant injection numbers, no catastrophic shutdown details.

Just "blow up." Dead men had no reason to be specific.

None of the crew was warning him anymore. They weren't telling him it couldn't work or what was breaking down. They knew he wasn't stopping.

Kirk found himself wishing to just get it over with. Any instant now, boom. If they couldn't stop the Romulan, better they just blow up. If they lived, and the Romulan made it to Gullrey, then there would be war. The *Enterprise* would be here to testify.

He didn't want to testify. To start a war. He would rather blow up.

Strange. If Valdus's original plan had worked, there probably wouldn't be a war. Nobody would quite understand what had happened. The Federation and the Romulan Empire might have fallen into another hundred years of distrust, but that would have been all.

Now there would be war. A planet dies, a starship lives to tell why.

He almost wished the ship would hurry up and explode.

But she didn't. She held together. They pushed and pushed, and she held.

Warp nine point three . . . nine point four . . . nine point five . . .

The narrow red line kept on glowing out, forward from the ship into the infinity of space.

Under the science station the wiring trunk blew open, sending sparks and bits of material against Spock's shins, then on the other side at engineering subsystems another one went. The crew flinched and jumped out of the way. They glanced at Kirk, but he didn't budge. Didn't even look.

His heart kettledrummed in his ears. He knew it was the same for all of them.

"Phasers overheating, sir," the ensign at weapons reported.

"Maintain fire," he said. "Scotty, take every safety off everything."

"She'll blow up, sir."

"Then let her blow."

Minutes. Long ones. To just stare at the screen with nothing to do but think.

Spock and Sulu were pulling the phaser tighter and tighter, even narrower than a fishing line. Micromillimeters. Nobody had ever done that before. Could it reach far enough? Would it even stand up to particles in space?

The phaser only had to drill through for an instant. Just an instant. All that energy concentrated on one tiny point . . . through the shields, through the outer hull, the inner hull, through the containments . . . all it had to do was strike that lithium hydride packed around the warp core. A match on gasoline. Fusion was ready to start. All he had to do was start it.

Even a partial detonation—enough to start a chain

reaction. Two or three grams beginning to fuse . . . it would all be over in a microsecond . . .

"Approaching the Gullrey solar system, Captain," Chekov said. "We'll be there in . . . three minutes. He will beat us by one minute, twenty-six seconds."

The starship screamed in their ears. Bolts exploded around the bridge as pressure tried to release itself by breaking the least important parts first.

Two ships, state of the art in two cultures, blasted through open space at killing speed, sutured by a fine red line.

Spectator Ship *Gamma Star*

"Look at that!"

"Wow!"

It was a good thing everybody happened to be looking at the finish line just then. Anybody gone for a hot dog or to the bathroom missed a hell of a show.

A giant tangerine-colored blast of ball lightning with a white cloud inside spread in a sudden thorn tree of energy. Huge and blinding but for the distance, still sparking bits of metal illuminant and radioactive gas blew outward, hot in spite of space, the ten billion decimal candles of spitting phosphorus shards couldn't decide whether they wanted to burn up or freeze to death.

Moving at immeasurable speed, the savage light show fumed out a cometlike white tail for a few seconds—long enough to paint space and make quite an impression.

And as if that wasn't enough, the crowd gasped when a Federation starship suddenly bolted through the giant plasma cloud, plunging out at high speed, spitting red-hot sparks and leaving a donut of atomic heat expanding behind it.

Everyone rejoiced. She was beautiful! Every line of her white wineglass body was as vivid as an architect's pencil drawing, seductive and broken-in, flying the best she knew how. The viewscreens flickered and buzzed, trying to keep up with her.

In their minds they all heard it—*Swoooosh*.

As she slammed past them, they cheered and laughed and ducked tiny yellow-hot bits of spark that showered their ceiling-high viewscreens.

Jubilation pealed through the spectator ship. What a race this had been!

As the sparks died in the cold of space, a skinny great-grandmother asked, "Was that in the program?"

Nobody answered her. Nobody really cared. The outrageous pyrotechnics were still fresh in their minds, and they couldn't wait to see it all again on the stadium screen at the closing ceremonies.

The white starship suddenly veered—very sharply—to avoid the planet of Gullrey, then seized out of speed and appeared to be shivering as it dropped to sublight faster than anybody thought was possible.

A vacationing shuttle pilot shook his head. "I didn't know any ship could stand that!"

The man beside him shoveled popcorn into his mouth and nodded, "Those starships are tough."

"Was that an emergency shutdown?" a twelve-year-old kid asked his teacher.

"Naw," the teacher said. "They're okay. Just showing off."

"I dunno," the kid muttered. But he didn't want to argue his way out of a good grade.

The applause settled down to ear-to-ear grins as the crowd watched the starship drift along on momentum, not even applying thrust, until she simply drifted gracefully across the finish line, with her wings high.

Applause erupted again as the spectators watched the starship drift between the two committee ships, officially finishing the race.

The performance was extravagant and madcap, something people of all kinds appreciated, especially when they'd come hundreds of parsecs to see it.

As one father herded his children through the crowd, away from the enormous viewscreens, he glanced back at his wife.

"Starfleet sure knows how to put on a great show, don't they?"

EPILOGUE

Chapter Twenty-three

Closing Ceremonies, Monn Oren City, Gullrey

"AND IT'S WITH the greatest of joy, and in the name of our broadening interstellar community, that I present the First Place Platinum Plaque and possession of the *El Sol* Doubloon to Captain Miles Glover and the crew of *New Pride of Baltimore!*"

The newly reelected president of the Federation wasn't the dynamic type, but there was something accommodating about him that the throng of spectators appreciated. He was thin and economical of movement, his hair a tumble of gray curls, his faded blue eyes much slower than the brain behind them, failing somehow to reveal a people-wise intelligence that had won him a reputation for being able to read minds.

Everyone knew that just by being here he was honoring them, the starship race, and the Rey, because he very rarely left Starbase One. And here he was, about as far from there as he could get in friendly space.

Behind him, a thirty-meter viewscreen had just shown the parade of ships that happened yesterday, and before that the balefire explosion not explained by the newscasts until this morning. Now everybody knew.

They knew about the sacrifice of at least two innocent lives, maybe more, and the destruction of the Romulan ship, though nobody had a clear idea of what exactly had happened. The reasons, apparently, had died with the Romulans.

At least, that was the public line.

Jim Kirk sat with his officers in the first ten rows of seats, mantled by thousands of others in the huge stadium. All over the Federation, the ceremonies were being broadcast on screens.

He watched with perfectly settled emotions as the energetic Miles Glover jaunted up to the podium to accept the *El Sol* Doubloon on behalf of his cheering crew, and bowed to the applause of millions.

Suddenly Kirk was glad he didn't have to be up there. All he wanted to do was sit here with Spock on one side and McCoy on the other, and let his shoulders relax, and nurse the knuckle burns he'd gotten from touching the wrong things on Nancy Ransom's ship. Around for rows and rows of the competitors' section, were the captains and crews of all the racing vessels. He liked the feeling. He glanced past McCoy and his own officers to where Nancy Ransom sat with Mike Frarey and the officers of *Ransom Castle*. They were cleaned up, but somehow no amount of cleaning would take the rough edge off them, especially with Nancy wearing a telltale neck brace.

Oh, well . . . they were alive and they were here. Two points for the good guys.

Beyond them, Hans Tahl and his crew from *Great Lakes*, T'Noy and hers from the *Intrepid,* and not far down there were Ken Dodge and the officers of the *Hood* wearing sashes of honor—everybody looked good enough to get married.

"The trophy for second place," the president continued, "goes to Captain Kmmta and the crew of *552-4.*"

After another round of cheers, the president handed the trophy to an Andorian woman who approached the podium, then explained what he was doing.

"Due to the life support-requirements of the captain

and crew of *552-4,*" the president explained, "they are watching from their ship, and the trophy is being accepted by Ambassador Yeshmal, Federation representative to the Tholian Assembly."

The Andorian woman took the trophy, bowed somewhat extravagantly, and went back to her seat without glancing at the thousands of faces watching her.

"Third place award," the president said, "goes to Captain Sucice Miller and the crew of the *Ozcice,* the host entry!"

The crowd went wild. The idea that the host planet had managed to show in the first Great Starship Race was especially invigorating for everybody. Of course, there were jokes about the race having been rigged, but nobody really believed it, and beyond that, nobody cared.

Everybody had a good time, right?

Kirk sighed. His crew had earned a good time. He hoped they were having one now.

"Part of decent competition," the president went on, "is the trick of deciding whether to stop when another ship has distress, or to take advantage of that distress and gain ground. In all fairness, most competitions consider it fair to leap over a fallen entrant, and let authorities handle the injuries. One vessel in particular went above and beyond the call of competition, even beyond the call of duty, by risking their own lives on behalf of a fellow entrant. Despite the fact that some might say this is their job, certainly it is no mere job to place your own vessel in danger on behalf of others. Nor is it the simple call of duty to stretch all capabilities beyond limits . . . for the sake of a planet of strangers. A special award, my friends, newly created just last night by the Race Committee at the request of Captain Nancy Ransom and the crew of *Ransom Castle . . .*"

His voice boomed in the audio equipment, resounding across the stadium, across the planet, across the Federation.

He looked down, to his right, into the competitor's seats, and he held out a hand.

"To Captain James Kirk and the crew of the *U.S.S. Enterprise,* we would like to present the Spacemanship and Sportsmanship Award."

Before Kirk could even think of getting up to acknowledge the completely unexpected honor, Nancy Ransom pushed out of her chair and went to the podium. She took the award from the president and walked it down the aisle to where the *Enterprise* officers were sitting.

And she handed the big platinum medal to Kirk without a word.

Entire sections of the competitors' seating areas rumbled to their feet, and the rumble was drowned out by the roar of cheering. Somewhere in the vast audience, somebody waved a handkerchief, and almost immediately the trick rippled across thousands of spectators. In a few seconds everything from handkerchiefs to gloves, tissues to children's sweaters was being waved in honor of those who had lent a hand.

In spite of the cool Gullrey spring, everybody was a lot warmer when the crews sat back down and the president was able to speak again.

"We who merely watched the race and were so joyously entertained by it must from this day forward remember the true definition of sportsmanship. Therefore we must remember . . . *Enterprise.*"

After Kirk and his officers had taken their reluctant bows and the raging applause finally faded into the Gullrey skies, the president spoke again into the booming mike, "We the living citizens of the Federation happily welcome the planet of Gullrey, whose people have so enthusiastically embraced our people and our many ways. You must, as we all must, accept the unsavory events of this race and take those as a prenotification that there is a price to liberty. It has been said that the price of liberty is eternal vigilance. That is true. You have lived at the edge of a sector that Federation people have defended with their lives. Now we will extend our boundaries to defend you also, and you are no longer strangers. We expect you to give up your secluded innocence and to share the responsibility, the pain, and the great rewards . . . of freedom."

As he paused, four Federation dignitaries left their seats. They'd already been introduced—Doctors Beneon and Vorry, the two scientists who had been the first Rey to see life from any other world, whose perseverance in watching the sky had earned them that reward, and Captain Ken Dodge and his first officer, who had followed their instincts and answered a faded blip that most spacefarers would log and ignore.

The four stepped to the front of the podium. Together they raised a five-meter banner of silver stars and a star chart on a navy blue background—the shimmering seal of the UFP.

The president moved his thin body to the banner, careful not to trip on the stage steps, reached over the top hem, and attached a bright golden star to one quadrant of the banner's star chart grid.

Then he stepped back to the microphone.

"Gullrey, welcome to the United Federation of Planets," he said. "Welcome to the future."

The balefire torch erupted across space, one giant convulsion of gas, fire, and crystals made a wild white tail of brilliant radiation and seemed in complete control of its own blast until the starship blew through it and changed the ball into a ring.

On the taped picture there was also applause and cheering, recorded on one of the spectator ships as the unexpected final show occurred.

Then the screen winked out. The computer politely regurgitated the cartridge, then went silent.

Jim Kirk took the small recorder cookie out of its slot, and backed off a pace.

"I thought you should see what happened. If it were my ship," he said, "I'd want to be sure."

On the bed in the Rey hospital room, plainly aware of the two Starfleet guards on this side of the door and the

301

four on the other side, Valdus let his head lean back on the raised pillows.

"Thank you," he managed.

Kirk gazed down at him and couldn't keep empathy from chewing at him.

His own ship was undergoing repair. Would be for a long time. There hadn't been enough power left on board even to keep the Romulan in the brig or under guard in sickbay. So they'd brought their prisoner here, to a hospital on the host planet, the first bit of interstellar crime to stain the shores of Gullrey.

But he wasn't worried about this planet, or even his own scorched and bruised crew. He was worried about Valdus.

This was the worst thing that could happen to a ship's master. To be left alive after his crew is dead and his ship destroyed. The worst of all. To go on living.

He looked at Valdus's tired eyes and the sallow skin behind the beard that was meant to be fierce, and somehow this person didn't look like either a bastard Vulcan or a venomous Romulan. This man was a culture all by himself.

Completely separate. Maybe something new.

"What will happen to me?" Valdus asked, without looking at him.

"You'll be transferred to the *Starship Intrepid,* sent back to Starfleet Command, probably tried, probably incarcerated. Someday you might be sent back or traded in a diplomatic maneuver."

"I hope not. I'll go back disgraced."

"Or a hero." Kirk found himself offering a charitable grin. "You never know how these things play out. The long run can be very long, Commander."

They paused together without any more parrying, and any trace of animosity that might have remained between them just didn't seem to be there anymore. There also wasn't anything to say. Kirk knew he certainly wouldn't have accepted comfort if he had to live beyond the lives of his crew, and there was no point foisting comfort on Valdus just to make himself feel better. Where this incident was concerned, neither one of them would ever feel any better than this.

He tapped the computer cookie on his palm and moved toward the door. The two guards stepped aside, but at the last second, he stopped.

"Commander," he began, "there's one thing I want you to believe."

Valdus turned his head to look at him.

Kirk ticked off a couple of seconds until he could warm the Romulan's expression with his sincerity.

"We have no intention of conquering the Romulan Empire," he promised.

The commander raised a single brow—a gesture Kirk found familiar.

"Then you've lost," he said. "Because we have every intention of conquering you."

Maybe the lights were dimming. Or the sun was going behind a cloud. A threat? Portents and predictions? Vultures in the trees? Serpents under the bed?

Maybe.

Jim Kirk grinned his snake-eating grin. "But not today."

Chapter Twenty-four

Enterprise

"FEELING BETTER after a night's rest, Mr. Spock?"

"Very well, thank you, Captain."

"Your report?"

"At least two months' round-the-clock repair at a starbase. Starfleet is arranging for a hyperlight tug, and we are scheduled for dry dock at Starbase 16 in ten days. The warp nine strain, plus the hot metal bombardment and electron shower as we came through the remains of *Red Talon*, necessitate major repair."

"Yes, of course. Convey my apologies to Mr. Scott."

"I already did, sir."

"Oh . . . thank you. Send a message ahead to Starbase 16. I want Scotty to supervise the repair himself and I don't care how much the base engineers squawk about it. Authorize leave for the crew for the duration of repair."

"Very well, sir."

"And I don't want anything replaced that isn't in pieces."

"I beg your pardon?"

"The *Enterprise* just showed us how tough she is. Her spine, frame assembly and exostructure turned out to be a lot stronger than we thought. Even stronger than her designers thought. I don't want any of that strength repaired out of her. I don't care if they have to glue her together like a jigsaw puzzle. Make sure she's the same ship when they're done."

"That is . . . most discriminating, sir. I'll oversee the step-by-step repair plans myself."

"Thank you, Spock."

"You're quite welcome. Also, there was a private communiqué this morning to all participating Starfleet officers, from the president. On behalf of the Federation's many independent systems, worlds, countries, companies, and individuals . . . he thanks you for not winning the first Great Starship Race."

THE STAR TREK PHENOMENON

- [ ] **ABODE OF LIFE**
  70596-2/$4.99
- [ ] **BATTLESTATIONS!**
  74025-3/$4.99
- [ ] **BLACK FIRE**
  70548-2/$4.50
- [ ] **BLOODTHIRST**
  70876-7/$5.50
- [ ] **CORONA**
  74353-8/$4.95
- [ ] **CHAIN OF ATTACK**
  66658-4/$5.50
- [ ] **THE COVENANT OF THE CROWN**
  70078-2/$4.50
- [ ] **CRISIS ON CENTAURUS**
  70799-X/$4.99
- [ ] **CRY OF THE ONLIES**
  74078-4/$4.95
- [ ] **DEATH COUNT**
  79322-5/$4.99
- [ ] **DEEP DOMAIN**
  70549-0/$4.99
- [ ] **DEMONS**
  70877-5/$4.50
- [ ] **THE DISINHERITED**
  77958-3/$4.99
- [ ] **DOCTOR'S ORDERS**
  66189-2/$5.50
- [ ] **DOUBLE, DOUBLE**
  66130-2/$4.99
- [ ] **DREADNOUGHT**
  72567-X/$5.50
- [ ] **DREAMS OF THE RAVEN**
  74356-2/$4.95
- [ ] **DWELLERS IN THE CRUCIBLE**
  74147-0/$4.95
- [ ] **ENEMY UNSEEN**
  68403-5/$4.99
- [ ] **ENTERPRISE**
  73032-0/$5.50
- [ ] **ENTROPY EFFECT**
  72416-9/$5.50
- [ ] **FACES OF FIRE**
  74992-7/$4.99
- [ ] **FINAL FRONTIER**
  69655-6/$5.50
- [ ] **THE FINAL NEXUS**
  74148-9/$4.95

- [ ] **THE FINAL REFLECTION**
  74354-6/$4.99
- [ ] **A FLAG FULL OF STARS**
  73918-2/$4.95
- [ ] **GHOST-WALKER**
  64398-3/$4.95
- [ ] **HOME IS THE HUNTER**
  66662-3/$4.99
- [ ] **HOW MUCH FOR JUST THE PLANET?**
  72214-X/$4.50
- [ ] **ICE TRAP**
  78068-9/$4.50
- [ ] **IDIC EPIDEMIC**
  70768-X/$4.99
- [ ] **ISHMAEL**
  74355-4/$4.99
- [ ] **KILLING TIME**
  70597-0/$4.99
- [ ] **KLINGON GAMBIT**
  70767-1/$4.50
- [ ] **THE KOBAYASHI MARU**
  65817-4/$5.50
- [ ] **LEGACY**
  74468-2/$4.95
- [ ] **LOST YEARS**
  70795-7/$5.50
- [ ] **MEMORY PRIME**
  74359-7/$5.50
- [ ] **MINDSHADOW**
  70420-6/$5.50
- [ ] **MUTINY ON THE ENTERPRISE**
  70800-7/$5.50
- [ ] **MY ENEMY, MY ALLY**
  70421-4/$5.50
- [ ] **THE PANDORA PRINCIPLE**
  65815-8/$4.99
- [ ] **PAWNS AND SYMBOLS**
  66497-2/$5.50
- [ ] **PROBE**
  79065-X/$5.99
- [ ] **PROMETHEUS DESIGN**
  72366-9/$5.50
- [ ] **RENEGADE**
  65814-X/$4.95
- [ ] **REUNION**
  78755-1/$5.50
- [ ] **RIFT**
  74796-7/$4.99

822A-02

THE
STAR TREK
PHENOMENON